On Me, Myself,
& Everything Else

This book is a work of fiction. Names, characters, places, and incidents either are products of the author's imagination or are used fictitiously. Any resemblance to actual events or locales or persons, living or dead, is entirely coincidental.

Published by Charmily Rose LLC
http://www.charmilyrose.com

Text set in Century Old Style

Printed in the United States of America

ISBN 13: 978-0-578-02537-7

To Emily & Brittany,
for helping me publish my first book.

To my family,
for their love and support

and to whom I would suggest
skipping certain parts of this story :-)

On Me, Myself & Everything Else

Cece Kae

CharMily Rose

Foreword

One of my main motivations for this book was to give a voice to a girl that I feel is underrepresented in modern literature. I have felt that the voice of young black women in fiction today is overwhelmingly falling into the category of "street/ghetto lit." Not to knock it, but that's not me, and if I don't see myself in those books, then there are too many other girls like myself who feel they don't see themselves there, or in any other books either. As an author, I want to change that, to create a new voice and alter the dynamics of what we see as modern black literature.

I also sought to develop a character and a story that people of various backgrounds could empathize with. I wanted to write a book that could easily cross into mainstream fiction while still being true to itself, and I'm confident that I accomplished that. Although the character is a young, black female, people of any race are able to relate to her feelings and life situations. I even wanted the cover to have a racial ambiguity to open this character's story up to a new audience, because even though they say you can't judge a book by its cover, we very often do.

It's inevitable that people will think this book is about me, but I assure you that you have not just read—or are not about to read—any deep, dark secrets of my life. Even so, I'm sure you won't be disappointed. Enjoy!

The first time I ever truly saw myself, when I first became aware of my self in the world, was in a photograph. I was looking through an album, and I stopped to study a picture that was taken of my dad and me on my tenth birthday. We were sitting on the stoop of the house that I lived in at the time. His arm was around my shoulders with a lit cigarette in his hand. My mom was in the background, smiling at the scene before her. What struck me was the look on my face; I was staring directly into the camera with pleading eyes, my plump cheeks shiny wet with tears, mouth slightly open with no words as I was in such disbelief. Even my ten-year-old self knew that it was a lie, though I may not have been able to articulate it. My affectionate father, my smiling mother, all a lie. Being made to believe it was okay that I woke up each morning without a father and fell asleep at night listening to my mother cry: a lie.

Six years after the picture was taken, all of the emotion from that day came flooding back to me. I ripped the photo in half, deepening the fault between my father and me. No one should have to look back on shit like that, I told myself, and I went out to buy a camera with all of the money I'd saved from my after-school job. No one would fabricate my reality anymore; I would create my own.

Years upon years later, I'm still going strong. I was hooked on self-portraiture from the get-go. I had never been the girl to sit in front of the mirror for long periods of time, but seeing myself in my own photos never bored me. I could find one beautiful moment and capture it forever. Those close to me say it's become a narcissistic obsession, the way I've taken to photographing myself. I wouldn't go that far, but I'll admit it's given me a healthy dose of confidence that some people can't handle. It felt good to be able to show myself what beauty really is instead of having the rest of the world feed me a definition in which I did not fit.

I dashed to the other side of the lens and plopped my naked body in the chair. And I really did "plop" myself, as there was a suction kind of noise when the chair received me. I composed myself, smiled wide, then puckered seductively to give my lips a warm-up, and stared intensely into the camera. Shutter release, muscles relax. I looked in the mirror at myself, my wild curly hair and string of pearls, contemplating putting some underwear on. Not that I was exposing any of my naughty parts to the camera, but you know, they say sometimes less is more, and I believe that sometimes. I should've taken the heels off before I tried to step into the panties, but I just didn't. Gravity won over my balance, and I smacked my elbow on the edge of the dresser on my way down to the floor. Inevitably, there came the sound of someone trying my bedroom doorknob, which I'd locked as soon as the inspiration to do a photoshoot hit me.

"Are you okay?" It was my mother. "What are you doing?" If she knew, she would've lost her mind.

"I'm *fine*." Her unseen presence made me want to put a bra on as well, which was a feat that far surpassed uncomfortable considering my throbbing elbow.

"Are you sure?"

"Mom, please, I'm fine."

"What are you doing?"

My inspiration was gone. I quickly pulled on a t-shirt and shorts, dismounted my camera from the tripod, and opened the door. "I just tripped on my shoes."

"It sounded painful, the way you hollered. And that *bang*."

"Yeah, it was, but I'm *fine*."

"Well, I got some dinners from the church."

"Chicken or fish?"

"Both."

"Sweet potatoes?"

"Yeah. Macaroni and cheese, too."

"I'll be down in a minute." I closed the door and sat on my bed to upload my new pictures onto my computer, most of which were gorgeous, especially the last one I took. Just some more great photos to add to my collection—I can't help it if my best subject is me. Don't get the wrong idea here: this is no pornography we're talking about. This is a website, designed and operated by yours truly, featuring my personal poetry and blog entries, along with a (rather risqué) gallery of photos—which my mom knows about. Trust me, she loathes the mere idea of it. I've never felt like I was more of a disappointment to her than when she discovered my site, so I try to keep it as distant from our relationship as possible.

My sister and her daughter were sitting at the kitchen table. Leslie, my niece, picked at her inch and a half piece of whiting, placing tiny shreds of fish on her tongue and pulling them into her mouth. She looked up when I came in and gave a big grin. I forced a smile back. She held up her hands to me, displaying sparkling pink French tips.

"Me and Mommy got our nails done," she said, smiling and batting her eyelashes.

"Mommy and I," Deena corrected her daughter. "Sit up straight and stop wriggling around—unless you want to practice. I brought your music."

"Okay," Leslie replied, shrugging.

The threat hadn't gone the way Dee intended. "Just finish eating."

Only two Styrofoam containers were on the table. Two dinners for four people, of course. It's always been that way here. Maybe if my mother had gone to school before having a family on her own, we'd have had more food. I sat across the table from my sister and piled food onto my plate.

"Mom didn't eat yet," Dee said, watching my portions.

"Put mine in the fridge," Mom hollered from the living room.

Deena, showing off how responsible and selfless she is, got up from the table, fixed Mom a plate, and covered it with foil. When she bent over to put the plate on the bottom shelf of the fridge, her clothes pulled away to expose the tribal tattoo across her lower back. It's an ugly thing, which she tried to pretty up years after she first got it by getting Leslie's name in script right above it. A sweet gesture, I suppose, but I can't imagine it's much of a turn-on for the guy hitting it from the back.

You'd never know it now, but Deena and I used to be best friends. Since we're so close in age, you'd think we fought a lot, but we rarely did. Instead, we bonded over our plan to overcome our circumstances. Through the majority of our childhood, we lived in shit-hole apartments and bad neighborhoods. Our lives depended on receiving welfare and Mom working menial, dead-end jobs. We came to the conclusion that she'd had us too young (she gave birth to Deena fresh out of high school and to me three years later); therefore she couldn't go to college of any kind in order to get a better job.

Deena and I made plans to start a magazine after both of us graduated us from college. Since I always loved writing and putting stories together, we decided that I would be the "head writer." My sister wanted to be the "fashion and boy person." Obviously, we weren't entirely sure what roles were to be had at a magazine. Now I know that I'd be editor-in-chief while my sister wouldn't be shit because I'm sure those dreams of hers have since been deflated, or were popped along with her cherry. We promised each other we wouldn't be like her. We motivated each other to do better, and stayed at the tops of our classes throughout most of our high school years.

Until Deena met Charlie. I don't know exactly what he did for a living, but it was something that they never spoke of that brought in a lot of money. I was with them when they first met. Deena and I were walking home from the bus after school. She was wearing a jean skirt and these red, cork wedges that mom told her not to wear to school. I, too, had a bad feeling about those shoes when she bought them. As we were about to cross the street, an old-school, black Caddy with gold rims pulled up at the stop sign. The black window sunk into the door and Charlie stuck his big head out. He ran his tongue across his gold teeth and called out to my sister.

"Ayo, slim, com'ere for a minute."

My sister went over to the car and leaned into the window. With her red heels and miniskirt, you can only imagine what this looked like. She turned to me and said, "Come on, Cleo! Charlie's gonna give us a ride home."

"We live four blocks away. That is hardly necessary," I told her.

"I'll see you there then!" she said, walking around to the passenger side of the car.

"Wait!" I groaned, and got into the back seat. I didn't want to send her off alone with him, plus, it was hot outside.

In the front of the car, he talked in a deep voice, giving her compliments, running his fingers along the seams of the red tube top Mom told her not to wear. She giggled "you're so crazy" while I grew more angry in the back seat. When we pulled up in front of our little row house, Deena turned to face me and told me to go in the house.

"Well, let's go," I said.

"Take my key, Cleo, and go. Just go in and close the door. I know you gotta pee anyway, you always do after school."

"What about you?"

"I'll take care of her," Charlie said, smiling at me, turning my stomach. Deena giggled.

"It's the middle of the day!" I said in disgust. I grabbed the key and stormed inside without looking back. I went into our room and slammed the door. Fifteen minutes later, I heard her come in and go right to the bathroom. I heard the sink running, and then she came into our room with one hickey on her neck and one at the top of her breast. My mouth hung open.

She tried to cover the marks with her hands, saying, "Shut up! And don't look at me like that."

"Like what?"

"All judgmental!"

I wasn't judging her, but I knew what just happened. What had happened was, my sister had become lost. Lost from our original plan, instead of following her own goals and determination, had succumbed to "the power of the penis," as Alexyss K. Tylor would say. Too soon they gave themselves over, my mother and my sister, giving themselves to another person—some man—before they even knew themselves. That leads, as you can see, to a life of servitude, if not to him, then to his offspring, with or more often without his help.

So Deena lived for Charlie for a number of years. That is, until he died a year after Leslie was born, when his car was run over by a runaway garbage truck. I was glad. He was an asshole; I know he hit my sister regularly, and he verbally abused her in front of absolutely everyone. Although it's farfetched, I like to think my sister had something to do with the faulty brakes of that garbage truck, but I think that might be giving her too much credit.

I licked the sweet potatoes from my fork, savoring the very last bits. It was delicious, but the tiny portions were hardly satisfying. As I finished washing the few dishes that were in the sink, I could hear music playing in the living room. I dried my hands on my shorts and walked into the room to find Leslie doing a disgustingly cutesy-peppy-happy dance to some remix of *I'm a Little Teapot.*

"Leslie, no!" Deena shouted, pausing the music. "*Here* is my spout." She jerked Leslie's arm into place. It looked painful, but Leslie had a smile frozen on her little face. "Do you want that crown? It's not for me. If you want it, you have to work for it."

"I do want it," Lele replied, poking out her bottom lip.

Deena looked at me, shaking her head. "What am I supposed to do with her?"

Stop parading her around like a show pony.

"You know she won Ultimate Grand Supreme at the last one two weeks ago."

"How could I forget?" I pretended to stick my finger down my throat as Leslie did a twirl with her hands on her non-existent hips.

"You could be more supportive," my mom said.

"Of beauty pageants? You're kidding me. They have more support than they're worth already. Why a five-year-old needs false teeth, eyelashes, and hair is beyond me."

"To win," Leslie replied honestly, oblivious to my tone.

"Thank you, Lil' Mama," Mom said, giving her a pinch on the cheek and a kiss on the forehead.

"Fuck this, I'm going to work."

Leslie's hands flew up to cover her ears and her mouth made a perfect "O". I soaked in the shocked and disgusted looks on the faces of my sister and mother and laughed myself upstairs. I changed into my black work pants and white tank top. I threw the yellow polo that completed my uniform into the messenger bag and pulled my hair back into a bun. When I opened the door to leave my room, I found Deena there, ready to turn the knob.

She smiled sweetly. "We're both adults, Cleo. And mom, of course, is, too. So you're not shocking anyone by cursing, just contaminating the mind of a five-year-old. That's… far from commendable, and I know how self-righteous you are."

"Wh—"

"You look… okay today. I do wish you would start wearing makeup though. You could be so pretty." She handed me a Bloom brochure. Bloom is a cosmetics company that, next to Lele's pageants, consumed my sister's life. Every couple of weeks, she'd start throwing new catalogues at everyone and urging us to buy crap. She was a machine when it came to recruiting new customers, collecting payments on time, and delivering the products to those who ordered them. Yeah, good for her. Too bad she didn't have a life.

My blood was boiling when I got to work. Not only was I still pissed at my sister for the stupid comment she made, but also it was so humid and sticky outside. Begrudgingly I put my polo over my tank top and headed out into the store from the stock room. Customers dotted the aisles sparsely, which was a relief. I planted myself at the end of a check-out lane and began bagging some lady's groceries. Someone grabbed my ass from behind. I turned to see Janine walking by.

"How nice of you to show up," she said, taking her place behind a register.

"They only gave me four hours today. Not that I'm complaining."

"Lazy. I've been here since two, and I'm pregnant." She always has to mention that she's pregnant. Of course the lady in line started cooing over her, asking how far along she is and stuff. Janine is another one of them, those females who aren't about anything except whatever it is their man is about, and then only about being a mother after that. So while Janine may be working at Keiman's Supermarket to support her family for the next two decades or so, I'm gonna be doing me, far from here, making my own shit-load of money for me, myself and I.

Something heavy landed on my shoulder, and heat radiated from it to my neck, ear, and cheek. "How's it going?" my manager asked, rubbing my shoulder in a way that border-lined sexual harassment.

"Fine, Paul."

"I need you to restock the cereal shelves. Can you do that for me?"

"Yes, Paul." I dragged myself off to the stock room and began loading the flatbed. Janine wasn't far behind me, rubbing her belly and humming to her unborn baby. She stood and watched me work. "Can I help you?"

"Yo, aren't these hot?" She put her foot up on the flatbed to show off the white, high-top Keds she'd had airbrushed with a picture of the Puerto Rican flag and her name on the side. "To match these." She leaned her head forward and pulled her curly, crunchy hair aside so I could get a glimpse of her gold-tone hoop earrings with an image in the middle, similar to that of the one of her shoe. "Hot, right?"

Hot mess? Well, "Yeah."

"I know, right! Tell your sister to hook me up with some more lip gloss."

"You didn't pay her for your last two orders."

"I know, Cleo. You know how things were last month though. We're good now. Me and Junior moved back in with my mom. It's all good."

That's a damn shame.

"Yeah, she's glad. But look. You know that new girl, Tonya? Girl, me and Junior was comin' in from the movies real late a couple days ago, and she was in the house with my brother, all the lights off. We walked in, pitch black, turned the lights on, they're scrambling around on the couch, tryna get dressed real fast! Now today, I was vacuuming, found a damn thong right under the couch! It got stuck all in the nozzle and shit, me and Junior were *dyin'*!"

"I hope she's standing right around the corner and hears your trifling ass."

"Girl, shut up, calling me trifling. I was looking at your website, you little Internet slut."

"Janine, don't even! You know there's more than that to me. The pictures are just bait, just to entice people to stay a while and maybe they'll actually read something."

"I know girl, I'm playin' witchu. I replied to that last blog, about how too many men run through here buyin' Magnums like they need them, cuz you know everybody don't need all of that!"

"For real."

"Girls, are you working or chatting?" Paul asked as he walked by.

Janine snickered, then whispered in my ear, "Girl, he switches harder than I did before I got pregnant. You know I just waddle now," and headed off.

I tried to finish up my reading as quickly as possible as the train approached my stop. I continued reading as I walked to class, glancing up every few sentences so I wouldn't bump into anything. Of course I was the first to arrive at my classroom, even before my teacher. I took my usual seat on the far side of the room. Students trickled in, giving awkward, tightlipped smiles or raising an eyebrow to acknowledge me. I could tell I was the only one—besides Claire, the instructor—who really wanted to be there. It was a required course for all of us English majors, and although I'd already taken it once, I was allowed to take it again as an elective as long as I took it with a different instructor. This class in particular was made more accessible for students of other majors to take as their English literature elective, and it was much more interesting so far than the original course I'd taken. Claire arrived and the class was underway. Forty minutes later, she pointed to me. "Yes, Cleo? Always something profound to point out."

"Well, it's more of a question."

"Okay."

The door flew open and slammed against the wall. The culprit raised his eyebrows apologetically. "My bad." He made a noisy procession to the back of the room, smacking faces, shoulders, and arms with his backpack along the way.

"You were saying, Cleo?"

"I forget."

"Travis, can I see you after class?"

He looked up, surprised, like *who, me?* Yes, you, idiot! "Uh, sure," he replied, as if he could not seem to figure out why.

This hideous girl named Joslyn raised her hand. I'm not just saying that because she wasn't cute, but because she just looks disgusting. I'd never seen a belly ring on a hairy gut like that in my life, and I'm sure it wouldn't have killed her to apply some lip balm. It's really a shame because I love the name Joslyn. "Isn't it possible that she was gay?"

"Uh… it's highly unlikely considering the time period," Claire replied.

"She just didn't like him!" I blurted out. "He was a pompous asshole, he would've ruined her anyway."

"Ruined her?" Claire repeated.

"Yeah, I mean, she's so self-reliant and everything, he couldn't handle that. He would've ruined her."

"So she should be lonely instead?" some other girl asked.

"That, or find some guy to serve her needs, one who wouldn't smother her."

"How very hypocritical," Travis chuckled from the back. "You think she should do to some man exactly what she won't let some man to do her."

"Thanks for putting words in my mouth, but that's not what I was saying."

I stood outside of the classroom, waiting for Claire to finish making idle threats. Although it was ridiculous for Travis to be late to every class thus far, she was too cool to fail him straight away. I would've failed him, absolutely. He almost walked by me, but I grabbed his arm. I surprised myself more than I did him, as I didn't expect to like the way his arm felt as much as I did. His arm was slender, but muscular, and my hand had slipped just under his sleeve, so I could feel his warm, smooth skin and delicate, little hairs on it.

I snapped myself back to the moment, but realized I had no idea what to say. I stammered, then pressed my lips together to gain control. "I think you misunderstood me."

"I think I didn't. It was hypocritical, that's fine. Realize it was an asshole statement and call yourself on it."

"Excuse me?! You think you can talk to me like that?"

He laughed as Claire came out of the classroom. She waved to us and disappeared into the stairwell. "I'm kidding! I see where you're coming from, but that doesn't make it right. And that's okay, you don't have to be right *all* of the time. But I'll tell you what: you definitely got it right when you chose that skirt this morning." He licked his lips.

Incredibly, I was so shocked and embarrassed that I just walked away. Minutes later, after replaying the situation over and over in my mind, I was flooded with things I could've—should've—said to him.

I went into the bathroom, needlessly kicked a stall door open, peed, and then washed my hands. Studying myself in the mirror, I had to agree with Travis. Not to disregard the fact that he was being a pig, it was also a fact that I looked damn good. I put half of my hair into a ponytail and let the back half hang loose, then pushed my boobs together more before walking out. The girl at the sink next to me kind of sneered at me, then snickered. I did the same to her, skinny bitch. I hate when girls think they're the shit because they have no ass. I just don't get it.

Listen, I'm really not trying to be conceited, but I know for a fact that I'm highly appreciated physically by men. The reason I feel it's necessary to point this out is because I am very obviously not a size two, so one may not see me and immediately realize the attention I can draw. I'm not even a four or a six. By no means am I skinny, but by no means am I blob either, just so we're clear. While so many girls seem to beat themselves up for not looking like sickly, stick-thin supermodels, I embrace my thick thighs and large breasts like the blessings that they are. I'm not afraid to show myself off. I've realized that the sooner I learned to love myself, the sooner I realized how much I'm loved. Mainly by men. And when I say men, I'm more-so talking about Black men. So I guess it does work out in my favor that I happen to be a Black girl, with a body that attracts the kind of men that I'm attracted to, a body that a lot of women wouldn't have a clue what to do with, and would waste their lives away trying to diminish.

I have often considered why Black men seem to be so appreciative of more curvaceous women. Ask any man: confidence is sexy. How many times have you seen a plus-sized Black woman in something that was probably not made for her—let's say, a leopard print pantsuit for example—but she works it out, and you can't tell her *nothing*. Yes, it may be a hot mess, but don't lie, you wish you were that bold.

In the mainstream, skinniness is next to godliness, so when women aren't given the chance to feel beautiful at *whatever* size within their community, that lack of confidence and void of self-love exudes from their beings. And nobody wants to be around all that do-I-look-fat-in-this bullshit. I know all white people aren't this obsessive about stick figures, and this is not to say that many Black women aren't body conscious, too—a minority community can't help but to be influenced by the mainstream culture—but a stick-thin Black girl who really wants to be that skinny is rare. Our men want at least a little something to hold on to, some hips or ass, thighs or *something*. (This is also not to say that men of other races are completely unappreciative, but I can count on three fingers the number of white men that have hit on me in person. The Internet is a whole different story—not that I would go that way in either case.)

It's a self-feeding cycle of self-confidence influencing the preferences of men and the preferences of those men influencing the self-confidence of the women. I wrote a great blog about it all once, which wasn't nearly as well accepted and praised as I thought it would be, but I'm well aware that most people aren't on my level intellectually. Most of the readers usually only care to read about sex and stuff like that.

I called Derek immediately after work. I waited outside the supermarket after everyone else left, swatting gnats and other flying critters away from my head. I couldn't stop thinking about Travis and all the bitchy things I wanted to say to him. I didn't even see Derek speeding through the empty parking lot in his duo-tone '94 Civic. He stopped right before me and leaned across the seat to unlock the passenger-side door.

"You weren't waiting alone for too long, were you?" he asked, looking at me through his glasses, which reflected the windows of the supermarket behind me.

"No. You got here fast."

"Well, a girl was raped two nights ago down the street. Raped and killed."

"Wow. No one told me, and I walked home from work every night."

"They found the guy, but still... I was worried about you."

"Please with that, Derek."

He pressed his lips together and stared at the road ahead. Sometimes he gets too emotional, pretending there's something between us that there really isn't. He reminds me of a turtle, his personality. Like a turtle who wants to be a stallion, which is not possible. Physically, he's more like a mountain lion, but his gorgeous physique doesn't give him personality points, especially with only a so-so face. None of that is helped by the fact that he's actually too close for comfort, that is, unless no one finds out about us. He's a family friend, and I know there would be so much pressure if they got involved.

Derek unlocked the door to his apartment and I went straight to his bedroom. I stripped from my work clothes, down to my bra and panties. Derek came in, turned off the light, and got into bed with me. I let him kiss me on the lips, then all the way down. I played with his ears and rubbed his head until I was no more. He came up to lie beside me, and I just then realized that he hadn't even taken my panties off, just pushed them aside. I laughed to myself.

"What?" he asked, kissing my shoulder.

"Remember the first time, when you were so nervous because you had no idea what to do? Now you're a pro. I mean really good. I mean like *damn* that was good. I thought my panties were off!"

"I know your body like the inside of my own mouth by now."

Scary.

"Hungry?"

"That isn't some double entendre, is it? Because I really am starving."

"No. I bought pizza earlier."

"Sure, I'll have some."

He left for the kitchen as I sat in his bed, staring at his white walls. I listened to him open the fridge, close it, take out a plate, put some pizza on it, place it in the microwave… He stood in the doorway. "How hot do you want it?"

I had to fight my lip from curling up in disgust. Couldn't he just do something without asking me first? "Warm."

"But not hot?"

"Forty-nine point seven seconds should do it."

He rolled his eyes and returned to the kitchen. Sometimes I feel bad, because he's so nice, but sometimes he's too nice, and that's just annoying. It's a lose-lose situation: he'll be too nice and I'll be repeatedly annoyed until I explode, or I can tell him when he's getting on my nerves and he'll have his feelings hurt for a couple of seconds. So I consider being a bitch the lesser of two evils, next to exploding.

Derek placed a tray of Hawaiian pizza and cream soda in front of me on the bed. He leaned against the headboard and began reading some car magazine.

"Since when do you eat Hawaiian? Or drink cream soda? Or read car magazines?"

"Well I know you like that stuff. The car magazine… I got a job at this garage, keeping books and stuff."

"So you have like three jobs now?"

"Four."

Four jobs. Taped glasses. Tiny apartment. Old ass car. Ordinary, cheap clothes. I wondered what he did with all the money, but I didn't ask. Honestly, I didn't feel like hearing his voice anymore. I munched contentedly on my pizza, which he'd heated up to a perfect temperature with my instruction. I carried the tray back into the kitchen and washed my dishes. I left the tray on the counter. Derek was still reading. I straddled his legs and he put the magazine down straight away. He still was fully dressed while I was in my underwear. That happened a lot, me making myself extra comfortable while he remained fully clothed in his own home.

"You're too gorgeous," he said, running his hands over my shoulders and down my back. I took his glasses from his face and put them on the two stacked milk crates that served as his nightstand. Already I felt like I was doing too much, so I dismounted him and lay on my back. His skin was shining like a new penny, dewy with sweat as he loomed over me, rocking back and forth, trying to lock eyes with me, but I wasn't having that. I kept closing my eyes or glancing away or looking down between our bodies. My bra dug into my armpit; it hurt, but I kind of liked it. I wanted the light off. It was kind of cute the way he stuck his tongue out the side of his mouth as he concentrated.

After lying there for a minute, he got up to get me a warm, wet washcloth from the bathroom. I thanked him, wiped off, and handed it back to him. He was back in bed before I even found my panties and put them back on. I took off my bra and then pulled on the Philadelphia Eagles t-shirt he'd laid out for me. It had to be ancient because it was the bright, grassy green they used to rock back in the day, not the sophisticated, jewel-tone green they wear nowadays.

"Cleo," Derek sighed.

I didn't respond. I laid my head on the pillow and tried to get comfortable.

He turned the light off. "Don't you ever think about us?"

"About what?"

"Us."

"But *what*? Stop being vague."

"That I love you, and if you love me, too."

"Derek, please. You always have to do this."

"Well, honestly, Cleo, why shouldn't I do this? Look at us! Look how good I am to you. I should at the very least be able to ask."

"You know it would never work."

"Why not?"

Because you're annoying, you know nothing about current events because the news is too upsetting for you, you don't read any serious books, you're annoying, you're too sensitive, you talk about dumb stuff, you're annoying…

"Are you scared?"

"Derek, please! What would I be scared of? You're really getting on my nerves. You make me not even want to come see you."

"Ha. Come see me?"

I know, I know, I said it like it was some kind of an honor to have me over. Honestly, as ridiculous as I knew it was, I knew that he really did feel that way.

"Derek, let's not ruin tonight. I enjoyed your company and now I just want to sleep." He didn't say another word, but for some reason, I still couldn't get to sleep and that really pissed me off. I started to regret ever calling him. I was really wishing I was in my own bed, but I wasn't about to walk so I made the best of the situation. "Are you asleep?"

"No."

"Good. Neither am I. Wanna go again?"

"Cleo, this is crazy."

"I'm not trying to have a deep discussion right now, I just want to have sex. Can you handle that?"

He could.

I got up before eight the next morning and tried to sneak out. Derek caught me just as I was slipping out of the bedroom door. I went back inside and sat on the edge of the bed. "Can you hurry? I have to get home. I really could just take the bus."

"Don't be silly. I really wanted to make you breakfast, but hey."

"I'm not hungry anyway."

"You might have been by the time I cooked it."

"No."

En route to my house, Derek pulled into the parking lot of a diner. I wanted to glare at him, but I couldn't stand to look at him. Begrudgingly, I got out of the car and followed him inside. We claimed a booth next to a window and sat across from each other.

"I thought—no, I *know*—I told you I have to get home."

"You're lying."

I was lying, but he didn't know that. How could he? "How can you possibly know that?"

"I know you so well. You're going to love the pancakes here, trust me."

"How I can enjoy anything is beyond me. I told you have to get home."

"You will! Calm down, my God." He reached across the table for my hands. "Cleo, can we just do what I want for once? And all I want is for you to taste the best pancakes you've ever had in your life."

"Have it your way? Does this look like Burger King to you?"

I hated to admit it to myself, so you know I didn't dare tell him that those pancakes were indescribably delicious. They were like butter in the form of cake, with amazing warm syrup, they were orgasmic, like my taste buds had climaxed.

"How was it?" Derek asked on the way to the car.

"Okay." I was lying. They were not okay. They were extraordinary. I wished it hadn't ended so soon. It was like a little piece of heaven, eating those pancakes. But I couldn't tell him that. I licked my lips during the entire ride home, savoring every little taste of butter that was left on them.

My house was empty. I looked at the calendar that hung in the kitchen to find that Lele had a pageant to compete in at that time. That meant that my mother and sister were together, probably dogging me out as they so often do when they get together. They only talk about me or Lele, which clearly says that they both need to get their own lives. It's pathetic, and these are the women I have to look up to. It's a wonder I'm turning out to be so stable.

I took a shower, then lay across my bed in my robe to update my website on my laptop. There was plenty of mail from people (men and women alike) who just wanted to tell me how sexy I am. Those types usually get no reply, unless they say something extra, like "you have the most gorgeous eyes/beautiful lips/cutest nose I've ever seen." Since those people took some time, I, too, take some time. A few critiques on my poetry and replies to my blogs. Then one message with a subject line reading: "oh my god…" I clicked on it to read the body, which stated "YOUR SO FAT." I burst out laughing. The idea that someone thought it was worth their time to tell me I'm fat, probably with the intention of hurting my feelings, was nothing short of hilarious. Say what you will, but I couldn't help but to reply, letting him know the immediate response and thought I'd had about the situation. I thanked him for the good laugh and for reminding me of what ignorant people there are in the world.

A few days later, he replied, "your welcome, fat ass."

Ignorant indeed. He used "your" instead of "you're" two times in a row. I didn't feel that he deserved the enlightenment of my correction, so I left it at that.

I uploaded the pictures I took a couple days earlier, the tasteful nudes with the heels and pearls. They looked better in black and white, classier. Grayscale is in no way pornographic, or at least I could use that with my mother if she happened to lay her eyes on them. Although the content of my website hasn't come up recently, I'm sure it will eventually, as her hatred for it ebbs and flows. I don't see what the big deal is, but I'm clearly not my mother, and thank God for that. To be honest, I think it's close-minded and hypocritical that I should be condemned for taking some pictures while it's just fine for my sister to have had a baby two days after her high school graduation. I guess it's a sin for a woman to embrace any sense of her sexuality unless it's tied directly to procreation? Or do you think it could possibly be because she followed directly in my mother's footsteps? Yes, both of them were pregnant in their senior pictures, and can you believe they bond over shit like that?

Not me. No, not me. I'm determined to achieve something greater than pushing out a child.

Don't get me wrong, motherhood is great; it keeps the world going and all that stuff. I understand that people love their kids; my heart is not made of ice. It's just that too many women lose themselves when they have kids. I'm sorry, but I like myself too much to get wrapped up in all of that.

I sat in front of my mirror and looked at myself. I decided that maybe Deena was right and I should get some make-up. My pictures were becoming a little repetitive, and I could start a new thing, with the headshots and stuff, trying out different looks and what-not. I flipped through the Bloom brochure, folding down pages every now and again, until I heard commotion downstairs. I pulled on a t-shirt and shorts and ran down there.

Leslie was in her gown and sash, crying on the couch. Mom and Deena were in the kitchen, trying to argue quietly for Leslie's sake. There was a small tiara in the fruit bowl on the kitchen table.

"What's up?" I asked.

They both glared at me, then ignored me.

"Give her a break," Mom said to Deena. "The child is tired."

"I'm tired!" Deena shouted, then checked herself. "We've been training so hard, how can she not get it?" she whispered.

"She's over-tired, she can't perform like that."

"What do you suggest, Mom? Less pageants?"

"Duh."

"Not gonna happen. I bust my ass to raise money for her outfits and gowns and all this other shit. These judges are gonna see her and know her, and she is gonna win. Either you're with us or you're against us."

I tried to stifle my snickering, but it was no use. I doubled over as I let out a hearty "ha."

"This isn't funny," Mom said, shielding her smile from Dee. "Honey, you know I'm not against you, but I don't want my granddaughter run into the ground. You know how you used to do in school, study so long you couldn't sleep, then do bad on a test. You know a healthy amount of rest can make things so much better."

"A 'C' isn't bad."

"Oh, now a 'C' isn't bad? You thought it was at the time. I guess now that you're not the center of your own attention, it's not a big deal?"

"That was until she met Charlie. Just throw a man in the equation to throw her off her game. You know she can't resist."

Deena kicked a chair at me, so hard that it lifted off the ground and toppled over sideways at my feet. Then she immediately pushed me aside to get through the doorway, stumbling over the chair, and joined Lele on the couch.

"What happened?" I asked Mom.

"She got ninth place. Out of twenty-five."

There was a knock on the door, which I went to answer. It was Leroy, Deena's father. He took his white hat off of his bald head and stroked his graying mustache. Imagine if someone taped a piece of silver duct tape on an over-sized Milk Dud."Deena here?"

"Yes."

My mom shoved me aside and held the door open to let him in. "Leroy, hello."

He came in wearing white slacks, blue suede shoes, and a baby blue jersey knit tank top, like he was trying way too hard. It looked like the kind of thing a woman my mother's age might find attractive and hip, which she obviously did. He gave hugs to his daughter and granddaughter, then told them and my mom that they all looked lovely. I must have become invisible by then. Through her sniffling and snotting, Leslie told him about the pageant, with some interjections by my mom and Deena. Then Leslie just leaned into him, sniffling and still and sucking her thumb.

Deena snatched her hand out of her mouth. "You want buck teeth? Huh?"

"So, Leroy." My mom combed her fingers through her hair. "How have you been? Busy? You haven't stopped over in a while."

"Well, I… only come to see my girls, and I haven't seen their car around lately."

Shot down.

"So, Lil' Mama, what do you want to eat? Anything, anywhere." Leroy whisked my sister and niece out the door. I heard his rusty Caprice rattle and roll away.

"Mom, do me a favor."

She looked at me with a blank expression.

"Never appear so desperate ever again." I felt bad for saying that as soon as the first word left my mouth, so I ran up to my room before I could see her reaction.

Placing each can of corn on the shelf one at a time, I couldn't help but think about what a waste of myself this job was. I know for sure that I was smarter than most of my superiors, but I was on the same level as some of the slowest people I'd ever met in my life. It frustrated me. Then to see Janine up at the register, smiling and rubbing her belly while I did hard labor… it was infuriating. I threw a can to the back of the shelf just to satisfy myself with the sound of the two metals crashing against each other

"Having fun?"

I looked up. And up, and up. And I smiled, because before me stood one of the most handsome men I'd ever seen in person, or at least for quite some time. His skin was smooth and brown, looking like it would taste just like a Hershey bar if I licked it. His eyes, his gorgeous gray eyes, sparkled under the florescent light. But those eyes, those gorgeous gray eyes, they dimmed in comparison to his smile. I stood straight, trying to look as attractive as possible.

"Can I help you?"

"Yeah, honey."

Was that "yeah (pause) honey" like he's looking for honey or "yeah, honey" like he's looking for me and he likes what he sees and think I'm sweet and wants to take me—

"Where is it?" He smiled.

"Where? What?" I melted.

"I got it." Up walked this blue-eyed, flat-chested, flat-assed hussy, wearing disgustingly tiny jeans shorts and dangerously high heels, pushing a cart of one jar of honey, wearing about two pounds of make-up, and with her tracks showing through her stringy, streaked, brassy hair.

Are you kidding me?!

They both looked at me. Did I say something? I turned away and began stocking the corn shelf like a madwoman, boiling under my yellow polo. I envisioned myself hurling a can after them and knocking her out, then hitting him in the head as well, but only to knock some sense into him. Then we could stand over her unconscious body so I could point out why what he was doing was so wrong.

Let me tell you something to explain my feelings, which may at the moment seem outrageous: I am damn sure *not* the mule of the earth.

When I say that, I speak for *all* Black women, who have been treated that way throughout history, doing the dirtiest jobs that no one else wants to, and being treated like we deserve nothing more. Taking care of white ladies houses and babies so they can sit and be "pretty." Getting raped by "massa" in the middle of the night only to be ignored or abused by him during the day. Constantly bombarded with opinions that have been revered as fact for far too long that the definition of beauty is pale skin, blue eyes, and silky, straight hair, which can only leave my brown skin, dark eyes, and kinky, black hair (or *Black* hair) to be anti-beauty. I watched a whole lot of television and movies as a child, and that really fucked up my perception. For the longest time I thought I just didn't fit the definition of a pretty girl and that I would have to go through the rest of my life being the undesirable one. Well fuck that, because I know now, beyond a shadow of a doubt, what I am: I'm no one's mule and I *am* beautiful.

I'm not, as it may seem, strongly against interracial relationships. I'm an open-minded individual, and I'm well aware that love sees no color, blah, blah, blah. My issue is why an ugly ass white girl would be chosen over a cute Black girl by some Black men for the mere fact that she's white. It seems that if one were to create a scale displaying levels of attractiveness from least to greatest by that school of thought, it would go: *unfortunate-looking Black girl, so-so Black girl, pretty Black girl, gorgeous Black girl, finer-than-any-woman-you've-ever-seen Black girl*, and next level up would be *ugly ass white girl*, and so on. Like whiteness trumps all.

You know the term "pass for white"? I hate that shit! Pass? What the fuck is that about? So if being white—or at least being perceived that way in society—is passing, that means what? Being Black is what? Failing? At life? At being members of society? Being beautiful? Again, fuck that.

So, Black men, unless she's some incredibly gorgeous, top-notch, bomb ass white girl, keep it out of my face. And don't even come at me with that "personality" speech, because I'm really not tryna hear that shit. You and I both know what it's really all about, so let's just leave it at that.

I saw Janine coming and stuck my head deep into the shelf. Unable to take a hint, she placed her hand on my back and started talking. I wanted to crawl completely onto the shelf and lay in the back with a wall of canned veggies to hide and protect me.

Janine ignored the fact that I was hiding from her and began yapping away. "Anyway, did you see that girl in the coochie cutters? My God! Her nasty ass was like hanging out the bottom. I wanted to vomit. Her shirt was cute though."

It was not cute. It was a red mesh halter-top with a metallic-looking heart pattern thing going on.

"I know, I want it. I want her boyfriend, too."

"You think that's her boyfriend?" I asked doubtfully, trying to fish out some reassurance that they weren't a couple. Especially after I'd embarrassed myself by acting like a bumbling idiot.

"Yeah. Or her pimp, but that would be really out of character for a pimp and ho to go grocery shopping together. Well, they only bought honey, and you never know what that was for, but for your own reference, honey is a mess in the bedroom. Or the couch, or the tub, or the back seat. You know!" she laughed, slapping my hand. I didn't know, I still don't. Clearly, Janine did. "Let me get out of here. I promised my mom I'd cook dinner."

I looked at my watch and decided to go for my break a couple minutes early. I walked outside with Janine, where Junior was waiting for her in their busted Ford Escort. The raggedy metal parts were rattling loudly from the bass of the radio. The back window, taped into place, was shaking violently, threatening to crash into the back seat of the car. However unlikely, I hoped to God that they would get a new car before the baby came. It would practically be a crime to put anyone in that back seat, let alone an infant. Janine blew me a kiss before they drove off, like she always used to do in high school when Junior would so kindly give me a ride home.

Sitting on the bench outside of the employee entrance, I made a call to a friend.

"Wuddup? This is J. Cru. Leave one and I'll holla. Peace." I didn't leave one. A half a minute later I received a text message.

WUT UP MA

I wrote back: *nothing much, just thinking about you. Are you busy?*

IN THE STUDIO MA

When will you be done? I get off of work in 2 hrs.

LEMME CUM SCOOP U UP THEN

That's fine. I'll see you then.

I sat wondering if I really wanted to see him. I shouldn't have called. Then again, what could it hurt? I was only going to go sit in my room on the computer or something if I didn't chill with him. At least I would be socializing.

J. Cru was born Jason Cruson. J. Cru is his rap name. He thought it was an ironic play on the preppy apparel label, you know, because he's so hardcore and all. I thought it was stupid. He would flip out if I ever called him Jason, but there was no way I was going to call him J. Cru, so I usually didn't call him anything. Even his mother called him J. Cru, which I thought was silly. I also thought it was silly that he took himself so seriously and still lived in his mother's condo. Luckily for him, she was away a lot and he could pretend like he owned the place. He tried to play like he owned it the first time he ever invited me over, but I could tell by the décor that it was his mom's. To top it off, she was watching TV while wearing her bathrobe in the living room the next morning. I didn't care about the lying—I actually thought the situation was funny. I was only there for one thing, so who owned the place didn't matter to me.

Jason had me waiting outside for nearly half an hour. I could've walked home within that time. His blacked-out Expedition came barreling through the parking lot like a giant panther or something. No, a panther is too graceful. That beast of an SUV would have to be a grizzly bear. I climbed up into the passenger seat, where he immediately took the back of my head in his hand and gave me a great, wet kiss on the mouth, then went to town on my neck, which he knew was the key. Just as my eyes were beginning to roll back, he stopped kissing me and stomped on the gas. I was tingling with anticipation. I forgot that he was late.

It was torture, riding all the way to his apartment. I just wanted to be there already, naked, being worshipped. I was craving it. There was no room for conversation over the roar of his sound system, which was blasting a J. Cru original. I was surprised when I found myself nodding my head to it. I looked over at him, wondering why he had sunglasses on. It was almost eleven o'clock at night. His left arm, which stuck straight out to the steering wheel, was covered in tattoos, as was his right arm, which sat on the arm rest, capped off by a massive watch, encrusted in what looked like diamonds. He caught me looking and smiled, exposing his diamondy grill. I say "diamondy" because I have no clue how to tell a real diamond from a fake one. On the account of his big ass, tricked out truck, I'd say his jewelry was real, including those big ass diamond earrings and the chain. Considering he lived with his mother, I would say that none of it was nearly as expensive as he would have people believe. So I was on the fence.

When I got out of the car he took me by the hand. Very quickly he led me upstairs, inside, through the living room, and into his bedroom. He closed the door and took his shirt off, but left his chain and glasses on. He looked like he was ready for a photo shoot. I was down for that, but I already knew there was no camera available.

"You want a drink?"

"Sure."

He left and returned shortly with a bottle of Hennessey and two tumblers. He poured some for both of us and then started making a playlist on his iPod. I took a sip of my drink and nearly died. I didn't know it was like *that*. Damn! I turned away from him so as not to embarrass myself. I tried to allow myself a small cough of relief without becoming a hacking mess. I snuck a look at him with my watery eyes, relieved to see that he was too busy to pay me any attention. Then I got up and practically ran to the bathroom, where I allowed myself to turn into a coughing fool, gagging and gasping for air. I cupped my hands under the running faucet and slurped cool water from them. I took a seat on the toilet to pee and recuperate.

I cleaned up my eyes with a wet paper towel and took my pants off. There was some lip-gloss in my pocket, so I smeared that on my mouth. I took my hair out of its bun and shook it free, letting the curls become loose and wild and—I hoped—sexy. I'd already taken my polo off after work, so I returned to his bedroom like that, hoping that he would think my sudden disappearance was deliberate, if he even cared.

Jason watched with a smile as I headed toward his bed, toward him. He guided me to stand in front of him while he looked me up and down hungrily, running his hands over all of my body. "I love these," he said, hooking his thumbs into the waistband of my boy shorts.

"Good. Now take them off."

There was no conversation when we were done, no I-love-you bullshit; we both just went to sleep.

Claire handed back our latest homework assignments, edited with green pen because it's the exact opposite of red. She was good for things like that. I flipped through, seeing more green than I liked.

"So, I guess that ends our discussion for today. You know the homework. If anyone wants to come talk to me about anything, feel free."

I definitely took her up on that. I packed my things very slowly, making sure to let everyone else out of the room before I approached the desk she was sitting at. It wasn't a teacher's desk; this room had no teacher's desk. It was a student desk/chair combo, which she pulled out of the rows and columns formation that the rest of us sat in and turned it so that she would face the class while she sat there.

"Hey, Cleo. What's up?" She took off her glasses and put them in her curly, red hair. They almost got lost.

"You keep 'correcting' the word *Black*." I actually used air quotes there.

"Yeah... you keep capitalizing it."

"It's a preference," I said.

"Hmm. Well, I'm not sure if it's correct."

"It's my identity. I don't know where I'm from; it's practically my nationality! If it's who I am, I think it's deserving of some capitalization. My ancestors were brought here in chains so I know nothing of the culture they left behind. I could've been a queen for all we know!"

She looked a little frightened about my tangent, like I was about to start preaching some Black Power stuff.

"Listen, I'm not going off about the Man keeping me down. I'm not mad at white people. I personally don't know anyone who owned slaves, so I have no grudges. But, like… where is your family from?"

"My mom is German and my dad is Irish," she answered.

"Yeah? That's good. See, I don't know that kind of stuff. Yes, I'm of African descent, but Africa is just so big and diverse. Who isn't African if you look back far enough? And what do I know about *Africa*? Probably less than you do. So while you get to claim *two different* European countries, I'm going to keep capitalizing Black, since that's what I identify with most."

Now she was leaning forward on her desk. "That's fascinating, Cleo. Really deep."

"You think so?"

"Yes, absolutely. I never thought of it like that. Well, I've never had to. It's definitely food for though. Okay, you have my blessing to continue with your capitalization."

I almost thanked her, but it didn't feel right. "Okay," I said.

"Your order is in!" my sister sang, poking her head into my bedroom. I peeked over the edge of the comforter. There were several hours to go until it was noon, and I had been looking forward to sleeping in until at least one on my day off. "Come on! I want to show you."

"Okay, Deena!" I screamed. "Get out!"

"Eew, bitch." She closed the door.

Try as I might, there was no chance of me getting anymore sleep. I dragged myself to the bathroom for a shower, threw some raggedy clothes on, and headed downstairs. Mom and Deena were bagging Bloom orders at the kitchen table. Lele was dancing and watching music videos in the living room. I fixed myself some cereal and joined Lele in the living room.

"You like this song?"

"Yes," she said, still dancing. "I love it, in fact."

"Okay! Please! Please, Lele. Would you mind putting something else on?"

She poked out her lip but obliged.

A couple minutes later, Deena called me into the kitchen. She ushered me into a seat, smiling broadly. The table was covered with white paper bags filled with orders yet to be delivered, except for a small corner, reserved for a few things she'd ordered for me. I was nervous.

"What exactly are you going to do?" I asked cautiously.

"Relax," Mom said.

"For real," Deena added, putting her hand on her hip. "You think I don't know what I'm doing? I'm an effin' pageant mom!"

"That's what terrifies me," I pointed out, getting up from my seat.

Deena put her hands on my shoulders and pushed me back down. "Look at this color palette; it's pretty natural."

"Pretty natural? Is there really such a thing? Either it's natural or it isn't."

"Will you shut up and cooperate for once? The most daring thing we have here is gold, and that's practically a neutral."

"Since when?"

"Ugh, Cleo! With a name like that, I'd think you were *born* wearing eyeliner! Can I please just do what I do and help you realize your full potential?" Now you know I had to really restrain myself from laying it on her for that hypocritical little remark, and I was glad that I did.

The sensations of having make-up applied felt strange to me, paying so much attention to such small details as eyelashes, which I'd never given much thought to. Well, I thought they were small details, but I was wrong. The eyebrow waxing and plucking was worse than expected, but well worth it. When I looked in the mirror, I was stunned. My eyes were beautiful, lined with black and a hint of gold, which was practically a neutral but made my eyes pop gorgeously, like constant but subtle fireworks on my face. My lips were so glossy they practically looked as if they would ripple like a pond if touched.

"Are you done admiring yourself?" Deena asked. "My arm is about to fall off."

I took the mirror from her hand and held it closer to my face.

"I guess you did good," Mom said to Dee.

"So you like it?"

"Yes," I replied, with a hint of *duh* in my voice. "I kind of love it."

"Aw!" Dee put her hand to her chest. "I love you!" She wrapped her arms around me and I quickly turned my head so as not to mess up my gorgeous, new face.

As soon as their attention was focused on something else, I snuck away to my bedroom and locked the door. I set up my tripod and camera, then tacked a white sheet onto my blue wall perpendicular to the window where all of the afternoon light was streaming in. I pulled the blinds all the way up to remove any shade or filtering of the light. I took my t-shirt off and pulled my bra straps down; the pictures were only going to be from the shoulder up and I didn't want anything distracting from that face.

Perfecting my make-up practically made me late for class; I arrived only five minutes early. Much to my surprise, Travis was sitting in the seat right next to mine. Technically that was okay because nobody ever sat there, but it made my stomach turn. Then I remembered how good I looked and stood a little taller as I walked his way.

"I'm sorry about the stuff I said before that may or may not have offended you."

"Not," I replied without looking at him.

"Is it chilly in here or what?"

I rolled my eyes and looked his way. "Apology accepted." I finished with a big, cheesy grin.

After taking role, Claire announced that we would be doing joint presentations instead of taking a final exam. I was the only one who didn't seem pleased with that decision. I hated to put my grade in the hands of others, especially knowing I was smarter and could write a better paper than anyone there. I was especially pissed when she paired me with Travis. He followed me out of the room after class. He was really nice, even though I was trying so hard not to give him that window of hope.

"Have you ever read the story she assigned us?"

"Nope."

"Me neither. She says it's very interesting though and we should have fun with it."

"I'll bet."

"You look very pretty today."

I stammered my footsteps and kept going, hoping he hadn't noticed.

"Did you do something different with your hair?"

"Straightened it."

"I can tell. It's gorgeous. And your eyes are beautiful; they're like *bam*. I don't want to sound like a perv, so I won't tell you how sexy your lips are."

I couldn't help but smile, but I covered it with my hand. We stopped at the exit.

"I want to apologize again," he said, gently taking my wrist and moving my hand from my face. "I was a jerk."

"I'm over it."

"Good. So you won't turn me down when I invite you to my place? To work on the project, of course."

"Oh! That…"

"I live with my parents, very non-threatening environment…"

"Oh, it's not a problem. I carry pepper spray."

He laughed silently with a smile and squeezed my hand before turning to leave. A couple strides later, he turned and said, "By the way, I'm glad we're partners because I love your writing!" as he continued walking, but backwards.

I pushed through the exit doors with urgency to get as far from him as possible. Was he serious? If he was serious, that was sweet, but if he was kidding... I put a lot of myself into my writing, and for him to mock me would give me license to kill.

I took a bus to Red Lobster after my last class. The bus was empty except for me and this white man who looked about thirty years old, too old to be flipping through the Yu-Gi-Oh cards he was holding. He kept looking over at me, and it was beginning to really get on my nerves. Very dramatically, I snatched my bag from the seat beside me and held it close to my chest, you know, to add some balance to the universe. I thought it was a nice counteraction to all the white ladies around the world clutching their purses extra tight at the sight of a perfectly innocent Black man in baggy pants. I laughed inside.

My mom was sitting in the waiting area alone, watching the lobster in their tank. She stood when she saw me and we followed the hostess back to our table.

"How was class?"

"Okay, but the teacher wants us to do presentations instead of taking a final exam. Group presentations at that. I'd rather sit down, take a test, and be done with it."

"Me, too. Do you know what you want?"

"Shrimp alfredo."

"That sounds good. I don't know what I want though. I do know I want cheesecake for dessert." She took her glasses out, put them on, and started looking the menu over again. "You'll never guess who called me today."

"Deena?" I figured that was a good guess, at it was almost impossible that she hadn't.

She looked up at me. "Well, yes, but that's not who I meant." She tucked her glasses in the breast pocket of her pink scrubs. "Give up?"

"Of course."

"Larry."

I stared blankly.

"Your dad." She waited for an answer that I didn't have. "That's big news, Cleo! I haven't spoken to him in a year. You haven't seen him in..."

"Nine years." I shoved half a cheddar bay biscuit in my mouth and gulped down some water. "Did he ask for me?"

She nodded. "I told him how well you're doing, how grown up and responsible you are."

"Not *about* me, *for* me."

"Oh, then no, he didn't ask for you."

"Not surprised. What did he want anyway? Why are you telling me this?"

"Crazy as this sounds, he wanted to stay at the house."

"I hope you told him he must be out of his fucking mind and hell no he can't stay in our house."

"Watch your mouth, Cleo. First of all, you shouldn't be using that language. Especially not in front of your mother. Have some respect. And we're in a restaurant."

I shook my head, narrowing my eyes at her. "You told him you'd think about it, didn't you?"

"And if I did?"

"You did."

"Well, then you'll have two people to avoid, so you'll need to sleep around twice as much. Are you gonna sleep out every single night of the week instead of every *other* night, just to keep out of the house?"

My jaw dropped. "You're so weak. You're so weak that you'd let *him* come back? Are we talking about the same man? The one who I met twice in my life and has never offered you a dime to help raise me? The one who stole all my birthday money the last time you told him he could stay with us? Not only my birthday money *on my tenth birthday*, but also the TV and car in the middle of the night."

"The cops found the car. Anyway, he's been in rehab."

"He's—HA! Oh my God. God! Excuse me, Julie!" I said to the waitress. "Can I get that shrimp alfredo to go, and get a separate check please?" I looked at my mom and shook my head. "Please don't do this to me. You clearly don't care about your own self, because that should've been the first thing to immediately make you tell him to get the hell outta here. Considering that, *please* spare *me*."

"People change, Cleo. He's your father. You don't even think your father deserves another chance?"

"Will you stop calling him that?"

"Well, he is and there's no changing that."

"I couldn't give less of a flying fuck about that asshole."

"Selfish and dramatic. Is that really all you have to offer? Have you no compassion? Not even for your own father?"

"What father?" I put my money in the little folder with the bill, picked up my Styrofoam box, and left. I stood at the bus stop with my iPod on and pretended that I didn't see my mom when she pulled over to the side of the road. I took the bus to the subway and rode that to Derek's. There was no answer when I knocked on his door so I called his cell phone. He told me that he was on his way and would be there in about twenty minutes. He was there in ten. As soon as he got out of the car, I wrapped my arms around him and cried. I cried for a while. It wasn't until I went into the bathroom that I remembered my make-up and it looked horrible. I washed my face and joined Derek on the couch.

"Wanna talk to me about it?" he asked.

"No."

"What's in the box?"

"Shrimp alfredo."

"Want me to heat it up for you?"

"No. You can have it."

It looked good when he returned with a plate of it. He fed me a forkful and wiped me off with his napkin.

"On my tenth birthday—this is only the second time I'd ever met my dad, mind you—he took my birthday money, our TV, and our car in the middle of the night, and we never saw him again. What really gets me…" I breathed deeply to keep from crying. "…is that my mom *let* him. They thought I was sleep, but I could hear them. She let him! I still don't know what to say about that because it really kills me, so I play dumb with her. If she couldn't protect herself, then whatever, but why couldn't she protect me? She's so weak."

"Well, it's hard being alone. She may have had a less strong moment, but that doesn't mean she's a weak person. She had the strength to raise you and your sister on her own."

"My dad called today to ask if he could stay with us and she said she'd think about it. How's that for weak?"

"Well, she had the strength not to go and say 'yes.' She's lonely, Cleo, I understand how she feels."

That sparked something in me to head home immediately. If loneliness was the problem, I was doomed if I left her alone in the house. My father could call or, worse, stop by and never leave. "Can you drive me home?"

"I was looking forward to your company, but I guess it's for the best."

My mom was watching TV on the couch, still in her scrubs. "He's staying with his son's mom, so you rushed home for nothing."

I was at a loss for words. I didn't know she could read minds. Creepy. Derek hadn't pulled off yet, I could still—nah. "What are you talking about?"

"I could see it on your face." She turned the TV off and went upstairs. Her bedroom door slammed shut and that was the last I heard of her for the rest of the night.

I looked out the window to see that, of course, Derek was gone. I hated to think that he was right, that my mother was lonely. That never feels good. I even started feeling guilty about spending nights out. Get over it, I told myself. I can't go feeling bad for having a life just because she doesn't have one. Besides, there's absolutely no excuse for letting *him* stay here to any degree, even if it was just a maybe.

I knocked on her door. "Mom?" I didn't know what I was doing. I tried the knob, surprised that it was unlocked. Mom was sitting in her bed, wiping her eyes with a tissue. I wanted to run the hell out of there, but I didn't. Instead, I said, "I understand that you're lonely."

"Really? You? Miss Social Butterfly of the Night? Miss Internet Attention Whore? Miss–"

"Wow." That shocked me. But what was she going to say next? "Forget it, okay?"

"Okay."

"No, look: I'm lonely, too. My dad's a fuck-up, you're disgusted by me, my sister abandoned me for a boy, and my best friend did the same. So I'm sorry if I like the attention, but it's really because I'm lonely. So, yes, I *do* understand what it's like not to have anyone. Unlike some people, I'm just not willing to give up my self to fill the void."

"I'm sorry," she said. "I never imagined my life like this. I thought I'd have a great husband, a house in the suburbs. A great family where I could give my kids whatever they wanted and needed."

"What about yourself?"

"That is what I wanted for myself."

How lame. "Well, have fun trying to get that fantasy out of Larry."

"That's not what I was trying to do."

"Subconsciously. Look, Mom, that ideal is so passé. Women do things with their lives nowadays. Move on."

"To what? What do I possibly have to move on to?"

"This is not for me to figure out. I think I really just came up here to apologize for acting so uncouth in Red Lobster, then to make sure you were okay, which you are. So… see ya." I got out of there before the situation got any stickier.

That is exactly why I'm the polar opposite of my mother and sister, because that leech-like dependency on a man to make oneself happy is sickening. It's crushing, and will leave you in ruins if it seeps too deeply. I retreated to my bedroom and locked the door. I felt like she needed to be quarantined as she was just reeking of that idiotic, self-sabotaging, male-centric enslavement.

I went onto my website to read the wonderful things peo-ple had to say in order to boost myself up from the way my mother's mood was dragging me down. And my site visitors did have some wonderful things to say, unlike: "Dame, ma, can I holla?" Now you know that's a damn shame. I don't respond to things like that, random spouts of unnecessary slang that reveal no clear-cut intention, especially with such poor spelling, and not even with a cute face to distract me from his abominable English.

Not everyone is an idiot though. I do appreciate people who read my writing and respond thoughtfully, like Janine almost did to one of my poems.

This is my body || Cover it? Why?
Cuz you don't get the secret || And you look at me surprised
When I take the road less traveled
And declare how || I love my thighs?
So big, so much unlike || the standard model type.

No, my tummy isn't flat like hers || but has never let me down.
So just cuz I'm not skinny || I should denounce my crown?

I should tell myself I'm ugly? || Tell myself I'm not a queen?
Just because my body's bigger || it should all go unseen?

As for these breasts || which I used to resent
Well, I've come to let them be.
So if my cleavage bothers you... so what? || I've got to let them
breathe.

Janine's comment was: "Wow, that was deep. You are blessed be able to put words on paper like that. Normally I wouldn't understand how you feel, but since I got pregnant I know how you feel to be huge."

There was a note on the message board from Jason. It was just some copied and pasted junk advertising his own bootsie website. I deleted it, then went to bed.

Travis took the seat beside me in class again. He was forty minutes late. He ignored me the entire time, so I pretended that I didn't see him either. But, my God, did I see him. I couldn't stop stealing sideways glances at him, piecing together the details of his profile, his vanilla-wafer-cookie-colored skin, and those juicy lips he kept licking. His hair was kind of a weird color, a couple shades darker than the sand at the Jersey shore, and he kept it cut close to his head. His whole look, his color scheme, was very monochromatic and smooth, like banana pudding. I really wanted to look more closely at his eyes, which I'd caught a brief glimpse of at other times. I nearly forgot that he may have made a sarcastic remark about the writing I'd shared in class.

My heart started pounding as we reached the end of our time. I was starting to become angry with myself; I am not one to sweat a boy. Boys sweat me, I get what I want, and then I'm out. I pretended that I didn't hear him calling my name down the hallway. Being that he had at least eight inches on me, his stride was a good deal longer than mine and he caught up to me in no time.

"Can I interest you in a seat?" he asked.

"Oh, no thanks."

"Please? I'm out of breath from chasing you." He wasn't.

I took a seat in one of the many armchairs in the lobby. He took the seat beside me and I finally got a good look at his eyes… but not a good idea of what color they were. Kind of a very gray hazel with flecks of gold or something. I didn't want to stare so I had to keep looking away and back, but each time I looked back again, I felt this weird pang in my heart, then a floating feeling, like I was hit with a tennis racket so far into space that it just floated continuously away until I stole another glance, and it was hit again.

"Well…"

"Um… huh?"

"Saturday?"

"Saturday?"

"Do you want to come over to work on our presentation? At my house?"

"Oh." Where the hell had I been? "Uh, no. I have to work basically all day Saturday."

"What about Sunday?"

"I work Sunday morning, but I get off at twelve."

"How about I pick you up around three and you can stay for dinner?"

"Is that okay with your mom?"

"My dad's the cook. Technically, my mom's the cook—professionally—so my dad usually cooks at home."

Two parents. Wow. I couldn't remember the last time I went to a house with two parents.

"You don't know where I live," I said, throwing out any lame excuse.

He took out his phone. "So tell me."

"Why don't you just pick me up here, at school?"

"Cleo… I'm not gonna stalk you."

I knew that was right, especially after he saw where I lived. I won't say it was a complete shit-hole, but there were some blatant shit-holes in the surrounding area, and I could tell that he was used to something more. Anyway, I gave him the address, which he typed into his phone. I took a deep breath to give myself a jolt of confidence, to snap back to my regular self. "What did you mean when you said you 'like' my writing?" I asked, unable to stop the neck-rolling and head-weaving.

He laughed. "Why are you so defensive? I'll loosen you up."

"Excuse me?" I leaned away from him.

"I meant that you have some interesting points of view. And your poetry was mad deep. I'm not gonna sit here and front like you're right all the time, but it's interesting. It shows you have a brain and talent, and that's sexy, if you don't mind me saying so. That's what I meant when I said I 'like' it." Copying me, he used his fingers to make quotation marks.

I know I was blushing mad hard. "Thank you," I mumbled.

"Well, I'll see you Sunday at three. Peace." He jumped up, threw me a peace sign and a mean mug, and walked off.

My insides were doing flip-flops. I liked it in a way, but hated that I couldn't control it. I didn't give him permission to have that kind of effect on me. Yeah, and why did he have that effect on me? I took out my compact mirror to apply some lip-gloss, then looked at my reflection. "Shake it off, Cleo. Now."

There was a thud behind me that made me jump. I turned to see Paul with a box at his feet and his mouth hanging open. "Did you do this?"

"Yes," I replied.

"Can you read?"

"Excuse me?"

"Did you bother to look at the ad this week, Cleo? The *boxes* of canned goods are on sale, not the *individual* cans! Where are the packs of eight?"

"All I did was put out what was already loaded onto the flatbed, like you *told me to do*."

"Did you check what was on the flatbed?"

"Did you? Who loaded the thing anyway?"

"There's no use playing the blame game. Clear this end-cap."

"Can't you just change the sign to the right price?"

"Clear. The. End. Cap. Understood? If you can't handle this, tell me now."

Can't handle this? *You* can't handle it, you pompous bitch. I know you're the one who had the wrong stuff put on the flatbed, now you wanna blame *me* because I didn't check *your* work? Or the work that you delegated? Sorry, asshole, that's not my job. I know, it's weird, isn't it? You probably barely got out of high school, yet I'm stuck working for your dumb ass. Just wait until I get my degree and educate myself right out of this hellhole. I'm gonna come back here with a slew of someone else's bad ass kids and be the most difficult customer you've ever had the displeasure of aiming to please.

I knew I was wasting energy slamming the cans around the way that I was, but I was too pissed off to be any less dramatic. Halfway through undoing what I'd already done, this kid named Roy brought another flatbed from the back room. He was extremely red in the face. I couldn't tell if it was because of his pimples, if he had rosacea, or if he was just really hot or something. I thought it might be the latter because he had huge pit stains, but I still wasn't sure.

"Here's your friggin' peas," he said.

"Excuse me?"

"Paul said to reload the flatbed with *boxes* of canned goods, that I did it wrong the first time. I did what he told me to do!"

"Same here."

"That sucks." He got down on his knees on the opposite side of the flatbed that I was loading up and started helping me. "What's your name again?" I turned my left breast his way so he could read my nametag. "Cleo. Is that short for Cleopatra?"

"No. Its just Cleo. My middle name is Patricia though, so it's Cleo Patricia."

"That's cool. My name's Roy."

"I know."

"It's short for Elroy."

"I didn't know that."

"Nobody does. It's a pretty stupid name."

"I don't think so. But you know what is? Paul."

He laughed. "More like stupid man, if you ask me."

I laughed. "So what's his deal? Do you think he's married? Sometimes I think he's gay because I couldn't imagine him with a woman, but imagining him gay would make him too interesting."

"I don't think about it," Roy replied, rolling his eyes.

"Don't tell me you're a homophobe," I groaned. "If there's one thing I can't stand..."

"Ha! Yeah, right!" Janine exclaimed from behind me. "One thing? One thing you can't stand? Which one of the million can you possibly hold above the rest?"

"An eavesdropper who invites herself into the conversation without being asked or wanted there."

"I can take a hint." She stuck her tongue out at me and waddled pregnantly into the back.

"What's her name again?" Roy asked.

"Janine. We were best friends in high school until she got a boyfriend and now she's all knocked up."

He laughed. His laugh had no sound. He closed his squinty eyes tightly and smiled wide as his shoulders shook up and down. Just seeing him laugh made me laugh as well. "I know how that goes. Do you have a boyfriend?"

"Nah, not really. Do you have a girlfriend?"

"Yeah. We've been together for almost two years."

"Damn. How old are you?"

"Eighteen. I'll be a senior this fall. She's seventeen. We want to get married right after graduation."

My open heart slammed shut and the wanting that I'd felt to get to know him screeched to a halt. I understood that he wasn't the most attractive guy on Earth and she was probably no looker either. They probably thought they could do no better and needed to lock each other down as soon as possible. Lame.

"Don't you want to live for yourself for a while? You'll be going from your parents to your wife in an instant."

He shrugged. "I love her."

"What's her name?"

"Anamae."

Gag. "Pret-ty."

"Thanks."

"Roy and Anamae. Okay. Do you wanna go to college or anything?"

"Don't quite know."

"Time's winding down, wouldn't you say?"

"Sure would."

"What about Anamae? What does she wanna do?"

"Be a stay-at-home mom."

"Good. For. Her."

"Yeah, I think it'll be nice."

Nice. Real nice.

"This is like the first time I've ever talked to anyone at work."

"How long have you been working here?"

"About two months. You?"

"Too long."

"How long?"

"A year," I answered, hanging my head in shame. "And it's driving me crazy. Literally." I showed him my wrists, where I had scars from lifting boxes and stuff.

Roy laughed and showed me his wrists. "Sometimes I wonder if people will see all these marks and think I'm suicidal."

"Same here. But I hope they do, just to scare them, so they'll feel like they have to be nice so I don't kill myself or something."

"You're horrible!" he chuckled.

Before long, the end cap was set up nicely with the correct items under the sign. "Thanks for your help, Roy."

"It's really no problem. I enjoyed myself." If I'm not mistaken, he blushed when he said that, then turned to go.

Janine was sitting in the break room, reading a magazine. She rolled her eyes when she saw me. "Tryna play me like that."

"Well… it's true."

"But what I said was true, too! You are an intolerant bitch." She dropped the magazine on the table and clasped her hands over her belly.

"I'm gonna say that's your pregnancy talking and let that one go, because if I let you have it I'm not sure that I'll be able to stop."

She laughed. "Why do you think you're so great?"

I left the room and could hear her laughing behind me. How dare she talk to me like that? I never gave her any shit about doing her. I never said, Janine, why are you so stupid that you got pregnant by a man with a house arrest monitor on his ankle while neither of you had a job? Why are you so lame that you *and* your baby's father are living with your mother? Why are you such a bitch that you uninvited me from going to Wildwood with you so you could take him instead? Yeah, that last one was in high school, but that doesn't make it any less foul. I was so excited to spend all day at the beach and all night on amusement rides. That tore me up.

Junior was waiting for her outside. You can't see outside from the break room and I wasn't about to do her any favors, so I didn't say a word.

My mom, Deena, and Leslie arrived home at the same time that I was arriving from work. They all looked happy and were chatting away. Not one of them took notice of me; they closed the door just as I reached the walkway. I found that the door was locked and started banging on it. Deena opened the door and sneered at me. I sneered right back. I went straight up to my room and changed into normal clothes. I really hate yellow shirts now.

Leslie was strutting around the living room for my mom and sister, clutching her bouquet and blowing kisses. I rolled my eyes and went to the kitchen where, unfortunately, I could still hear them sighing and gushing over how beautiful she was. She was cute, yes, but also kind of freaky, especially in all the pageant gear. Her fake hair looked like it weighed as much as her twiggy, little body.

I poured myself a bowl of cereal and carried it up to my room. I really wasn't in the mood to be around them. All I really wanted was for Sunday afternoon to hurry itself up.

There was a knock on my door. Mom poked her head in. "We're going to dinner. Wanna join us?"

Not in the mood to be around them, but not crazy enough to turn down a free meal. "Sure." I climbed into the back seat of Deena's Altima with Leslie, who was still wearing her crown.

"Look." She opened her mouth and wiggled one of her front teeth with her tongue. "Isn't that cool?"

"Yeah." I turned away and stared out the window.

"Lil' Mama got second place," Mom said proudly, turning to look at me.

"Runner up," Leslie said.

"*First* runner up," Dee corrected her.

"*First* runner up," Lele repeated. "Mom, why is it called runner up?"

"Because if something happens to Christine Stevens and she can't fulfill her duty as Little Miss Shining Star—God forbid—you would be the first to ***run up*** and take her place." Deena said all of this very matter-of-factly, so much so that I wondered if she believed herself. Hell, I even wondered if she was right, until I saw the sideways glance that my mother gave her.

Leslie's choice for dinner was a place called L.B. Diner, which she always wanted to eat at because it had her initials. Leslie took her father's last name, Breckman, while the rest of us are Jones'. I, having just eaten cereal, was in no mood for more breakfast food. I ordered the fried shrimp meal and a chocolate milkshake, for which Deena gave me a look.

"Fried shrimp? Chocolate shake? Take it easy there, slim. Weren't you just eating at home?"

"Deena!" my mom exclaimed. "Is that nice?"

"Let her go, Mom. Let her be an ugly bitch. It'll come back to her."

Deena rolled her eyes. "I'm just tryna help you out."

"By making me feel bad about myself? That's so good of you, Dee. And just so you know, being smaller than me certainly doesn't make you cuter than me, because cute is one thing you're not."

"Cleo!" My mom stared at me with wide eyes.

"Shit, you're not even skinny for that matter. Face it, you're looking like a full-blown pageant mom by now, too busy fussing over your little princess to take a comb through your own hair."

Leslie had her hands over her ears and was staring into her lap.

"I cut my hair and went natural to get in touch with my true self, thank you."

"You cut your hair so you could spend less time on your pathetic self and more time living vicariously through your daughter."

"Enough!" Slamming her palm down on the table, Mom looked back and forth at us. "This is utterly disgusting. Get over yourselves and shut up. This is a family dinner and you're messing it up. Especially you, Deena. We're supposed to be celebrating your daughter's success, not picking useless fights. What's wrong with you? Cleo, take Leslie outside for a minute."

I sat on the curb while Leslie walked on it like a balance beam. I wished I knew what they were saying inside. Nearly ten minutes later, Deena came to the parking lot and ushered Leslie inside.

"I'm sorry," she said to me. "Not just for what I just said, but for everything. I'm sorry that I abandoned you and did pretty much exactly what we promised never to do. It turns out that this path doesn't have to be such a horrible thing, it doesn't mean I'm doomed. We're doing very well, as you can see. I know you worry about that."

She was wrong. I didn't worry about that. It actually pissed me off that her life was going so well because now, especially with Charlie out of the picture, there was no room for me to say "I told you so."

"Mostly I'm sorry for being a shitty big sister. I don't know why I put you down so much. I get mad for disappointing you and then it makes me say things… Okay?"

"Okay? No, not really. What exactly just happened?"

"I'm telling you that that's not going to happen anymore. I promise. Okay?"

"Okay."

"Your make-up is flawless, by the way," she said, holding out her hand to help me up from the curb.

Work was unbearably long on Sunday morning even though I was kept busy the entire time. I wished I'd had a remote control for my life and could just fast forward to three o'clock. Impossible, unfortunately. Janine gave me the cold shoulder as much as she possibly could, which was pretty much the entire time. When she first walked by me in aisle four, she smiled and waved and started to say something. Then a look crossed her face like she suddenly remembered something, and she stared straight ahead with a furrowed brow and lips pursed tightly. I just rolled my eyes and went on with my business.

Paul asked me to start bagging groceries, so I went to the end of Janine's line just to be all up in her face. She was pretty good at pretending I wasn't there, even when I called her name. The customers looked at us suspiciously then, so I just gave them a sweet smile to make it clear who the bitch was.

I left ten minutes before my shift was actually over and hurried home. I took a shower, straightened my hair, and applied my make-up. My ensemble was simple but cute: a white tube top with a red, patent leather belt cinched at the waist, and jeans tight enough to hug my curves but not tight enough to give me a muffin top. I realized then that I needed to go shoe shopping. It was a choice between black flip-flops, silver pumps, or denim espadrilles. The most logical choice was the flip-flops, especially considering how I'd already gone a little over with the belt. I wished I'd gotten my toenails done. It's not that my feet looked nasty, but French tips would've been adorable. Then again, it's not likely that he'll be sucking my toes, I said to myself. Well, not yet. I crossed my fingers.

I sat on the couch as close to the door as possible. I kept glancing out the window. As soon as I would sit back down, I'd second guess myself. Was that him? No. Oh, wait! No. What was that? No. It was already three after three. Where was he?

There! My heart jumped into my throat and remained there as an uncomfortable lump. I reached for the knob with a trembling hand. What was wrong with me? Thank God I didn't wear heels, I would've been a disaster.

I hate to use the term, but his '85 Cadillac was nothing less than candy apple red, with red rims and white leather interior with red, suede piping—a whore for attention. An abomination in my eyes: another case of conspicuous consumption; another Black man trying to prove his status by showing off with fancy things when he really had nothing to back it up. I was just surprised that Travis would subscribe to that school of thought; he seemed like he came from a good family with better intentions. But I let it pass; we are not our cars, and although his car looked to be an asshole, Travis had proven himself otherwise thus far.

"What's up?" he asked, turning his music down as I got into the car.

"Nothing," I replied.

"You like Bob Marley?" he asked, turning the music back up a little.

"I never really listen to him."

"Ah, I see. Me either. My dad left this in my car. He has his own but likes to trade me sometimes."

Lucky. I only wished I had cars to trade.

"I must say, I don't get it. You would think I'd love the guy. Maybe I need to smoke before I listen to it."

"Oh." Wow. Okay.

Travis lived at the end of a row home not too far from South Street and the river. He parked in the garage, which was at the back of the house at the basement level. We walked around to the front door where he knocked loudly because he didn't have his key on him. The door was opened by his mother. When I laid eyes upon her, I felt like I was dressed like a ho. She was a little bit shorter than me but she stood with much power and grace. She had smooth dark skin, big, black eyes, and a very neat, very round Afro. She wore a brilliantly blue dashiki and modest gold hoops in her ears. Her eyebrows were shaped to perfection. There was a little bit of gold gloss on her plump lips, which parted to reveal the most perfect set of white teeth I'd ever seen. I was literally stunned by her beauty.

"Mom, this is Cleo."

"Hello, Cleo." We pressed our cheeks together as she hugged me. Hers was a silky soft pillow. "Make yourself at home. I hope you've kept your promise to stay for dinner. Take your shoes off and leave them by the door. You can call me Kina. Are you gonna give her a tour, Travie?"

Travis rolled his eyes. "Are you serious?"

"Fine, I'm sorry. Retreat to your den, as per usual. I'll call you when dinner is ready, which may be a while. Your father is still shopping."

I followed Travis from the beautiful, little foyer with its pristine white walls and golden chandelier, up the stairs to his bedroom, or shall we say *suite*. In his room was a queen-size bed, a loveseat, a plasma screen TV, an office space, and a full bathroom. He told me to have a seat on his couch while he used the "men's room." I wondered if he said that because he didn't want me to use it. I also wondered how light his dad had to be, because if I described Travis as a Nilla Wafer, his mom would definitely be an Oreo, just the cookie, not the cream. Well, maybe her perfect teeth could fill in for the cream.

There were clothes, papers, trash, and everything else all over the floor. He clearly wasn't concerned with impressing me. A bag of weed was sitting right on top of his closed notebook computer. There was a porno DVD box sitting on the floor beside my feet. *Big Booty Beauties*. Okay.

He came out fastening his belt. "Whatchu lookin' at?"

I picked up the box and showed him. "Extra research for our presentation?" I asked.

He laughed and took it from my hand. "What the hell is this?" He tossed it onto his bed and took a seat on the couch. I wished he'd toss me onto his bed. Why did he have me way over on the couch? Oh, yeah, we were doing a project. "Weird story, right?"

"Well, yeah."

"But?"

"You read the story, didn't you?"

"Well, yeah."

"But?"

We both laughed.

"Cleo!" He rubbed my shoulder vigorously. "I know this is awkward, but we have to do it. Why you actin' shy? Let me have it like you did in class, *before* I apologized. Do I need to say something to get you worked up? Women are nagging bitches and they need to stay in the kitchen. How's that?"

I rolled my eyes. "Nice try. Even you know that's too ridiculous to believe." I took a deep breath to calm myself, then nearly jumped out of my skin when I noticed someone staring at me from the corner of my eye.

"Sorry to interrupt," Kina said, her head poked into the room.

I hiccupped. Loudly. And it hurt.

"Do you guys want anything? A snack? A drink? I do have some shrimp kabobs."

"Sure," Travis said. "And cream soda."

I hiccupped again. "And—" Hiccup.

"Water," Kina finished with a kind smile.

I nodded, then turned to Travis as his mom left. "Your mom just serves you and your company like that?"

He shrugged. "Yeah..."

"My mom would *never ever* do that."

He shrugged. I hiccupped. We sat in silence until she returned a couple of minutes later. She carried a tray over and set it on the couch between us.

"Travis." She walked over to his desk and picked up the baggie. "What is this?"

"Weed, Mom."

"I know that! What is it doing here? How many times do I have to tell you not to bring this filth in here? You don't smoke, do you, Cleo?"

I hiccupped and shook my head.

"Have some water, honey. A big, big gulp. There you go. Travis, I'm pissed about this. Don't think I won't call the cops on my own son." She took the bag and left, closing the door behind herself.

Travis got up and locked the door. "She's frontin'. She's gonna go tell my dad, he's gonna pretend to get mad, then he's gonna smoke it himself. I don't care, I have more. So, what were you saying?"

"Your mom just has shrimp kabobs laying around?"

"Yeah, they're good. She marinates them, grills them, then freezes them for me to have whenever."

"She's like supermom. Or you're just super spoiled."

"Well, she's a professional chef, with her own restaurant and several books, so..."

"But still. What does your dad do?"

"He's a pediatrician."

"Wow, you guys are practically Huxtables."

He laughed loudly. "Hardly! Anyway, I don't wanna talk about my parents. Back to rape fantasies."

"Mmm, my God, Travis!" The shrimp were delicious. They were buttery-delicious with a refreshing hint of lemon. I never tasted shrimp like that before or since that moment.

Travis raised an eyebrow. "That was sexy."

"Shut up," I muttered, trying not to smile.

"For real. Anyway, back to this stupid project. I had no idea what this stupid story was about. What did you think this was about?"

I started rambling on, spewing off some research I'd done online to get a deeper understanding of the reading. I didn't even know what I was saying, just regurgitating. I don't think he had any idea what I was saying either. He was just sitting there, staring at me.

"You're so smart. I find that so sexy."

I smiled shyly, trying to hide my grin with my glass of soda.

"When we were going at it in class that day, I just wanted to make out with you to shut you up."

"You shut up," I giggled.

"For real. Even when you're talking nonsense it sounds so right." He stared into my eyes. "Can I tell you something?" His eyes sparkled, more green now than I'd noticed before.

"Uh, sure."

"I think you like me."

"Ha!"

He smiled. "Yeah, for sure."

"What makes you so certain?"

"I saw how jealous you got when you saw that porno on the floor. You only want me lookin' at you, huh?"

"Oh, please!"

"I'm playin'. Can I tell you something else?"

"Of course," I replied.

"All that stuff you were just saying, about the injustices between men and women or whatever, I don't know about that. I mean, yeah, it exists, but I don't think we need to put it in our report. Maybe gloss over it quickly, but that's not the story of Little Red Riding Hood."

"It's called reading between the lines. There's more to a story than word-for-word what's on the paper. This isn't the typical fairy tale, it's written to make you think about things like that."

"Yeah, but it's kind of awkward, don't you think? Who wants to hear us talking about what women aren't allowed to do because of the pressures of society when we could just mention it quickly, and then mainly focus on how it's just a twisted fairy tale?" He reached to the floor to answer his vibrating phone while I was left kind of speechless. "Yo. Yeah, yeah. Yup. Okay! See ya." He closed his phone and put it in his pocket. "You're wanted downstairs."

"Just me?" I was terrified. What could she want?

"Both of us. Dinner's ready." I followed Travis down to the kitchen. "Dad," he said, to the man in the fridge, "this is Cleo. Cleo, my father, Terrence."

I hoped I didn't look as shocked as I felt, because Terrence was a white man. Quite a tan white man, but white. He had salt and pepper hair on his head and in his goatee. He had the same gorgeous eyes as Travis, which grabbed me for a moment, but I pulled back. He was very good-looking, there were no two ways about it, but I was blind-sided. I looked around for Kina to make sure I hadn't mistaken her appearance. Clear as day, there she stood in a blue dashiki and Afro, setting the dining room table.

"Nice to meet you," Terrence said, holding his hand out to me. He stood a bit taller than Travis, and Travis was easily over six two. "He told us you were coming. He also showed us how pretty you are. I thought one of the two had to be a lie—either that wasn't your picture or you weren't really coming over. He sure proved me wrong." What a charmer.

I was putty. Until I realized what he'd said and I immediately froze up. "What picture?" I looked sideways at Travis.

"The one on our class page, with our email addresses and stuff. You know."

"Oh, right!" I felt like a balloon in my chest had deflated then. You know I thought he was talking about my personal site. I was comfortable with it, but not comfortable for it to be the first impression his family got of me.

Travis led me to my seat in the dining room and pushed my chair in for me (with much effort, it was almost awkward). His parents sat at the ends of the table and Travis sat across from me. Terrence poured each of us a glass of wine. The food looked delicious. When I wasn't silently obsessing over how amazing the steak, scallops, string beans, and rice were, I was wondering about Travis's parents. How did I not know? How? Now that I did know, Travis's coloring was just screaming at me from across the table: *Mixed! Mixed! Mixed!*

"How's the project going?" Terrence asked.

"Good," Travis said.

Well, I corrected him silently.

"Well," his mother said. "You mean it's going well. Cleo, what do you want to do after school?"

"You mean as a career?"

"Yes."

"Well, I'd like to be a wildlife photographer, travel Africa for a while." Now where the hell did that come from? I'll admit it, it was something I'd briefly considered once while watching this show about lions on the Discovery Channel, but I never expected to speak of it aloud. I was incredibly embarrassed. I think her dashiki was making me think strange thoughts of the motherland.

Travis look at me with a raised eyebrow, then stuffed his mouth with string beans and rice to keep from laughing.

"Fascinating," Terrence said. "So you're a photographer?"

"Uh, yes. I love photography."

"Nice to see someone who knows what she wants to do, huh, Travis?" his mother asked him.

"Yup, great."

"Travis is undecided," she told me. "Maybe if he spends more time around you he'll get his head right."

"Well, I'm not absolutely sure what I want to do. I really… don't really know yet," I admitted.

"Oh, I see," Kina replied, sounding slightly disappointed. "What do you like to do then?"

"Photography, writing, money."

"Accounting?" she suggested.

"No, I'm not really into math. I'm actually majoring in English."

"So what's all this stuff about touring Africa and taking photos?" she asked.

I was so very embarrassed that I'd said that. Why the hell did I even say that?

"Stop grilling the poor girl!" Terrence said to Kina. "Have some more wine and loosen up, it's Sunday evening."

I was so relieved for that.

"On a lighter note," Kina sighed, "guess who came into the restaurant yesterday evening?"

"Who?" we all asked.

"That guy from the Sixers."

"What guy?" Terrence asked.

"You know I don't watch sports or pay attention to who plays them. One of the waitresses told me he was a basketball player."

"How do you know he plays for the Sixers?" Travis asked.

"Well, I just kind of figured."

Terrence and Travis laughed. I just smiled.

Kina rolled her eyes. "Shut up. Y'all know I don't care about stuff like that, but it could've been any headlining opera singer and I would've known them right away. You can't say that for yourselves."

"Wow, Mom, like anyone likes opera."

"Excuse me, son, but opera is one of the most beautiful forms of art a person can experience. If you would allow yourself to be a little more cultured you might understand that. Step your game up, okay?"

At that, I did laugh.

"Don't humor her," Travis said to me. "She's crazy! You should've seen her going on and on when she met that *Lord of the Dance* guy. You would've thought she'd met Jesus Christ himself."

"Shut up! Michael Flatley is the stuff. Cleo, have you ever seen *Riverdance*?"

"Can't say that I have."

"Oh no," Terrence groaned, chuckling.

"Do you—"

"No, Mom, she *doesn't* want to watch *Riverdance* with you!"

"Travis, why did you even bring that up?" Terrence asked. "You know once she gets on her *Riverdance* thing she can't quit."

"No, I thank you, son. I haven't watched it in a while and it would be the perfect thing to finish off a lovely day."

"See?" Travis said to me, pointing his fork at his mother. "Crazy."

"Why are y'all such haters?"

"Mom, please stop talking like that!" Travis howled with laughter. "You're embarrassing yourself."

Terrence nodded in agreement. "Something seems kind of off when you're sitting here, swooning over Michael Flatley, *Lord of the Dance*, then using the term 'haters' in the same conversation."

I was dying.

"Is that weird?" Kina asked me. "You think it's fine for me to talk that way, don't you?"

I nodded, still laughing, but silently.

"Thank you, honey. It's nice to have another woman in the house. These two little boys just gang up on me constantly. I know what I'm talking about, but they think I'm crazy."

"Crazy people don't know they're crazy," Travis pointed out.

"No, but crazy people do continue to call their mothers crazy, and seem to convince themselves that she won't beat their asses. So what would he be, Dr. Terrence, delusional?"

I sat, eating, watching, laughing, beaming. They were so fun. I wished my family was fun. There was Kina being herself, and Terrence being himself, and both of them being themselves together. It was strange to me, but beautiful. I didn't want to leave. The last thing I wanted was to leave. I wanted to stay and be part of the family, like that perfect girlfriend that the parents just love to love. That's what it started to feel like. I offered to help clean up, but Kina and Terrence insisted that I shouldn't lift a finger… but it would expected of me the next time, Terrence said jokingly with a wink.

Why couldn't my family be like that? The only reason I could think of was money. My mom was pretty much always in a bad mood *because* of money. Like I said, she didn't have money because she never had great jobs, because she couldn't further her education, because she had kids too soon, because she had sex too soon, because she was looking for love in all the wrong places. So love and money. While my mom seemed to lack both, Travis's mom had them in abundance. I felt it wasn't fair. We all want our moms to be happy. But what can we do? Really? Especially as children, most of us can't just wipe out their financial woes. Nor can we make some man, our fathers or whomever, treat them and love them as they should be loved and treated.

Travis dropped me off at home. I thanked him and went inside. My mom was laying on the couch, watching TV. I knelt beside her and gave her a hug.

"What was that for?" she asked, clearly surprised.

"Because I love you. Even when I stupidly forget to act like it, I love you. And I appreciate everything you've done for me."

"Wow, honey, thank you. I love you, too." She kissed me on the forehead, then went back to watching TV.

I took a seat in the break room across from Roy as he dealt the cards for our Go Fish tournament. "How's Anamae?" I asked, wiping soda off of my upper lip with the back of my hand.

"Good, good." He looked into my eyes. "I'm lying. I think she hates me."

"Aw, why?"

"This is kind of embarrassing, but she had me go to the store to buy her pads and tampons. I didn't know it would cost so much and I didn't have enough money on me, so I bought the generic brand."

"Did she tell you a specific kind to get?"

"Yes, but I couldn't remember all those descriptive details."

"Oh boy."

"All the wings and absorbent cores, scented, unscented, plastic applicator, cardboard, no applicator—I don't know! It was confusing and terrifying. So, since I was kinda low on cash anyway, I figured I'd just go with the cheap ones. When I gave them to her, she cried and yelled at me.

Called me stupid and worthless, then told me to get out of her sight."

"Well, yeah, you messed up. Some girls are really specific about what they use. Not to mention that she was probably just in a bad mood because she was on her dot. I doubt she hates you though."

"So glad I'm not getting my period," Janine said, walking in with her nose up.

"Oh, lucky, lucky you. But you do get to push an eight-pound baby out of your coochie. Not really an equal trade if you ask me, but you know my period is never really too bad cuz I stay on that pill."

"Are you tryna say I should've used birth control?" she accused me, weaving her head back and forth.

"If that's what I was tryna say, Neen, I woulda said it."

Her expression suddenly softened. "You haven't called me Neen in so long! Aw, I miss that. Anyway, we're having a barbecue baby shower at my mom's this afternoon if you aren't busy. We're getting a DJ and everything, it's gonna be so hype!"

"You must not be expecting a gift to give me such short notice."

"Money's cool. I can put it in the baby's college fund."

"Ten dollars isn't gonna do much for an education that costs several tens of thousands."

"Mm! That much? Well, damn, no wonder I don't go." She laughed. "Anyway, please be there. Four PM." She blew me a kiss as she left.

Roy rolled his eyes. "That was awkward."

"What?"

"You guys… like I wasn't even here… talking about periods and child birth and the pill… then practically getting into a fight, then making up cuz you called her *Neen*… like I wasn't even here."

I laughed. "She's crazy. Seriously insane. But she's especially been off the wall since she got pregnant. See what all those hormones do to a girl? Just like Anamae. Give her a minute, she'll come around."

"I hope so."

"She will! Don't worry about it." Especially since she probably can't do any better anyway.

I left work and went straight to the shower. It was 4:11. I walked around to the back yard of Janine's mom's house. There were cute decorations, balloons and streamers in pastel colors. The DJ was setting up on the concrete patch by the fence. Janine was sitting on the deck with her feet up, giving out orders to her family.

"You made it!" she shrieked. "We're running a little behind though."

"I see." I handed her the card I'd bought. There was no money, but I did write an I.O.U. for me to baby-sit. Cheap, I know. That's one reason why I wanted to get the hell out of there as soon as possible. "I'd better go."

"What? Why? You just got here. And you just might get a prize for the being the first to arrive!"

"Oh, for real? But that's not really fair cuz I'm early, so give it to the next person."

"You're not early, we're just late. Please stay! You're like the only one I can stand nowadays. Everyone has been driving me crazy."

It's probably reciprocal.

"I know, right? I don't know what's up with them."

I sat on the wicker seat beside her. I took the card and placed it on the wicker end table to take her mind off of it. "Are you expecting a lot of people?"

"Oh, so many! You know I have a big family, so does Junior, put it all together and you've got one big mess."

One big mess you want me to sit in the middle of.

"Right. But that means lots of gifts! I hope people took advantage of our registry, cuz I don't want no corny stuff."

"Of course not."

"Aunt Donna, you made it." Her aunt stooped down to hug her. "This is my friend Cleo."

"Hi," I said, looking at her hairline. It was thinner than the hair on my forearms, peeking out from the edge of her wig. I couldn't see her eyes behind her big, tortoise shell sunglasses, so I just took in her outfit. She was wearing noisy, lime green track pants and a black t-shirt with a cat on it. Seven of her fingers were embellished with gaudy, fake-looking rings. She nodded at me and pressed her skinny, hot pink lips together, but uttered not a single word. She went over to greet Janine's mom.

"Who's that big pretty girl on the deck, lookin' like she swallowed a basketball and glowing all the while?"

Excuse me?

"Tina, you made it!" Janine squealed.

Tina stepped onto the deck and struck a pose. Her legs went on for days, from her tiny denim hot pants to her red patent leather, peep-toe, platforms with six-inch heels, stripper shoes if there ever were such a thing. She wore a vest as a shirt that matched her hot pants, with a little hint of areola sticking out the top. Classy. I looked away when she bent over to hug Janine, but I could see Janine's brother staring right at Tina's behind from across the deck.

Enough. I told Janine I was going to use the bathroom. I walked into the house, passed by the powder room door, and walked right out the front. I nearly broke into a run when I reached the sidewalk, trying to get out of sight before anyone caught me. I felt kind of bad, but not really; people would start to show up and she wouldn't even miss me.

I sat on my couch, waiting for Jason. I really hated that he absolutely insisted on picking me up from my house. It was too risky—my mother or Deena could show up at any time, start asking questions and basically ruin the good, anonymous thing we had going on. I darted outside when he pulled up and climbed into the truck.

"What it do, ma?"

"I'm good, how are you?" I replied, checking myself in the mirror. Climbing all the way up into that seat always left me feeling disheveled.

"Good, ma. You look right, and you're titties look so damn good!"

I looked down to the see them spilling over my shirt. That's what I meant by disheveled. "Oh my—excuse me." I pulled the neckline up to its proper place, blushing.

"I'm not mad." He licked his lips and laughed. "You hungry?" He took a hard turn into the parking lot of a pizza restaurant. He took his phone out and called in his order. "What you want?"

"Nothing."

"I got you!"

"Nothing. Really, I'm not hungry." I really wasn't. I was actually feeling kind of sick. "Can I actually get a bottle of water?"

"Oh, now you want something. After I hung up the phone, dammit."

"Calm down. I'm sure you can just add it on when you get in there. A drink? I'm sure it won't be a problem. As a matter of fact, I'mma just go get it myself."

"Well go get it your damn self then, ma."

I got out of the car and went inside. It was stifling in there. They didn't carry any major brands, so I got a brand that I didn't recognize—but it's water, so why should it matter? Jason was getting out when I returned to the car. The door was locked, and he ignored the fact that I was trying to get in. I had to wait until he came back outside.

"Don't disrespect me in public," he said, staring straight ahead while driving.

"Huh? There was nobody around. Not that I even disrespected you in any way."

"There was a guy outside smoking. If people see a girl talking to J. Cru like that, who's gonna take me seriously?"

Damn sure not me, but who takes you seriously now anyway?

"Exactly. So… just don't. You know I'm not a really mean guy, but that's what people like to see, you know? They like to see somebody who won't take shit from a female, like I don't give a shit about you, ya know?"

"That's J. Cru. What about Jason?"

"Jason who?"

I rolled my eyes and stared out the window. We didn't exchange words for the rest of the night. We went to his room, where he smoked and then ate while I watched TV and drank my water. Once he finished eating, he moved all of his garbage to the floor, then began nuzzling my neck and creeping his hand beneath my clothes. I laid back on the pillow and participated with minimal effort. He ate me out, then had sex on me with his chin firmly planted into my shoulder, which was sore when he finished. He rolled another blunt and smoked it, writing in his notebook while I lied naked next to him with my eyes closed. I felt him stop writing to turn and look at me for a second every once in a while, then he would start writing again.

I couldn't fall asleep. I wanted him to turn the stupid light off, but I didn't want to disturb him while he was inspired. I briefly considered sleeping on the couch but didn't want to confront his mother if she happened to find me there. Maybe an hour after we'd had sex, he turned the light off and fell fast asleep. Then I couldn't stop wondering what he'd been writing about. Me? He had sex on me, then got inspired, and he kept looking at me while he was writing. What else could he have been writing about *besides* me? Probably some sexy, sexist stuff about how much I turn him on. Yeah. About my sexy lips and thick thighs. Yeah, most likely. I wanted to sneak a peek in his notebook, but I fought the urge by diverting my extra energy to a quick bathroom run.

I pulled his T-shirt on and went out to the hallway, only to run smack into his mother. And I do mean *smack*. We walked directly into each other as we rounded the corner from opposite directions.

"Excuse me," I said, looking down at the floor bashfully. Oh, how I wished I was wearing a bra and panties, especially since we ran into each with full body contact. She had to have felt my nakedness. "I'm so sorry."

"Okay," she said, and stood firmly for me to walk around her. Not *it's okay*, meaning *forgiveness*, but *okay*, meaning *if you say so*.

I ducked into the bathroom and locked the door. My heart was pounding so hard that I could feel my pulse even in my fingertips. I splashed my face with cool water and took long, deep breaths.

But why should I fear her? Jason invited me there! I don't care what she thinks of me. Why should I?

Perhaps because I kept thinking about Kina, and how nice she was to me, and Travis and how sweet he was, and why *shouldn't* I have that if I *could* have that?

I put on some more modest pajamas and crept back into Jason's bed. The next morning, I contemplated back and forth whether I should just dip out on him or wake him up for a ride home. It was raining something fierce, so I swallowed my pride and chose the latter.

"It's early," he grumbled, rolling over to turn away from me.

"No. Shit."

"When did you become such a pain in the ass? You used to be so cool."

I backed off for a minute. Pain in the ass? Me? For real? Oh, cuz I'm not doing exactly what you want me to do, you punk-ass-bitch-ass-fake-ass-wannabe rapper?

"Well, I *am* sleep."

"But you're talking to me, so you talk in your sleep? Come on, Jason, please!"

"Who the fuck is this Jason nigga you keep talkin' about?" he barked in my face, suddenly at full attention. "Show me Jason then! Huh? Go 'head, show me! That's right, cuz ain't nobody named Jason in here. Get outta here with that corny shit. Matter fact, I'll get you outta here my damn self." I flinched. I'm not gonna lie, I thought he might hit me.

Needless to say, the ride home was beyond uncomfortable. He didn't even turn the radio on, and we couldn't roll down the windows because it was raining so hard. The tension was so thick in the air I could barely breathe. I took very slow, careful breaths, trying to be as nonexistent as possible. Then I found myself giggling, quietly at first, then nearly choking to hold in my hysterical laughter as I thought about what a ridiculous person he was. Ludicrous, really, which is almost too close to being a compliment given his chosen career path.

"What?"

"Just thinking about my friend," I lied. "Sorry if I upset you. It won't happen again."

"It ain't nothing."

Deena was asleep on the couch with the television on and a buffet of food in Styrofoam containers spread out on the coffee table before her. She was watching some shop-from-home crap like she always does. Crap, it is, but I'll admit that it can be quite alluring. As I stood there, surveying the scene, I became almost completely convinced that I needed that sandwich grill. Before I became anymore delusional, I took myself up to my bedroom with every intention of changing into a big, comfy t-shirt and climbing into my own, comfy bed, only to find that Leslie was already there.

I was livid. I fought the urge to scream at the top of my lungs and drag her little ass out of my bed. I would've been better off staying with Jason's stupid ass had I known that my bed was being unnecessarily inhabited by some spoiled little creature. Seriously, she had her own bed in her own room at her house, something I never got to experience until Deena moved out after high school. Why did she have to be in *my room* in *my bed*?

I shook her—not too hard—then escorted her to my mom's room, to the full-size bed my mother should've invited her into from the get-go. Leslie and my mom were both groggy and needed no convincing. They were back asleep in no time. I shut and locked my bedroom door and began taking my clothes off. I searched in the dark for a soft, well-worn t-shirt and then climbed into bed.

I froze in shock, then a horrified scream shot from the depths of my throat before I even fully realized what had happened. I felt around my body, finding that, no matter where I touched, the sheets were soaked with lukewarm wetness. "Oh my God! Oh my God! Oh my God!" I felt like I couldn't stop screaming, but I did, just long enough to tell myself, "Well, get up."

I turned on my light and stared at the huge wet spot on my bed. Oh, there would be no rest in that house until some wrongs were made right. Or as right as possible. I flung my door wide open and shouted "DEEEENAA!" at the top of my lungs.

Deena and my mom both showed up looking less than half interested in my dilemma. "Yes?" Dee asked, rubbing her eyes.

"Your daugh-ter *peed* in my *bed*!" I shouted.

"Well, she's five," Deena explained with a shrug.

"No shit," I hissed through clenched teeth. "But I'm not, and I don't wanna sleep in a pissy bed! Why was she even in here? Don't you two ever go home?"

"Stop being like that, Cleo," mom said. "They haven't slept over in a while, you know that. Leslie wanted to sleep in your bed, she said you have the coolest room."

"Touching as that may sound, she pissed in my *bed*. I'm utterly disgusted."

"Well, it happens," Dee said, shrugging again.

"WELL CLEAN IT UP!" I screamed, beginning to cry.

"Sleep in my bed," Mom said.

"Yeah, good idea. Like the pissy princess hasn't soaked your bed, too." If it soaked right through my clothes, I'm sure Leslie must've been waterlogged like a motherfucker. I took off my t-shirt and underwear right there and put on another pair, adding shorts to the ensemble. The couch was my last resort. I left Jason's in hopes of getting into my own bed, only to end up on my own couch.

I woke up several hours later and took a shower. It was still raining. My bare mattress was driving me crazy, taunting me, as I got dressed in my room. Deena and Leslie were having cereal in the kitchen.

"Sorry, Aunt Cleo," Leslie said.

"Okay." Not *it's okay* meaning *forgiveness*, but *okay* meaning *if you say so.*

"She apologized," Deena said sternly, as if expecting something from me.

"I *said* okay. What do you want? I'm the victim here."

"Victim?!" Deena spat. "It's a little urine!"

"It was a lot of urine! She practically drowned me!"

Leslie giggled while Deena scowled. At least Lele picked up on the very little sense of humor I had about the whole situation.

"Shut up, Cleo. Lele, don't humor her. Eat up, we have to get to practice."

I was so tired that I fell asleep on the train and nearly missed my stop. It had been raining for days and the constant pitter-patter of raindrops was a nonstop lullaby. I popped open my umbrella and headed to class. As I passed one of the small cafés on campus, this girl grabbed my arm. I snatched it back and raised my eyebrow at her. She was tall and kind of goofy looking with big lips and a droopy eye. I couldn't remember her name, but I knew she was pretty popular around campus, I think because she was really good at basketball.

"Ya name Cleo, right?"

"Yeah."

"You in mah class, right?"

"Yeah."

"Lemme get a dollar?"

"No."

"Ain't you got no money?"

"No, I *don't have any* money." I turned and walked off. The classroom was empty, as usual. I took my seat and started to read the assignment for the next class. When the room was halfway full, the girl from the café came in with her little crony, both of them eyeing me. "What?" I said, loud and clear.

She flipped me the bird while her shorter friend rolled her neck and replied, "Nothing, you bourgie ass bitch."

The room got awkwardly silent.

"I'm gonna let you get away with that. Why? Because I was raised better than that, and it's really not your fault if you weren't."

"I can't *stand* how you be talking!" she said, pointing her finger at me like she was holding a handgun sideways. "All proper and shit. You think you some white lady. You think you better or something?"

"Are you serious?! We're all sitting here in college, being educated. Excuse me, but I like to *act* like I have some education. Don't get angry with me because I know how to speak English properly and I *do it*! Get angry at yourself for being ignorant enough to believe that because I use proper grammar I'm 'acting white.' What year is it anyway? Don't all Black people in this country have the right to be equally educated? I think so, and I'm damn sure going to express that right every chance that I get and not be hung up on some stupid idea that I need to prove my Blackness to you." I caught myself before ending the whole thing with "dumb-ass bitch."

"Day-um!" Travis howled, walking across the room. "Sit down, Alicia. No shame, no shame, but she really just killed you with that."

"She ain't say shit," Alicia said as she and the tall girl sat down. "You need to get out her ass though, 'fore you catch something."

"And you need to be quiet 'fore you catch something else." Nah, I didn't really say that. I wanted to, but I can't fight, so I held my tongue because I'd said quite enough. I felt that one more thing could send her across the room, fists flying at my face. And I looked so cute that day, like most days. It wasn't worth it.

"Come over tonight," Travis said.

My breath caught in my throat, like the carbon dioxide I was exhaling had suddenly and magically turned into marshmallows. Not the little ones you put in your hot chocolate, but the big ones you roast over a campfire to make s'mores. I gulped some water. "For real?" I asked, trying not to pant.

"Yes, for real."

"Shit, I have to work."

"Aww. Oh well. What about tomorrow? Do you work tomorrow?"

"I surely don't."

"Come over. Stay for dinner. Oh, it's my night to cook though, I forgot."

"So I'm uninvited? Is your food like inedible or something?" I was trying so hard.

"My food happens to be delicious. If you decide to assist me, I can't say for sure."

"I don't cook."

"You will. My dad said he was gonna put you to work and he meant it."

"Well, I guess I'm in."

"My parents will be glad to hear it. I'm actually *not* a great cook, and they'll be so happy to have someone watching over me." He leaned close and whispered, "That was so sexy the way you told her off." His low voice sent tremors through my ears, my heart, down my spine, and into my panties. I wanted him to stay right there, whispering in my ear, but I wouldn't have been able to handle it if he did. That little tickle at the small of my back would've driven me insane. I probably would have creamed my pants, had a heart attack, or spontaneously combusted.

Work was a bitch. All I could think about was that I could be over at Travis's house, laughing it up with him and his parents, working on our stupid project, maybe making out hardcore in his bedroom.

"What is *this*?" Paul shrieked.

I very slowly looked up from what I was doing. I didn't want to move too quickly and give him the satisfaction of seeing me jump to attention. "What?"

"I asked you to straighten this aisle up."

"I'm working on it."

"Did you do this section already?"

"Yeah…"

"Then why is this box crooked? This left corner is back practically three quarters of an inch farther than the other one."

"Don't you think it's possible that a customer may have picked it up and put it back since I last straightened it up?"

"Are you sassing me?"

"I'm just saying…"

"Okay, well look at this. And this. And… dear God… you straightened up the front and left the back a wreck?"

"It's hardly a wreck, Paul. I can't reach the top shelf that well! I usually ask Roy to help me out."

"Well, Roy's not here today, so what are you gonna do? Slack off, slacker?"

"I was gonna do all I could do and pray to God that you weren't in a nit-picking kind of mood."

"Well you should've started praying sooner, sister. I'm writing your little incompetent ass up."

"Do it."

"Is that a dare?"

"No, it's not a dare! What is this, kindergarten? I'm a grown-ass woman, which is precisely why I don't need you talking to me like a *child*. No, Paul, I'm not *daring* you, I'm *telling* you. Do it."

He quickly shut his gaping mouth and tried to play it cool. "You don't value your job, do you?"

"You're a smart one, Paul. Tell Tom on me, if you like. You know Tom, your *boss*. Despite what you may think, you're not the HBIC around here. He can keep me for the next two weeks or cut me off right now, this is my notice."

"A-are you serious?"

"This. Is. My. Notice." I stared him down without batting an eye.

Paul rolled his eyes and held out his hand. He was daring me. He thought I was bluffing! I took off my apron and draped it delicately over his fingers. I stood tall with my nose in the air and walked through the employee doors for the last time.

Up in my bedroom, I had a fit. I couldn't believe what I'd just done.

Yes, Paul could be a serious bitch sometimes, but why the hell had I just quit my job?! I took off my stupid work uniform in a fury, rolled everything up into a tight ball and threw it, unfortunately, at my dresser, where it scatted all of my lotions, nail polishes, make-up and other girly grooming items.

I picked one of my shoes up from the floor. It was a ridiculously ugly shoe, one that I never would've worn if we hadn't been required to wear all black sneakers. I hurled it at my wall, where it left a black mark. I kicked the other shoe, and it flew straight for my open window, banging hard against the screen and busting it from its frame. The screen must've been way old, because the shoe tore right through it like a pencil through tissue paper. My shoe was just lodged there, one half of it in my room while the front half was out in the world, just beyond the screen. I tried to pull it out with a surgeon's precision, but only succeeded in tearing the screen further.

Just what I needed, right? I went down to the kitchen to find some duct tape. My mom was just coming in the house. "What are you doing home?" she asked me. "I thought you have work today."

"Not anymore," I replied, and ran back up to my room. It was better than a lie, but I knew that it wouldn't fully suffice as an answer for her. She was not going to take the real news very well, I was sure of that.

Try as I might, I could not create a bug-proof seal with the duct tape because the screen kept popping out. I knew my mom would not respond very well to this either, especially considering all of the other expensive work that needed to be done on the house, so I chose not to tell her. I would just keep my window closed as much as possible, during most of the day, but definitely while I was asleep. It wasn't that big of a deal since it was summer time, hot and humid, and we usually had the central air conditioning on. But my mom turned it off at night sometimes to save on the bill, and I would have to remember not to open my window, no matter what. The idea of some big, hairy moth flying into my room and landing on my face or crawling into my ear gave me goose bumps already. Thanks a lot, Paul.

"You were fired?!" my mom screamed.

"I quit. I said I'd stay for two more weeks—as is the standard procedure—*or* they could let me go immediately."

"And *they* let *you* go. You were fired, you little asshole."

"I'll get another job."

"Where?"

"I don't know yet."

"Find out soon, because I am pissed. I'm pissed."

"Where was I going with that job anyway? Where? Nowhere!"

"To the bank, that's where! We don't have extra money lying around, sweetheart. You've got your head in the clouds cuz you're goin' to school, hangin' out with people who have nice cars, got you thinking shit is easy. Shit isn't easy, Cleo. You *needed* that job. I needed you to have that job! How are you gonna get loans for school if you have no income?"

"I'm not stupid! You think I think money grows on trees? Hell no, I don't think that! You think I'm oblivious?! What about you?! You're oblivious if you don't think I saw you crying on the floor when you were dead broke and didn't know what the hell to do. You don't think I was as fearful as you were, wondering where we were gonna live? Yeah, I'm in college now, and trust me, I appreciate it. But guess what? I was hungry just like you were."

I banged out the front door, leaving her in the kitchen to stew in her own rage. Yeah, I was mad. I was mad as hell, but I wasn't gonna let it get to me like that. How dare she tell me that I think shit is easy! Acting like I wasn't there when we didn't have shit to eat. Acting like I wasn't there, shivering my ass off when we had to heat the house with the oven. Acting like I never felt the embarrassment of going to the corner store with food stamps. No, shit isn't easy, but that's a lame ass excuse for just accepting the shit-hole predicament you're in.

I sat on the curb outside of Derek's apartment. I don't know how long I sat there, maybe it was even an hour. Luckily he came by then, however long it was. I was taking a chance by going over there unannounced; I really had no clue when he might be home.

His jaw dropped when he saw me, then his face lit up with a smile. He took my hand to help me off the curb then hugged me tightly with his face buried in my neck. He kissed my neck, then my lips, then hugged me some more. "Cleo," he sighed.

"Derek," I said rather cordially.

"I feel like it's been so long. You look good."

"It hasn't been that long, Derek, please. Maybe a week or so."

"Well, I missed you."

"Can we go inside?"

"Of course, babe."

I stopped sharply and looked at him. "Please, Derek, *please*. I'm stressed as it is."

He put his hand on my back and guided me inside. "I'm trying to soothe you."

"By calling me the pet names that you know I hate?"

"Okay, okay! Let's drop it."

I went straight to his bedroom and took off my shoes, socks, and pants. I tried to lie seductively across his bed in my tank top and panties, but he was taking too long for me to hold the pose. I got up and went to find him sorting through his mail at the dining room table. "Excuse me."

He looked up. "Damn. Look at those thighs. Damn, I missed you."

"Oh, really? I couldn't tell."

"I wanna kiss you all over."

"Oh, for real?"

"As soon as I write this check…"

I went back into his room, stretched across the bed and stared out the window. Or, shall I say, at my reflection in the window. It was too dark out to see anything outside of the apartment, except for the little rectangles of light from other people's windows. I was just starting to fall asleep when I felt Derek's weight on the bed as he crawled over me. He started kissing the back of my neck as he rubbed my back beneath my shirt. He unfastened my bra and turned me over.

"Beautiful."

I tilted my head with a closed-lipped smile. I removed my bra from beneath my tank top as Derek removed my panties. I rested my feet on his back and shoulders as he did what he does best, making me feel like the tastiest, most irresistible thing in the world. I shivered and shuttered, sweated, swore, and stuttered, until everything was released in one long, deep wave of a climax that nearly knocked me comatose. When my eyes squeezed shut from the pleasure he'd caused, I didn't have the strength to open them, not even as he removed my shirt and turned me back over.

The last thing I remember was him collapsing on top of my back. I wanted to tell him to get off because it was so hot and we were both sticky with sweat, but I fell asleep instead.

"Morning, sunshine." Derek pushed my hair back and smiled in my face. "It's so good to see you here in my bed in the morning."

Yeah, about that...

"You're so cute in the morning."

I looked at myself in the mirror. My hair had frizzed up during the course of the night, my skin was polished with sweat and grime, and my make-up had made raccoon eyes on my face. Cute? Not in the slightest. Sca-ry. I made a beeline for the bathroom and took a refreshing shower. As I cleaned my body, I decided to clean my life up as well. No more having random boys on call to sex me up whenever I was stressed. No more dead-end job. No more bitchy bitch. I looked in the mirror at my clean face and my slicked-back hair. The slick sheen of the ponytail would puff up soon, as water was my only styling ingredient, but I looked new and fresh for the moment, which was inspiring.

"Derek," I said at the kitchen doorway as he stood over the stove, making omelets.

"Yes, dear?"

I rolled my eyes and almost said something bitchy, but regained my composure. My intention was to tell him that I wasn't going to see him ever again, but suddenly that seemed way too harsh. He would be crushed. He would probably slam his face down on the hot stove to avoid the sheer misery of my eternal absence. And how would that look for me? Badly, for sure.

"I have to go."

"Eat first," he said, sliding a delicious-looking cheese omelet onto a plate beside some delicious-looking sausage links. "Please?"

I sat across the table from him and inhaled my breakfast. He ate slowly, with manners, cutting things up and chewing delicately. I put down my utensils, finished off my orange juice, and forced a smile. "Yeah. So. Thank you."

"Of course, baby."

"Yeah, well, about that…"

"What?"

"The whole baby thing."

He dropped his fork and his jaw and his eyes bloomed wide. "Baby?" He looked down at my belly, then up at my face, then down and up again.

"Oh, God, no, Derek! Are you crazy?! Shit. Hell no, *hell no*, hell no. Are you crazy? Oh my God. No."

"Oh." He looked relieved, but also disappointed. "Oh, okay. What baby thing are you talking about then?"

"You calling me baby! I don't like it. I really don't like when you call me anything but Cleo. It's kind of a problem for me."

"Really now?"

"Yeah. So… I'm gonna go."

"For real? Because of that?"

I nodded. "Among other things. But… I'm gonna go. So… bye." I got up from the table, pushed in my chair, cleaned my place setting, and left. It was a beautiful day outside, the perfect temperature, a bright blue sky, with cumulonimbus clouds floating by. A day like that could make even my grayest moods bright. I walked home, which took nearly an hour, but I didn't regret it, not even when I stopped in an unfamiliar corner store and had a run-in with Alicia.

She approached me, flipping her long micro braids behind her shoulder. "You live around here? I've never seen you before."

"Not really." I shielded myself behind the open glass door of the beverage cooler. It was an entirely different thing running into her outside of school, and I'm not even gonna act like I wasn't kind of scared.

"Didn't think so." She pushed the door shut, forcing me out of the way before I'd even gotten my drink out. "You and Travis are friends?"

"Something like that."

"Fuck buddies?"

I rolled my eyes. "No."

"You better not be."

"You like him or something?"

"Like I would discuss that with you even if I did. No, I don't like him. But he looks good, and you don't. I just hate to see two people on two vastly different levels of sexiness waste their time."

"What is your problem? I don't know you, so I don't know why you think you know me enough to hate me."

"I don't care enough to hate you, ho. What I do know is you're a stuck-up, brown-nosing bitch."

"I don't kiss ass to save my life. So, what? You're mad cuz I'm smart?

And cute? Please get a life."

"I wanna stomp your ass so bad, but it really wouldn't be fair. What good would it do anyway? Everyone would just feel all sorry for Miss Goody–Two–Shoes and I'd come off looking like the bitch."

"I'm so confused as to what this is even about."

"And let's leave it at that." She shoved me a little as she walked by.

I grabbed my drink from the refrigerator and speed–walked to the counter at the front of the store. I kept glancing behind myself as the store clerk rang up my bottle of soda and slowly counted out my change. I could see Alicia coming down the aisle toward me, her hand already in a bag of salt and vinegar potato chips that she hadn't yet paid for.

Hurry it up, man.

"Two seventy-five is your change," he said, dropping eleven quarters into my open palm. "Sorry, but I'm out of ones right now."

"That's fine." I shoved the quarters into my tight jeans pocket, which was way uncomfortable. I took my bottle and left the store. For the next couple blocks or so I couldn't help glancing over my shoulder after every few feet I covered. Alicia was never behind me, but her menacing words and behavior haunted me all the way home. Not even the perfect weather could release the tension I felt at that point.

Wasn't I too old to be dealing with bullies? I'd only been in one fight in my life with a girl other than my sister, but never ever over a boy and I was not about to start. I'd just have to duck Alicia whenever possible, or use my words and superior intellect to keep her at bay, and then physically hide behind our shared object of affection if she did decide to swing on me.

Travis picked me up at my house and drove us back to his house. He was smelling as good as he looked. "What's up?" he asked, turning the volume of the radio down.

"Well, since you asked." I cleared my throat. "What's up with that Alicia girl? Why does she hate me? I get the feeling it has something to do with you."

He laughed. "No shit. She hates every girl within three feet of me."

"Uh huh, why?"

"If you must know, we smoked together once. She ended up giving me head, which the poor girl practically begged to do. I wasn't tryna be her boyfriend though, and she took offense to that. Shit, it's not like I asked her to do it, so I don't really care."

"That's… pretty awkward."

"Must be for her. Again, I don't really care. On a happier note, how do you like salmon?"

"I do…"

"Good, cuz that's what we're cooking. With rice and a vegetable medley on the side."

"Do you guys drink with every meal?"

"You mean wine?"

"Yeah, wine."

"My parents usually do, yeah. I do occasionally. Not every meal though, just dinner. That's the only meal we have together though. So, what are your parents like?"

Whoa. Totally caught me off guard with that. I skimmed my imaginative library for a plausible lie. "I don't wanna talk about my parents," I decided to say.

"Oh, sorry."

"No, I'm sorry. You've shared so much with me, I shouldn't have this wall up. Okay, well, I've met my dad twice. He's an asshole, deadbeat type. My mom is… I don't know how to describe her. Distant, maybe."

"Oh." I could tell that he wanted to apologize again.

"It's okay, I'm so over parents anyway," I joked. "They're so last season."

He forced a laugh. "One day you'll get to show them how it should be done," he said enthusiastically.

I simply nodded in agreement, just as I nodded in agreement as he talked me through the steps of making dinner. I tried to take mental notes for future reference, but I have a feeling I couldn't recall a thing if I had to. Kina strolled through the kitchen a couple of times to see how things were going.

"Smells delicious," she said. "You'll have to give me the recipe."

"Funny," Travis replied. "We got it from this great book called *Kina's Cooking Companion.*"

"You should read it," I added. "It's *amazing.*"

"I've seen her before! Gorgeous woman."

"Kind of favors you," I told her.

"Oh stop! You really think so? She's *gorgeous*!" She walked out, laughing.

"Conceited much?" Travis sighed.

"Your parents are fun."

"Eh."

"Eh? They are! Trust me, you'd understand if you had parents like mine."

"That would be nice sometimes. I could do without the interference."

"You're crazy."

"Everyone wants what they can't have."

"I guess that's true." I set the table in the dining room. I stood rearranging the utensils, trying to figure out which setting looked proper.

Terrence came in and waved his hand across my work to throw me off. "Oh please! You don't have to do all of that! We don't know how they're supposed to go!"

"But your stuff is so nice, it just looks like it should be set up right."

"It's right just like that, everything piled up on the right-hand side. Unless you're left-handed."

"I'm not."

"Good then, cuz we don't allow those kinds in our home." He gave me a soft pat on the back. "Dinner better be as good as it smells or you two are taking us out to eat."

Travis rolled his eyes as he carried in the last platter. "It's good, it's good. We followed the recipe and nothing's been burned, so it should taste just like Mom's."

"Doubtful," Kina said, taking her seat. "You think I put all my secrets in that book? Puh-lease. You never tell anybody *everything*. Especially us girls." She winked at me. "Pour me a glass, honey. And fix me a plate, baby. Guess who came into the restaurant today for lunch?"

"Who?" Terrence asked.

"That news anchor on channel two. She did that segment on the dog fashion shows last night."

"And why did you even remember that?"

"I didn't, she told one of the waiters, who told me. She's new in town."

"You don't know anyone who comes into your restaurant," Travis said.

"Except—"

"Yeah, yeah, Michael Flatley."

She smiled. "Oh, dear God, the salmon."

"How is it?" I asked cautiously, preparing myself for the worst.

"Good, my lovelies, quite good. Maybe more marinade next time?"

"You marinated it last night," Travis said.

"Shush!" she replied. "Not in front of the guest."

"Can we really call her a guest now that we had her cook for us?"

"Damn right we can! I'm still going to offer her dessert when we're finished. Of course she'll have to run out to Rita's and get it. I'll have a custard myself."

"Mmm, I love their custard," I said.

"Are you serious about that, Mom?"

"Well, do you want dessert?" Terrence asked.

"Yeah."

"Then there's your answer," Kina replied.

I'll be damned if they weren't serious. They laughed about it, but laughed as they showed us to the door. Travis and I took a short walk over to South Street, talking back and forth. I had a strong urge to hold his hand but fought it with all my strength. It was like our hands were magnets, drawn to each other. No, it was more like his hand was a magnet, a big, heavy, solid magnet. My hand was more like a flimsy piece of metal unable to resist the magnet's pull. A couple of times I lost focus and my hand drifted over to his. Our skin made contact for just an instant, sending a rush of fluttery static throughout my body. Instinctively I snatched my hand back and prayed that he didn't find me awkward.

"I'll have a cup of vanilla and a cup of chocolate custard, with lids, in bags please," he said to the girl behind the window.

"What size?" she asked, yawning.

"Regular. Then can I also have…" He turned to me.

"Mango," I told him.

"A regular cup of mango and a regular cup of chocolate water ice."

"Thanks," I said as we headed back to his house.

"Thank my dad. Want some?" He held his spoon up to my face.

"No thanks."

"Come on, try it!"

"Okay, okay." Of course I would eat anything he fed me, but I was nervous that I would do something stupid, like not be able to resist licking from the spoon all the way up his entire arm, which I somehow managed not to do.

"Like it?" he asked.

"Not at all. Chocolate water ice makes no sense."

"Watch your mouth! The chocolate custard is my dad's. Me and my dad fiend for all things chocolate."

"Like me and your mom?"

"Ooh, nasty! But true, so true. We do love the chocolate ladies. Although I'd have to say you're more of a vanilla fudge."

"Oh my God."

"There's nothing *clearly* wrong with vanilla fudge, I'm just saying."

"Clearly wrong? I'm gonna change the subject and let that slide. You wanna taste?"

He responded by chomping down on my spoon. "What flavor is this?"

"Mango. You ordered it for me and you don't even remember."

"Mango? Eh, it's okay. I'll stick with chocolate though."

"Suit yourself."

"Suits me just fine."

Travis's parents thanked us for the custard run and retreated to the media room. (Yes, the media room. I know, right?) I, being a very slow eater, sat on the barstool at the island and finished off my water ice, which was pretty much mango soup by that point.

"We don't have much left to do for our presentation," Travis said.

"Yeah, I was thinking the same thing. Exactly what is there left to do?"

He shrugged as he leaned across the countertop towards me. His eyes just looked into mine for a couple of seconds until I got too scared and looked away. He snatched my cup up and swirled it around. "How are you still eating this?"

I shrugged. "I guess I'm done."

He dropped the cup into the trash can and then took my hand. My heart was pounding as he led me to the stairs, then placed his hands on my hips to guide me up before him. I took my usual seat on the couch as he locked the door. My mouth was a freaking desert. If only the excessive moisture from my armpits could've been redirected to my mouth.

"Way over there?" he asked. "You can sit on the bed if you want." He was super casual, just hanging out.

This was weird to me. Was it happening? Wasn't it? It had been a very long time since I'd had spontaneous sex, or had to wonder whether or not it was happening. I couldn't read him. He was sitting on the bed, comfortably, talking. About what? Pay attention, keep up.

"Can I kiss you?"

"Yeah!" I replied, a bit too eagerly. I couldn't help blushing, which only embarrassed me further.

"Where?"

A downpour down there.

He smiled, put his hand at the nape of my neck, and leaned in to kiss me. His mouth was so, so soft and he used the perfect amount of pressure, exploring my mouth with his tongue, nibbling my lips till they tingled. He leaned me back onto his pillow, still kissing. His weight on top of me felt so good, I wanted to grab him, but I was scared. Me, scared. I gently held onto his arms as he wedged himself between my legs.

He pulled back a little. "Where?" he asked again with a raised eyebrow and a coy smile.

"Anywhere," I told him, then thought of something better. "Everywhere," I gushed.

He touched his fingertips lightly to my neck. "Here?"

I nodded.

He traced his fingers down to my breasts, where he circled my nipple through my t-shirt. He nodded for me, then used his whole hand to slide under my shirt and bra to get a better grip. He kneeled down to brush his lips across my breasts, laying sweet, sexy kisses as he massaged them in his strong hands. He made an invisible trail down my belly, oblivious to or ignoring my (many) imperfections. I held my breath as he hovered over my fly, unfastening my pants excruciatingly slowly. He looked up at me and smiled.

"Here?"

I couldn't not smile. I lifted myself up a little so he could undress me. I reached up to take off his shirt. This time my hands thought for themselves, rubbing all over his body as we kissed and then moving fervently at his belt buckle.

He backed off a bit. "No, no. Not yet. You first."

I was so wet I almost felt bad for him, but he went down like a pro, doing everything my body was craving that I didn't even know I wanted on a conscious level. He showed me rhythms I'd never felt in my life, striking a chord I didn't know I had. I didn't need to keep my hands on his head to guide him along, so I gripped the sheets to keep from losing my mind.

Soprano shrieks escaped my throat and my eyes squeezed shut as he released all the feeling that he'd built up inside of me. And he kept going. Thinking I could take no more, I wanted to ask him to stop, but that last reaching of my peak had somehow turned me mute, or I guess he'd really just turned me out. With his guidance, we made a swift transition, with my face conveniently hovering at his fly. I got his clothes out of the way and gave him all I had, which he clearly appreciated. With my heart beating a rapid rhythm against my chest, I stared up at the ceiling from the foot of the bed.

Travis's face came into view a moment later. I wrapped my legs around his waist and pulled him deeper… and I must say he could reach deeper than places J. Cru could only rap about. He was reaching places I'd never felt, but I wanted him deeper still. I wanted to devour him. I was greedy. He made me greedy. And justifiably so, because the tremors that shook me that third time were a new sensation to me. Never ever had a boy made me feel so crazy, physically and emotionally. I was lost in him.

Travis rolled a blunt at the edge of the bed while I rested on the pillow, still coming down from the highs he'd taken me to. My heart was still aflutter and my skin was still tingling. A tear slipped from my eye and soaked into the pillow. I couldn't even explain that to myself. I was just so happy. I wanted to roll over and touch him, to rub his back, to kiss his neck, but I remained still. I felt like moving would make the experience disappear, like it was a mirage or something. It was dark outside, but I didn't know what time it was. I could only see by the blue light coming in through the window, which threw highlights on the glistening condom on the nightstand.

"What time is it?" I asked.

"Who knows?"

Hmm. So he couldn't be dying for me to leave, I thought.

"You have somewhere to be?"

"Not really."

"Good. So we can just chill for a while. You don't have to work or anything?"

"I quit."

"Oh, shit."

"But your parents won't care that I'm still here?"

"They don't know what we're doing."

"Well, that depends on what time it is."

He offered me a hit, but I declined politely. "They probably think we've been having sex this whole time anyway. I showed my mom our presentation and she was like 'Well, it looks done to me, so what are y'all doin' up there all this time?'"

"Oh, great. What did you say?"

"I shrugged." He started coughing like crazy and put the blunt out in the saucer on his nightstand. Daintily, he picked up the condom and dropped it in the wastebasket. I watched as he crossed the room in his blue plaid boxers. Watching his muscles move beneath his beautiful, smooth skin made me salivate… from all of my lips. He returned to bed with his computer. "I've been meaning to ask you…"

"Yeah?"

"When you first met my dad…"

Oh, no, where's he's going with this? Was I checking him out a little too much?

"You kind of freaked out about the picture I showed him on the Internet."

A lump grew in my throat.

"What was up with that?"

I turned the computer towards myself and typed in my URL. His mouth hung open and his eyes popped right out of his head. "That's what was up," I told him.

"No," he said, rubbing his chin and smiling, "That's what is up. Shit, if I would've seen these earlier we would've been having sex every time I ever saw you! At school and everything!"

"Shut up," I laughed.

"You're real sexy. No, you were already real sexy. Now you're real fucking sexy like *damn*. Who takes these pictures of you?"

"Me."

"I don't to sound like a such a pig, I mean, you look good, but it's great photography as well. You have a great eye. But, are you naked?!"

"Yeah," I said, almost inaudibly.

"What do your parents think? Or, well, your mom?"

I rolled my eyes. "Tscha. She hates it, of course, thinks it's wrong to put my sexuality on display like that. This coming from a lady who got pregnant in high school. Her and my sister, but they look at me like I'm Satan herself. Pregnancy is a *very* clear display of a woman's sexuality! Hell, that tells more about her sex life than just some pictures! Anybody can take some pictures, a virgin can take some pictures! But there's only one way to get pregnant. I hate that shit, but she hates my site, so I guess we're all squared away." I finally took a breath and realized that he probably didn't give a shit about my little rant.

"Wow, you feel pretty strongly about that, huh?"

"I have to. I would've taken it down a long time ago if I let her get to me." A thought popped into my head to check my cell phone. It was almost two in the morning. His laptop must've been messed up cuz it had me thinking it was only like eleven at night.

"Oh yeah, it was set to West Coast time when I got it and I never fixed it. I mean, if you're uncomfortable being here this late I can take you home."

"No, it's cool."

"We can go to school together tomorrow, if that's okay. You can wear something of my mom's."

The first thing that popped into my head was that blue dashiki she wore when we first met. Now I love being Black, but I can't be walkin' around in a dashiki. Come on now. It wouldn't even be convincing. "Uh, I don't know."

"She has normal clothes," Travis laughed, either reading my mind or my face. "I'll get you something."

"Aren't they sleep?"

"She has two closets. There are plenty of clothes in the guest room."

"Oh, *excuse* me!"

"Shut up," he chuckled, putting on a white t-shirt as he headed for the door.

I sat and checked the new messages on my site just to keep from obsessing about how amazing my life was at that moment. I was crushing mad hard. I like-liked him more than I'd ever like-liked anyone. He was just so perfect. Not flawless, but perfect for me, with whatever imperfections he might have. Stop obsessing, bitch, read your mail, 'fore you fall for him or something.

Travis returned. "Try this."

I got out of bed in my underwear, not even shy about it; his gaze warmed me. I stepped into the jeans and pulled them up… to my thighs and could go no further. Kind of embarrassing. I kept my eyes on the floor.

"I'll find something else," Travis said, quite nonchalant about it. He left and came back with a pair of black lounge pants and a pack of underwear. "They're new, don't worry. My cousin had to buy some when she visited, but she left them here."

The black yoga pants, which were meant to be somewhat loose, hugged my body tight, tight, *tight*, like a long lost lover. But I was confident that I could work it with the plain white tee that he gave me. I didn't get much sleep. The constant pitter-patter of my excited heart kept me awake most of the night. Every time Travis would move, I could feel his shifting weight and my heart rate would speed up all over again.

It was nice to wake up a little later than I usually have to since I didn't have to take the subway to campus. It wasn't until we got on I-95 that I remembered we had a presentation to do. I knew we had our shit together, we did a lot of quality work on it, but I was so far off in lala land that I'd forgotten to prepare what to say.

"It's all good," Travis said calmly. "We know the stuff. We can just talk."

I had a terrible knot in my stomach. I was almost glad that Travis drove so recklessly on the highway—if we crashed, we could hardly be expected to do our presentation.

"You must be my good luck charm," Travis said, pulling into a space right near our building. And who could be walking in our direction at that exact time but Alicia. I felt my heart pop up into my throat. I would've fled the scene if I didn't feel like I was going to vomit.

"It's a little early to be hanging out," she said, "and from the looks of those clothes I think it's safe to say somebody had a sleepover. You look like shit." She laughed loudly at herself. "Why wasn't I invited? Oh, right. I don't associate with assholes and fat whores."

"Shut up," Travis sighed. "Don't get mad about it, just move on. You can call people whatever names you want but you have to deal with the fact that nobody wants to be with you but your lesbian lover over there."

Alicia gasped. "Where did you hear that shit?!" she shouted, darting he eyes between us.

"Don't worry, Alicia, it's our secret."

She flipped her hair over her shoulder and walked off in a tizzy. Her friend was waiting by the door, and they went inside together.

"I told you how she was jockin' me, right? Well, she told me that if I would be her man, we could have a threesome with that Lindsay girl, that I could watch them go down on each other."

I couldn't believe he turned her down; I thought any man would agree to that.

"Of course I turned her down! I'm not for that shit. Especially not at the expense of being locked down with a bitch like Alicia."

"Does her friend know she made that offer?"

"Nope. Alicia said they'd never talked about it, but she could see in Lindsay's eyes that she wanted to. Bitch is crazy, thinks everybody wants a piece." He took my hand and we walked inside together. I was not expecting that at all, but relished in the fact that Alicia caught of a glimpse of us walking by. Well, until she dragged her finger across her throat like a knife. Then I wiped the smile off of my face and kept my focus straight ahead, only looking back once to make sure she wasn't stalking us.

Travis wasn't in class the following day. My heart slowly sank as we reached the halfway point of class and I realized he wasn't just embarrassingly late. Then I told myself, Oh, good, now you can pay attention instead of spending the whole class period planning on how to sneak peeks at those dreamy hazel eyes and that big, sexy smile. I'd already wasted away half the class worrying about and wondering what could be keeping him, so I figured it was time to really pay attention. Then my heart froze in terror when Alicia and I made eye contact and I realized not one person on campus cared enough to protect me from her. She gave the finger and I immediately averted my gaze back to the book on my desk.

Funny, Travis's absence only made me think harder and obsess more. Where was he? Maybe he wasn't as confident as he seemed, and he was mortified by the mediocre (in my opinion) presentation that we gave the day before, so he decided to spend the next class in bed. Unlikely. The only reason I entertained that hypothesis was because I kind of felt that way myself that morning. (Seriously, our report kind of sucked.)

Or perhaps he was so smitten with me that the mere though of my being sent his heart aflutter, and so it would just be torture to sit so near to me during class and not devour me on the spot. So all he could bear to do was to lie in bed and fantasize about being together.

Travis and I would have such beautiful children, I don't think the world would be able to stand it. You would probably be able to tell that they were mixed with a little something, but they would be so exotically unique that I don't think anyone would even dare suggest they were white. It would be like an honor to have Travis's babies. To think of anything more deeply intimate would be impossible. Two people merging together as one, not just physically as in sex, but for an actual *lifetime.* Life. To be completely real, I wouldn't even mind staying home to take care of them. I couldn't ask for anything more than just to have him call me *wifey.* Wifey? Where was this coming from? It was so unlike myself, but I couldn't deny how I felt.

I guess I was being a bit obsessive. I went home to my bedroom and stretched across my bed, debating what to do. I could call him. No. Don't. Don't look desperate. I could go over there. Hello! Trying not to look desperate here! Without a car, it would be quite a trek—completely desperate situation. Well, why not call?

Because I'm scared.

I was. I was so scared. I wanted to slap some sense into myself. I wasn't a virgin, so what hell was wrong with me? Why was I catching feelings for this cute, funny, charming, smart, undeniably and universally attractive boy? Why? Why? Why does anyone fall for anyone? It's stupid. Completely stupid.

I tried to convince myself of the absurdity of it all, but I just wasn't having it. It was too late for me. Too late to save my own drowning soul. I turned on the radio to mask the buzzing feelings of what-I-prayed-to-God-wasn't-love in my tummy.

I crawled around my bedroom floor on Saturday morn-ing, picking up trash and papers I'd haphazardly tossed about throughout the week. The next step in Operation: Clean Bedroom was to get all of my dirty clothes off of the floor, maybe wash them, and then vacuum. My ears perked up at the sound of a familiar name on the radio. I turned up the volume and listened to the "new hot track" about how many girls this rapper had and how none of them could ever be his wife. And then:

She get it from her mom
Momma gave it to her good
Cuz she's the thickest chick
You ever seen in the hood.
They say she kinda bourgie
Cuz she's bout her business, right.
But that's cool with me
Cuz she could never be my wife.

You know she's a smart girl
Cuz she give good brain.
The kind that give you chills
For days and days.
She don't talk much
Til she in da bed.
And don't ask her for [shit]
Til you give her some [head].
But I'll play along
Cuz that [shit] is tight.
But even none of that
Could turn a [bitch] to my wife.

I immediately knew that verse was about me. How could it not be me? Thick, 'bout my business, love to get head? My mouth hung open in shock and I stared at my radio as J. Cru moved on to the chorus.

"That son of a bitch," I said aloud to myself.

The radio DJ came in as the song faded out. "That was new-comer J. Cru, with *Ain't Ma Girl*."

"No shit I'm not your girl!" I screamed at him through the radio. "Did I ever ask to be, you fake ass wannnabe?" It was kind of sad, now that I look back on it. Me, sitting there, yearning for Travis, too scared to call, screaming at the radio, calling Jason a wannabe while he was clearly making big things happen for himself. But that song was just absurd. And how many girls did he have? I never thought it was more than a couple because he was *always* ready for me. That's why I kept him around. Yes, *I* kept *him* around, and here he was thinking *he* had *me*!

I picked up my phone and scrolled through my contacts list. But what would I say? I didn't have anything to say. I had plenty to say, actually, but no words to express any of it. And if I wanted to be completely honest with myself, I would have realized that I really only wanted to talk to Jason for some male attention, as a substitute for what I was not getting from Travis.

So maybe I should call Travis… I took my time scrolling to the T's. *Tasha, Thai House, Tiffany, Tool World, Travis.* It rang forever. I slowly died. Finally his voicemail picked up. I was relieved and elated. I didn't have time to drive myself crazy with what-ifs because my phone rang just as soon as I'd hung up.

"Hey," I said, trying to sound casual.

"Hey," he said casually.

"I just called you."

"I know. What's up?"

"You missed class the other day, and I haven't heard from you since. Are you okay?"

"I'm straight. I was just on chill mode."

"Okay. That's cool. Have you heard this new song called *Ain't Ma Girl* by this lame ass called J. Cru?"

"Yeah, I heard it yesterday. Why'd you call him lame? That shit is kinda tight."

"It's just weird cuz I know him."

"For real? How?"

"The second verse is about me."

Silence. Dead-ass silence. So very awkward.

"So! Have your parents asked about me?"

"No, you were just here like two days ago."

"Oh."

I guess he could sense my disappointment, so he added, "But I'm sure they will. Um, I guess I'll see you next week. Last week of class."

"Yup."

"Okay, bye." Click. Didn't even wait for me to say goodbye. Well that left me in no mood to even entertain the idea of calling Jason. My mind was simply reeling over what just happened. What the hell did I say? I could barely recall, but my gut told me everything I'd said was pathetically dumb. I did mention J. Cru. And I said the song was about me. Why the hell did I say that? Was I trying to make myself sound like some groupie whore? Because that's exactly what I just did. And I asked if his parents asked for me. Oh my God. I don't know why I said anything that I said, it just came out, like verbal diarrhea.

After sitting on my bed and obsessing for several minutes, I forced myself to shake it off. How unlike me to sit in my room and think about a boy. A boy. One boy. There were a dozen boys I could call up, all of which would probably drop whatever they had planned just to fuck me by midnight. For real. So I had no reason to sit and try not to cry, because I had no reason to cry. Over a boy. Over a dick. Over sex. I could have all the sex I wanted.

If only all I wanted was sex.

Lele was practicing in the living room, fake teeth a-shinin'.

"Good," Deena said, clapping her hands to the beat. "Hit those poses."

For the finish, she cart-wheeled into a split with her hands in the air, face frozen in that big, stupid grin.

"Break," Deena announced.

Leslie got up, dramatically wiped her brow, and came to sit beside me. "The big one is coming up," she told me. "You know, Little Miss Pretty?"

"Oh, of course," I lied.

"I hope to bring home the big crown for you guys."

"Excuse me?!" Deena shouted from the kitchen. "We're not doin' all this work to go in there on hopes!"

"Okay, okay." She secretly rolled her eyes to me, smiling. "We *will* win the big crown."

Deena poked her head into the living room. "Oh, honey, it's not about me, it's about you."

I rolled my eyes and Lele and I laughed.

"Will you come?"

"Where?"

"The pageant!"

"I don't know, it sounds pretty lame."

She held her hand up in my face. "Whatever. What's lame is you getting fired."

I gasped and caught myself before I let her have it. "First of all, I quit."

"Secondly?"

"Second of all, I'll find another job."

"Where?"

"What's with all the questions?"

"Grandma won't stop complaining about you not working."

"I don't give a shit anymore."

Leslie shrugged, got up, and went into the kitchen. Deena came out shortly, her nose in the air. "Stop cursing around my daughter."

"You mean the spy sent by Mom?"

"Whatever you wanna call her, she's a child, so the foul language is just uncalled-for. Anyway, I like what you're doing with your make-up. Your eyelashes look incredible."

"Thanks," I replied, confused and taken aback.

"You know, Cleo, if you need a job you could always come to me."

"Huh?"

"Selling Bloom. Duh."

I hadn't thought of that. Was she serious? She looked serious. And the job didn't look too hard. "For real?"

"Of course I'm for real. Just give me the word."

"Who would I even sell it to?"

"I'll give you Mom. What about Janine? Do you still talk to her?"

"Not lately."

"I mean you can sell to whoever has money and skin. Hell, just money for all I care. A great way to start off would be to have a party."

"A party?"

"So, are you in?"

"Umm..."

Deena was beaming with anticipation. Her glow was freaking me out. She had been stone cold a minute before. Could Bloom ladies just flick a switch and be instantly charming? "Come on, Cleo. It's a great opportunity." Smile beaming. Creepy.

I would be done with school in the next week, my bank account was in the double digits and dwindling, and I really had nothing else on my plate but Travis. I was dangerously close to becoming one of those girls that I hate, with no life but that of her boyfriend—and I didn't even have a boyfriend. This was my only chance to keep some respect for myself.

"Okay, I'm in," I said, holding my hand out to shake hers.

She waved her limp hand in my face and giggled in a Stepford wife kind of way. So not my sister. No wonder she made a killing; she was quite pleasant. I'd buy shit from her if I didn't know her. "I'll bring the stuff by later. There are just a few forms to fill out and you'll be on your way. I'll handle the party details, you just invite some folks, I'm not sure about the date yet, and I'll get back to you. Lele! Let's get started!"

It was the second to last day of class, so he had to show up. I couldn't stop staring at the door. Finally he came through, actually two minutes early. So I was overreacting a bit. He said "wassup" and took his seat beside me. Nothing special, just "wassup" with a slight nod of the head. Had he forgotten who I was? The amazing sex we had? Those sexy ass pictures I'd let him in on? How could he not remember me? Maybe I should've called more. I'd only called four times since I'd seen him five days ago. I had to fight myself to keep from calling more but maybe it wasn't worth the trouble. I should've let myself go.

As far as I could tell, he didn't look at me once during class. So you know I lapped it up when he finally turned to me after class ended.

"You wanna come chill at my crib?"

"When?"

"Now."

I had class now. My second to last day of class. But I hadn't missed a day yet, so what the hell. I followed him to his car and got comfortable in the familiar curves of the passenger seat. He started the car and the speakers started blasting music, the last few lines of the second verse of *Ain't Ma Girl*. I reached to turn it off but Travis pushed my hand away.

"I hate this song," I said.

"I like it. Were you serious when you said that you know him?"

"Yeah."

"That's wild. So you know a lot of dudes?"

"Huh?"

"I mean, you know this guy, so who else do you know, na'mean?" He shook his head. "Nevermind, I'm trippin."

"You are." What was he trying to say anyway?

"Yeah, whatever. I've just been thinkin' too much lately. I just haven't felt like leaving my room much. I've just been sitting and smoking, and sleeping."

"Oh, what's wrong?"

"I don't know, I'm cool."

"Okay, but if you need me…"

"Yeah, okay."

We went straight up to his bedroom. We sat on opposite sides of his bed. I stared at the TV while Travis rolled a blunt and smoked it. Whenever I stole a glance at him, he looked to be deep in his head. I wished he would open up to me.

Suddenly he reached over and draped his arm across my lap. I looked down at him as he lay on the bed, but his eyes were closed. He was completely still for the remainder of the Spanish-speaking sitcom I was watching. Then he sat up and started kissing me. Once he started on my neck I was no good. The sex was a lot different this time though. He removed my pants and underwear, then pulled his down just enough. He didn't lick, touch, or even look at me down there. We just fucked. Well, it would be more accurate to say that he fucked me. I did get *some* pleasure from it, none of it physical, although it was clear that that wasn't really what was on his mind. I felt pure bliss wrapping my legs around his body, squeezing his arms, kissing his chest. But then it was over as quickly as it had started. He pulled his pants up, rolled over, and possibly fell asleep. I pulled on my panties and pulled up behind him. I couldn't stop yearning for him. The yearning was driving me crazy. Even with him right in front of me, I wanted him. He wasn't mine, I could feel that for sure. He was now even less mine than he had been a few days ago. But I refused to let go.

I got up and put some clothes on. I went downstairs to the kitchen, where Kina was sitting at the island on a barstool, drinking a glass of water and reading a magazine. "Hi," I said to her.

"Hi, Cleo. How are you?"

"I'm okay. Is Travis okay?"

Kina's eyes widened for a moment, then she put on an unconcerned face. "He'll be okay." She waved it off. "But how are you?"

"I'm okay," I repeated. "I'm having a small party so that I can start this Bloom gig that my sister hooked me up with. I would love for you to come."

"Well I would love to support you. When is it?"

"I'm not sure yet, we're still working that out. But I'm sure I'll see you before then."

Her facial expression was unsure, then nonchalant. "Okay, that's fine. Just let me know."

Terrence then walked into the kitchen. Kina looked right at him, sneered, rolled her eyes and walked out. "How's it going, Cleo?"

"Well," I said. "How are you?"

"Couldn't be better."

A loud smash of glass breaking sounded from the adjoining dining room. I hurried in to see what had happened. Kina was sitting at the table, with a soaked magazine and broken glass spread on the table before her. I couldn't really do anything but stare with my mouth open for a moment, then I snapped back to the present and asked if she needed a hand.

"No, Cleo, I'm fine," she said through clenched teeth. "Just go up and visit with Travis *please*."

I turned and quickly went back to Travis's room. I had initially gone downstairs to get a drink, but that clearly was not going to happen. I searched Travis's mini-fridge, although I knew that he was stingy about it. He was definitely asleep. I paced around, sipping a soda, trying out different seats, on the couch, at his desk, on the floor. I wanted him to wake up and be with me. We were wasting time with him sleeping. I wanted to know what was wrong with his mother. And his father hadn't paid her little accident any attention. I sat and stewed for about an hour before Travis rolled over and looked at me with squinty eyes.

"Hi," I said cheerfully, moving quickly to his bedside from his desk.

"Um, do you want a ride home?"

"Uh…"

"I mean, it's almost dinner time, your mom probably wants you home, don't you think?"

"It's like three… not that she actually cooks dinner for me."

"Oh, really? I thought it was later. Well, look, I have things to do so I really don't have time to hang out."

"Oh, really? Oh, okay. Well, yeah, I guess you should probably drive me home then."

It broke my heart to leave him. He pulled up in front of my house and leaned across to give me a hug goodbye. He looked a mess, really tired and sad. Beautiful, of course, but a mess. I wanted to wash his pain away.

Lick it away, if that's what he wanted. I held on a little too long, I guess. I felt him pull back after a moment and he just kind of raised an eyebrow at me. I fumbled for the door handle and got out of there quickly. It took everything in me not to stand on the sidewalk like a pathetic little puppy and watch him drive away.

My house was empty. There were party plans on the kitchen table, along with some Bloom employment forms for me to fill out. I left them as they were and went up to my bedroom. I turned on the radio, heard a snippet of *Ain't Ma Girl*, and turned the radio off. I was too confused to cry. So I laid in bed feeling sorry for myself until I fell asleep.

After my last day of classes, I came home to find my mother and father sitting at the kitchen table, eating hoagies and drinking beer, laughing and talking like the past twenty years hadn't happened. I immediately looked down at the floor because, from the way I felt, I was quite sure my stomach had just fallen out of my body. I wanted to run out the door but my feet were cement blocks, my legs as strong as toothpicks. Besides, they'd already seen me.

"Cleo!" my mother exclaimed as if happy to see me. She hadn't been happy to see me since… when was the last time again? "I was wondering when you'd be home. Look who's here!"

"Who?" I asked, standing at the doorway between the living room and the kitchen.

"I guess I deserve that," my dad said, shrugging. He stood up and walked toward me with outstretched arms. I stood like a tree and let him hug on me. No, because that would make him a tree-hugger, and I know there isn't a good or charitable bone in his entire vile being. "How are you?"

"I'd be a lot better if you would back up. Thank you."

"Cleo…" warned my mother.

"No, it's cool," he said, holding his hands up in surrender. "It's all good."

All good? All good! Well, shit, let's just forget everything you've done and haven't done because it's all good!

"Anyway, how's school?"

"I don't have time for this."

"I got you a hoagie."

"A hoagie? Gee whiz, Dad, a hoagie? All this time and you come back with an em-effin' hoagie." I *really* wanted to say "motherfucking," but given my audience, I figured it might be a bit too much. Also, I didn't want to give the sperm donor any ideas.

"Cleo, that's enough, now sit down." My mom pushed the chair out with her foot. "If we're gonna be a family we need to get along."

I kicked the chair back under the table, spilling a bit of beer over the sides of their clear plastic cups. "A family?! I haven't had a father in my family all my life, now you wanna play house?! Mom, that's crazy."

"You shouldn't talk to your mother like that," he said, his lame attempt at fathering.

"Okay, well since we're exchanging tips, here's one for you: you shouldn't use your family for all they've got and then walk out on your child and her mother."

He grabbed my wrist a little too hard. "That's enough."

I shook free and ran up to my room. I wanted to leave but I didn't wanna leave them in the house together. I was boiling with anger. How could she let him in our house, then sit there and let him talk to me as if he knew me? If I was a boy, I woulda socked him in the face, that bastard. And what was she talking about, saying "if we're gonna be a family" and shit? Was she crazy? Had the woman lost her damn mind? How could we possibly form a family with that man now, after all this time? I stripped down and climbed into bed, pulling the covers up over my head. I was embarrassed that I was crying, but I really didn't know what else to do. There was really nothing I could do. How could I stop my mom from getting stomped on? I already did all I could to let her know that I was totally against it, but besides that… well, what?

Surprisingly, I slept for hours. I must've been exhausted without having really had the chance to feel it. It was getting dark outside, but there was still a little bit of sunlight left. The house was very quiet. I laid on my back, staring up at the ceiling, which was orange from the setting sun. Slowly the orange faded, and as my senses sharpened, I began to hear faint squeaking noises, which grew ever louder. Then there was the heavy breathing and muffled moaning. I threw up a little in my mouth. I moved frantically around my room, trying to find something to make noise and drown out the sounds. I turned on the radio, but there was no use. The sound of *squeak–squeak–squeak–"Mmmmm"–squeak–squeak–"Yeeessss"–squeak–squeak–squeak* was on replay in my head and I could not get it out.

I dressed quickly and hesitated at my door. If I could hear it in my room with the radio on and door closed, when I opened my door it would only get worse. But I had to get the hell out of there. I couldn't bear to sit in the house where my parents were having sex. I opened my bedroom door, immediately threw my hands over my ears, and ran for the front door to let myself out. It was quiet on my street, and although I couldn't actually hear them anymore, I couldn't get the noises out of my mind. At least I was out of the house. Now where would I go? Of course the only place I wanted to go was to Travis's, but he had just kicked me out the day before, only after using me. Not to mention the strange funk that had settled over his entire household.

I waited at the bus stop for a short while. I stared towards the sky and tried to count the number of wires on the power line to distract myself. There were so many, and in my unsteady state of mind, it was so hard to count. By the time the bus came, I had only gotten up to seven on three different tries. I gave up, got on the bus, and rode to Deena's block.

I stood outside of her apartment for a minute or two before getting up the courage to ring the bell. I hated to ask her for anything, sure that she would throw it back in my face someday. I pressed the buzzer and stood waiting, hoping that she wasn't home. Of course she was home, her car was parked right there.

"Who is it?" she asked over the intercom.

"Cleo."

"Cleo?!" she exclaimed, then buzzed me in.

I panted up four flights of stairs. Her door was ajar so I let myself in. It was a modest place, white walls, brown rugs, two bedrooms, tiny kitchen. Lele was eating macaroni and cheese at the coffee table. She smiled at me then went back to watching television. "Hi," I said to her.

Deena came from her bedroom with a book in her hand, her finger keeping the page. She had her hair wrapped in a scarf and her face was shockingly devoid of any make-up. "What a surprise."

"Well…" I shrugged. "I couldn't think of anywhere else to go."

"Why did you even need somewhere to go?" she asked, squinting her eyes at me.

I shook my head and looked down at the floor, afraid that if I looked anyone in the eye, I would break down in tears. "My father is there."

"Oh boy."

"And I could hear them…" I didn't want to say it in front of Lele. "…you know."

"Oh, gross!"

"You're telling me. I had to get out of there."

"Do you want some calming tea?"

"Uh, no thanks."

Deena shook her head and took a seat in the corner of the couch. "That really sucks. Yuck. It's happened to lots people, I'm so glad it's never happened to me though. Horrifying."

I took a seat as well. "She was talking about being a family and everything."

"Oh, please. You know that'll never happen."

"She sounded pretty serious."

"Mom did, but what did Larry say?"

"Well, he didn't say."

"Of course he didn't, because I'm sure he has no intentions of staying. He's just catching up."

"He's disgusting."

"Well, yeah, but what can you do? Give it some time, the whole thing will blow over, and Mom will be back by herself."

"That's not what I want," I said defensively.

She gave me a strange look. "I wasn't saying you want her to be lonely."

"Well I don't. I don't want her to be lonely, I just don't want her to be a fucking pushover and let any man who is hardly interested just use her for whatever they want. Especially *him*."

She looked annoyed that I'd cursed but then let it go, and I was glad that she did. "So find her a nice man who will treat her well."

"I'm not going to find a boyfriend for my mother. How awkward is that?"

She laughed. "Pretty awkward, I guess. But I wouldn't worry about it if I were you. You know Larry doesn't have the heart to stick around."

"Easy for you to say. You've got a father who has his shit together, knows what he wants, and sticks to it. No matter how Mom throws herself at him, you don't have to worry about him ever coming back to ruin her all over again. I, however, got the shit end of the stick, and I have this disgusting crap bag for a father who just drags her along for his own sick pleasure. I am part of him! That makes me want to crawl out of my own skin."

"Sure, he helped make you, but that doesn't mean you have his characteristics as far as being a jerk goes."

"I wish he would just die."

"Cleo!"

"I do!"

"You can't say things like that. The world wouldn't be any better if he were dead."

I cocked my head to the side and narrowed my eyes at her. "Can you honestly sit here and say that to me?"

She shook her head. "So maybe a few women would have a weight lifted from their shoulders…"

"More than a few, I'm sure. Who knows how many brothers and sisters I have in the world? Mom has told me of six other ones that she knows of, spread throughout the city, all by different women."

"Damn, I didn't know that."

"I could pass people on the street every day and they could be my brothers and sisters."

"Oh please."

"It's true! And he doesn't do shit for them either. Fuck him."

"Okay, Cleo, that's enough. I let you get enough of your cursing out, but now I think you need to stop, or at least wait until Lil' Mama is out of earshot." She reached over to the end table and picked up a notebook.

"I'm not listening," Leslie said.

Deena rolled her eyes. "These are just some details of the party I was looking into. I think we should have it next Saturday, which is nearly two weeks. I mean, it's not a huge thing, so I think that's enough notice. Is that okay for you? I mean, what could you possibly have to do, right? Did you fill out those forms I left on the kitchen table?"

"Yeah," I lied.

"So have you been inviting people?"

Not really.

"Good. You want as many people there as possible. I did get some invitations, and you should still send them out to the people that you already told by mouth. Lele, if you're finished eating will you go get that stack of invitations on my dresser?"

She got up and ran into the bedroom.

"I'm going to invite some of my customers, too, but all of the profit from the party will be yours. I've done well enough this month, so I'm not too worried about it. I get new customers everyday anyway, so it's cool."

"Wow, thanks." It was really nice of her to hand off all of her customers to me, if only for one campaign. I wrote out invitations to every woman I knew who might be interested, including Janine and Roy's girlfriend. We spent the rest of the evening watching *Lifetime* movies and planning the party. It was nice hanging out with her like that; I really missed my sister. We didn't say very much to each other throughout the night, but I hoped she felt the same that I did, which was relieved and so glad that we could still be friends after all. I wanted to ask her if she missed me, but I'm not the sappy type.

"Are you gonna sleep here?" Deena asked.

"Yeah, if you don't mind," I replied.

"Of course I don't," she said. "Come on, Lil' Mama, let's get Cleo some blankets."

Lele returned with a sheet, a blanket, and a pillow. I could hear Deena talking on the phone in her bedroom. Leslie helped make up the couch for me. Then she even tucked me in and handed me the remote control. She sat on the edge of the couch beside me and looked sincerely into my eyes. "I'm really sorry about your daddy."

"Thank you, Lele."

"I understand how it feels not to have a daddy."

"I know you do."

"So I know that you must be very sad about it, because daddies are special. I know you're so mad at him, because he's a bad dad, but I don't think you should ever wish your daddy to be dead." She was so right, and who was I to argue with her? She leaned over and hugged me. "You'll be okay. I pray for you every night, and God puts his angels around you, so you don't have to worry because it's in God's hands."

For a child, she was extremely wise, almost in a creepy way. I guess I hadn't given her enough credit for a being a very smart, very cool little girl. I gave her another hug and a kiss on the forehead. "Thank you, Lele. I really needed that."

She gave me the thumbs up and disappeared into her bedroom. As wise as she sounded, I also thought it was a little pathetic that she felt how she did, considering what a jackass her own father was. He was better than mine, since he at least stuck around, but he was definitely no contender for Father of the Year. In a way, maybe she was lucky for having never gotten the chance to get to know him well since I'm sure he would only have broken her heart more than a few times.

I returned home in the morning. There was a shitload of dirty dishes in the sink, soiled with eggs, breakfast meat grease, and pancake batter. The table was set with used dishes for two. I went upstairs. Mom's bedroom door was wide open. The bed was unmade, but no one was in it. No one was in the bathroom. No one was home at all. I went to her underwear drawer, where I know she always keeps a wad of cash. The money was gone, as I'd anticipated, and there was a clearing where it should have been. I shook my head and turned to walk out. My mom was in the doorway.

"What you looking for?" she asked me.

"You know."

"He went to get some milk."

"Get off it, Mom. Please. Are you kidding me? You're kidding me, right? You gave him fifty bucks to get milk?"

She ignored my remark.

I walked out and went to the living room. The DVD/VHS combo

player was gone. It was so ridiculous I laughed out loud. How could she sit upstairs like everything was okay when she was just robbed? Whatever. That was her business. I would be watching movies on my computer for a while then. No way was I going to replace that DVD/VHS player that I'd bought us for Christmas. If she was going to be foolish enough to let him take it, then she damn sure shouldn't expect me to replace it. No, as a matter of fact, I couldn't just stand there and say "whatever" anymore. I ran up to her room and threw the door open.

"What is wrong with you?!" I screamed at her, tears streaming down my face. "You let him take the DVD player?!"

"He needed the money, Cleo! He's your father, have a heart."

"Me have a heart? Tell him to have a heart! He hasn't lifted a fucking finger in his entire life to do anything right but conceive me!"

"Well what else does he need to do for you, huh? What does he owe you? He never asked for you to be born."

"I NEVER ASKED FOR ME TO BE BORN!"

She stared at her feet. "You're right."

Damn right I'm right.

"I'm the only one that wanted you. I wanted you in hopes that it would help to keep him, and I was wrong for that. And I'm sorry. If you need to blame someone, don't blame him anymore. Blame me."

I couldn't decide if she was serious or messing with my mind. I decided it didn't matter. "I'm sick of blaming you," I told her. I went into my room and closed the door. I *was* sick of blaming her, even though she'd just given me a real reason to do so, I just couldn't anymore. I felt horrible, looking at her sitting on the edge of her bed, beaten by love and life. If that was the truth, what she told me, then that was the truth. He didn't want me, I couldn't make him want me, and what did I need him for at this point anyway? Honestly, I needed him to stop taking shit from my house.

But it wasn't my house. It was my mother's house. And if she wanted to put herself out there like that, then I couldn't stop her. The only thing I could do at this point was to stop letting it affect me.

I didn't know how I was feeling. Empty? Confused? I was trying so hard to feel empty, but I was actually spilling over with emotions. Although I told myself I wasn't going to be mad at my mom anymore, it was kind of hard not to be. I didn't really want to watch any movies in the living room, but whenever I remembered that I couldn't, I got so mad that I had to force myself not to cry about it. Travis's sudden distance from me didn't help either. If it were a day in my past, I would've called up Derek or Jason and went to have sex. If it were a day even farther in my past, I would've called up any of the other ten plus men in my phone at any given time and see if they felt like taking my mind off of things. In my quest for monogamy, I was left lonely. I expected that the decision to cut off those men would leave me horny, but I never expected to feel so terrible emotionally. But if fucking was all it took to fulfill me, I wasn't nearly as deep as I thought I was.

I picked up a notebook and pen from the floor and sat cross-legged my bed. I put the pen to the paper and waited for the words to come.

The tears came first, then words flowed from my hand like water from a pitcher until the page was full of my feelings.

Do you know who I am?
Do you?
You must not.
I hate you, there, I said it.
There's one thing about me
That you may or
May not have known.
Do you know who I am?
You must not
Otherwise
You
Would
Not
Dare
To not answer when I call.
When I call.
Me.
ME.
Me calling you
Wanting you
Needing you
Loving you.
Loving you?
This is love?
But it hurts.
It can't be but

It must be because

Why else would

I be

Such a fucking mess?

And I hate that

I

Can become such a mess

Over you

Not calling me

Because, well,

Do you know who I am?

Do you?

Do you know the determination and creativity and intelligence and beauty and strength and sexuality and love

That I possess?

(You know, I have to remind myself of that stuff now

Cuz you've made me such a fucking mess.)

That did help some, to have everything there in front of me. Seeing the words always helps me to really get a good look at what I'm dealing with inside, and there it was. What was it, exactly, I wasn't sure, but it was definitely there.

I went to Keiman's Supermarket and searched the aisles for Roy. I found him stocking shelves and whistling to himself. I walked up and tapped him on the shoulder. He turned around and grinned when he recognized me. "Hey, what's up?"

"I'm good," I said. "How are things going here?"

"We're getting along, although the sun doesn't shine quite as bright without you here."

"Oh, whatever. Well, I just wanted to give you this invitation for your girlfriend. I'm having a little Bloom party to get some money, you know, to jumpstart my career. If you think she'd be interested in coming, I'd love to have her there. And don't be shy just because you're not a female, because I would love to see you there, too. There will be food and fun, and friends."

"I will definitely try to talk her into it. She's into cosmetics and taking care of herself, so I'm sure she would be thrilled to be there."

"Cool. Is Janine here today?"

"Yup. She went on a break a little while ago, but she should be back soon."

I held out Janine's invitation. "Just give her this for me, will you? Thanks."

I left and took the trip to Travis's house. In a way, I wanted him to be there so that I could finally see him again. On the other hand, I was hoping he wasn't there because I didn't really want to face him. What would I say to him? We hadn't talked in so long. How long? A week and a few days? I guess that wasn't *so* long, but I was missing him like crazy. But we had had that awkward goodbye after the last time he had me over, and he hadn't called to clear any of that up with me. But I hadn't called him to ask about it… I just didn't want to look desperate, even though I so completely was. I would've lapped up any morsel of attention he threw at me. This was what was going through my mind the entire way over to Travis's house. Utterly devastating confusion.

I hopped off of the bus and stood at the corner for a while, debating whether or not I should just cross the street and wait for the next bus home… or continue on to Travis's house. His car was not parked in front of the house, but of course that didn't mean it wasn't parked in the back. I walked up the stairs and rang the doorbell. It seemed like an eternity before the door finally opened. Some stranger answered the door. She looked familiar.

"Can I help you?" she asked.

"Hi, is Travis here?" I asked. Why did I ask for Travis? Why? I could've skipped over the whole Travis thing and asked if Kina was home.

"No, he's not. Sorry."

"Oh! Okay." Whew. "Is Kina here?"

"Yeah…" She looked back into the house and then cut her eyes back at me. "Who are you?"

"Who is it?" I heard Kina call from somewhere inside the house.

"Who are you?" she asked again.

"My name is Cleo, I'm friends with Travis but I know Kina, too. I wanted to invite her to my party."

"Your party?" She raised an eyebrow.

"Yes, a Bloom demonstration, if you will. You should feel free to come as well." Funny how my nervousness just melted away and I turned on the charm like it was nothing. I handed her the invitation with a smile. "Please do give this to her, she's been expecting it. And who are you?"

"Her sister, Nadine."

"Oh, okay, nice to meet you, Nadine. I hope to see you there." I gave one last big smile and got the hell out of there before I got any weirder. What had signing that Bloom contract done to me? It was like *Invasion of the Body Snatchers*. What was I doing? Schmoozing? I wanted to rinse my mouth out with soap. I felt so dirty. But good: it was money in the bank. Ideally, they would both come and buy lots of things from me, and be wholly satisfied with all of their purchases, and generally adore me as a person, and then convince Travis that I was the perfect girl for him. Sigh.

Okay, so I was pushing it. But when I thought about it, wasn't it already pretty farfetched that I would even be in this situation? As I sat on the bus and took a look at myself, I could hardly believe who I'd become. If Travis had this amazing power to make me swoon—*me*, and I'm so not a swooner—then what was so crazy about any of these crazy schemes I was coming up with to get him to fall in love with me? Nothing, as far as I could see at the time. If I could fall in love, then anything was possible.

Except being loved back. That just did not seem possible. What the fuck? Just when I learn to give my heart over to someone, I end up with this. This asshole who treats me like a princess one moment then like a whore the next week. Then I got so mad at myself for crying on the bus that I pressed the stop alert button beside the window frame and made myself walk ten extra blocks to get home.

En route to my house, I stopped at a Chinese take-out restaurant. Even in my punishment I couldn't resist over-indulgence. I walked right up to the counter and ordered a small chicken and broccoli with white rice and a shrimp roll. As I stood around, waiting for my food, I couldn't believe who I saw sitting in a booth over by the mirrored wall. By the way, it's hard to steal glances at someone who is sitting next to a mirrored wall; no matter which way they turn, they can see you looking. On one side of the booth sat this little boy in a black, velour track suit and a young, white woman in a pink, velour track suit. They were wearing matching Jordan's and gold rope necklaces. I won't dwell on that whole mess, because an even bigger mess sat across the table from them. My father. The girl was probably about my age, which was simply disgusting to me. Red flashed before my eyes, like the prom scene out of that movie *Carrie*, with the sirens blaring and everything. It was about to get bloody.

"Excuse me, ma'am," I said to her.

My dad's lips zipped and he tried to avoid the situation by looking elsewhere.

"Is this your son?" I asked her.

"Yes," she said, curling her thin, sparkly lip up in disgust.

"I'm sorry to bother you," I quickly threw in there. "Is this his father?" I pointed my thumb back at my father.

"Yes," she said, growing still more annoyed.

I smiled. "Well, I'll be damned! So this is my little brother?"

Now she was getting downright mad. "What the fuck are you talking about?"

"This is *my* dad, and this is *his* dad, so that makes us *brother and sister.*"

"Is she fucking with me, Larry?"

I turned and looked at him. "Am I, Dad?" I turned back to her. "So I guess you're kind of like my step-mom? How old are you anyway?"

"Twenty-one, not that it's any of your business."

"Twenty-one! Two years older than me. Holy shit, Dad. And your son is how old? Three?"

"He's two," Larry said defensively. "So if you think you're gonna catch me in some statutory rape case you're wrong, cuz we waited until she was old enough."

"Too much information, not that I give a shit. I'm sure she knows how old you are, Dad. There's really no hiding it, all the drugs don't exactly give you a youthful glow." It almost killed me to call him Dad, but I figured it was a nice touch to really drive the point home. I turned back to his girlfriend. "Just so you know, he steals. A lot. Ask him about my tenth birthday. For real. Shit, ask him about the other day! He wouldn't happen to have brought you a DVD/VHS player to your house, would he?"

Her mouth hung open in disgust.

I laughed loudly, mainly just for the attention, because wasn't a damn thing funny. "Dad! That is a damn shame." To her I said, "Now you know," and went back to the counter to wait for my food. I'm sure it was awkward for them to finish eating, the way I was standing less than ten feet away, watching and judging. But that's what I wanted. The very last thing I wanted was to let that man sit and eat in peace.

They left before their food was even halfway gone. She turned and looked at me, then started packing the food up in the aluminum and plastic containers. She took their son by the hand and led the way out the door. Larry followed quite pathetically, carrying a few shopping bags, the food containers, and her purse. It was weird to see him trailing after this girl. I would never imagine him to give himself over to a woman like that, considering how he still stomped all over my mother's heart. But maybe that's how he got them, made them think he cared.

I didn't say a word to my mother about my half-white half-brother or my good-for-nothing father. She was sitting at the kitchen table with the most pathetic look on her face, peeling a clementine and listening to Mary J. Blige's *Be Happy* on repeat. One of the most melodramatic things I'd seen since I can't even remember when. I put my food down on the table and sneered at her. "What are you doing?"

"Eating," she said, looking up at me. Her eyes were swollen like she'd been crying. I felt terribly for her for a moment.

"Were you crying?"

"I'm fine."

Not that I asked how you were doing.

"Thanks, baby. I'll be okay. I just need to go lay down."

"For some reason I feel like that's what you've been doing all day. Deena suggested this, and I was against it at first, but I really think you need to go out on a date."

She rolled her eyes. "Who would date me?"

Oh, great. Now I needed to give her some kind of affirmations to give her some confidence or something. I really am no good at complimenting anyone but myself. I took a deep breath and sat down. "Lots of men," I said. "What about dating online?"

"There are weirdoes online."

"Are you kidding me? There are crazy people in the real world, too, and look what you've ended up with so far. From the way I see it, there's nowhere to go but up."

She gave a small chuckle and looked down at her clementine sections. "I guess you're right about that." Then she collapsed onto the table into her folded arms. "I'm sorry," she sobbed quietly.

I reached across the table and touched her arm. "It's okay."

She looked up at me. A clementine section fell from her cheek. "No, really, I'm sorry for the times that I've put you through dealing with that man. The absolute *only* good thing he's ever done in his entire life was to give me you. And I mean that with all my heart."

I couldn't help but smile. I'd had the same exact thought about him, so it was good to be on the same track with her. "It's okay," I told her again, and I really did feel like it was okay. I wasn't mad at her. What was the use in being mad at her? She admitted she was wrong. She's human, and all humans are wrong at some point in their lives. Most of us are wrong a few times, at least. So could I really hold a grudge against my own mother for being human? For having flaws? For making bad decisions and wanting to be loved? Of course I couldn't. I don't see what kind of person could.

I tried to immerse myself in this whole Bloom thing, al-though I had to admit that I did find it kind of dull. Reading the books and everything made me feel kind of badly for my sister, that she actually believed in all of it. Maybe for some people it was real, for me, it was not. It was just something to keep me busy, to get me some money until I could find something else to do. But what else was there for me to do? Go back to school, and what? I criticized my mom for having no goals, but what was I passionate about besides my physical self?

Lurking behind everything I did were desperate thoughts of Travis. As I sat with my sister and agreed on all of the party plans, I was actually just thinking of him, comparing the two times we'd had sex, the many interesting and funny conversations we'd had, how sexy he was in everything he did, even when he was using me to get out his pent up aggression about something that he wouldn't tell me about. I kind of wished I hadn't invited his mother; that would only make it harder to stop thinking about him.

"So," Deena said, handing me a menu, "these are the meat and cheese platters I ordered."

"Oh, great," I replied. Those thin slices of meat and cheese did look delicious. If I had them in front of me at that moment I would eat all of them. I could feel my mouth beginning to water. I got up from the kitchen table and went to the fridge. There was only one slice of cheesecake left. I had three of the eight so far. If I finished off this last piece, it would mean that I ate half of an entire cheesecake within six hours.

And?

Deena looked at me accusingly, then went back to writing her little list. "You know, this is probably something *you* should be doing. And *that* is probably something you shouldn't."

"Any why shouldn't I?"

She took my fork and my plate. I took it back. "Because! This is beneficial to *you*… and *that* is not."

"You don't know how badly I need this right now," I said, shaking my head and savoring the creamy cake.

"Like a hole in the head."

"More like a whole in the heart."

"What?"

"Nothing." I never liked to discuss boys with my sister. Especially the way I pointed fingers at her for her bad choices, I didn't even want to put her in the position to give me that same treatment.

"Well, I got you lots of books, so make sure that everyone leaves with at least two. I also bought this stamp so you can easily put your name and number on the back of every book. I've set up a couple of games, so they can win samples. And samples lead to sales!"

"Oh, goody."

Deena rolled her eyes. "Will you please get into it, Cleo?! This isn't going to work if you show up looking like you don't give a shit."

"When the time comes, I will have on my Bloom lady smile. Trust."

"You better, because my ass is on the line as well. I can't be promoting you if you're going to let me down. What will that say for me? You know I don't push shitty product. Just look at Leslie. She's never less than her best, and you know why?" She placed a delicate finger on her chest. "Me."

"This is not a pageant."

"It may as well be. Do you know the kinds of prizes and recognition women get for making big sales? Amazing rewards! Vacations, cash, cars, you name it. I've already made the most sales in the district so far by a *landslide*. That's why I don't mind letting you take my sales for this campaign. The next one, you're on your own."

Mom came in with bags of groceries. For once I was thrilled to get up and help her put them away. Deena was putting me to sleep with such inane details. Washing carrots seemed so much more entertaining.

"How's it going?" Mom asked.

"Great," Deena said, "and I can't wait until tomorrow. I've felt like it's been taking forever to finally get here."

"Shouldn't Cleo be the excited one?"

"Oh, I am," I said dryly. "I am so excited."

"I'm getting kind of tired of your sarcasm. I'm doing this for you, you know."

"I know, I know. And I thank you dearly. Really, I do."

She looked suspicious, but I was being sincere.

I was kind of nervous as I let the phone ring. I went over in my mind what I would say to him. I guess I would just ask what he was thinking when he decided to put me out there like that. I'd waited so long, I wondered if he would even take my call. I was shocked when he answered.

"What up, ma?"

I almost called him Jason, but caught myself. Don't get the idea that I was suddenly sucking up to him, but I did want to keep him on the line, and with his newfound fame, he would probably have found it in himself to hang up on me if I had called him something else. "Hey… how are you?"

"I'm great!" he laughed. "What you think? I know you heard me on the radio, right?"

"Yeah."

"And now you wanna holla at me again?"

"No…"

"Yeah, right. Okay, so what are you calling for?"

"To see if part of the song was about me."

He was quiet for a moment, then laughed. "Yeah, that was you. Thick, bourgie chick that likes to get head. Yeah, that's you. Why?"

Hmm, I hadn't really figured out why I wanted to know, I just did.

"You want royalties or something?"

"Please, you know I'm not the kind of girl to run up on you because I want something."

"Besides sex or attention."

"Excuse me?"

"What, now you're gonna act offended? You know that's all you care about. You're selfish, you know? You never asked me about me, you were never interested in my music, all you ever wanted was for me to go down on you."

"What?!" I couldn't even find the words to express how upset he had me.

He laughed. "Don't act new, Cleo. You love sex and yourself, and you don't care about nothing else."

"Oh my God! I can't believe you think that!"

"Well, am I wrong? Did you care about me?"

"Well, not like *really* seriously, but we didn't have a serious thing. Did *you* care about *me*?"

"I could've, if you weren't so *you*." Oh, shit, he took it there.

"Here's the thing: it took dissing me on a song for you to get a hot single, so you should be *thanking* me that I'm *so me*." I hung up the phone.

I'd called him for some clarity on the song, but I only felt worse. He couldn't care about me because I'm *so me*? What did that mean? There was too much of me to be able to stand me? Okay, so I was kind of strong-willed and maybe a little bitchy and pompous sometimes, but I wasn't a bad person, was I? Did I really use people? I had to admit it, maybe I did, but I only did it to protect myself. I just didn't want to let my feelings get to me and end up like other women I saw, making themselves sick over not being able to have the man they wanted.

Look what happened when I finally did open myself up to someone: exactly what I said would happen. Travis broke my heart. Yes, it was broken, no matter how much I tried to convince myself that things would come back together soon. At least I knew one thing I could always do to make myself feel better.

I picked up the phone and dialed Jason's number again. "I'm sorry," I said as soon as he picked up. "If I did anything to hurt you, I'm sorry."

"Hurt me?" He laughed. "Do you know who you're talking to, ma?"

"J. Cru," I replied obediently, fighting back vomit. "Well, I really am sorry. You wouldn't feel like seeing me tonight, would you?"

"You know what?" He laughed. "I kind of would. And I have a surprise for you."

Jason picked me up from my house in about an hour. We didn't follow our usual route back to his place. He drove us into the parking lot of a new apartment complex with a view of the Delaware River.

"You moved out on your own?"

"Surprise," he said.

I followed him upstairs. He lived on the third floor, where there were extraordinary cathedral ceilings with sunlight flooding in through the floor-to-ceiling windows in his living room. I was very impressed. "You made this much money off of this one song?"

"I've been saving up," he said. Saving up. I never expected that from him. I thought he was all about being flashy and spending everything he had. I thought that's why he lived with his mother. Turns out I was wrong. Talk about a surprise.

I sat on the couch while he fixed us drinks of Hennessey and apple juice. I threw it back quickly. Jason sat beside me and rolled a blunt on his coffee table while I watched television, just like old times. Before long, he was on his knees in front of me, and I was holding his head in his my hands with my eyes rolling back into my head. After begging him to stop, we moved on to his bedroom. He still had all of the furniture from his old bedroom, but there were new silk sheets on the bed. They were kind of cold on my naked skin at very first contact, but they were like butter from that point on. I felt like I was just floating and swimming in his sheets, it was euphoric. I wanted a set for my own bed.

We didn't talk when we were finished, and the silence hit me hard. The only thing I could think about was Travis. I felt disgusting, literally and figuratively. The sheets were wet and I couldn't stand to lie there any longer. I got up from the bed and looked around for something to throw over myself. His t-shirt was lying on the floor, but it kind of turned my stomach to think of wearing something of his. I wanted nothing to do with him anymore. What was I thinking, coming here? What about Travis? How would I explain this to him? Who was I kidding? Why would I even have to explain this to him? He didn't give a shit about me anymore… assuming he ever really did.

I shut myself in the bathroom and took a quick shower. Then I went naked into the living room and got dressed. I sat on the couch, no idea what to do. This place was farther from my house than the apartment that he had shared with his mother. I didn't know exactly where I was, so I wasn't sure how to get home. I just sat on his couch in the quiet and waited. One of his notebooks was sitting on the table. I picked it up and opened it to a blank page in the back. I picked up his pen and began writing.

Why is it that
When I try to
Use a guy
For sex
I still feel violated?
Why does it feel like
He's fucking me?
If I picked up my phone
And called him,
Asked him if he
Wanted to "see me,"
Why am I
Getting fucked?
Him invading me, even though
I asked for it?
Plunging like a knife
Into my flesh
Exposing me, my insides
My deep, deep insides
That I've tried to hide
Even though
I asked for it.
Using a man
As my blade
To pry me open
And pour out the things
I try to keep in.
Is that what they mean
By cut buddy?
Fuck buddy?

Fuck is to cut
As what is to what?
No matter the what
I'm fucked.
Even though I
Asked for it
Cuz I thought
It would make me feel
Better about the other one?
You know…
HIM…
The one I can't have?
I tell myself
I love myself
Too much to ever raise
A knife to my skin
But would unzip a fly
Without a thought.
A user, a fornicator, a fucker,
And by default, therefore,
A cutter.

I woke up nervous. I took a shower and then stood in my room for nearly half an hour just debating what to wear without even taking anything out of my closet. I decided on a pair of dark jeans and a white t-shirt with brown sequined flip-flops. Clean and casual, great. Well, I thought so until I walked downstairs and Deena turned me right back around. "Flip-flops? Jeans? T-shirt? You're joking, right?"

"What then?" I asked.

She followed me upstairs, pulled out a khaki skirt, a blue sleeveless, button-down shirt, and a pair of ballet flats that I'd never worn. "That's cute. Put this on."

"You're kidding me."

"No I am not. Put it on, or I'll call it off."

"You wouldn't dare."

She rolled her eyes. "Just put it on! Please!" She walked out and slammed my door. If I was nervous, she was about to explode. I left my jeans on but went with her other suggestions. When I came back downstairs, she shook her head at me and rolled her eyes. "Close enough. Now get these trays out in the living room, get the plates and flatware and cups and all..."

"On it," I said, and saluted her, which she did not appreciate.

I took a back seat in the entire operation. I would answer the door, shake people's hands, tell them to have a seat and look through the books. Deena answered all the questions. Kina showed up fashionably late, although there was no real specific time to arrive. She was sharp in a red kimono and red lipstick that was gorgeous with her dark skin.

"Deena, this is Kina, my friend's mom. Kina, this is my sister, Deena."

They shook hands. "What a lovely name," Kina said to her.

"Why thank you," Deena said, patting her hair delicately. "I must say yours is quite nice as well." They giggled as Deena escorted her to the couch.

Derek arrived with his mother. He escorted her to the door, and stepped inside to see her in safely or whatever. I tried not to pay him any mind. He took me by the hand and led me outside. He closed the door to give us some privacy on the porch. I still tried not to look at him. I was feeling pretty horrible about ditching him the way I did, after he was always so nice to me. The fact that I sometimes found Derek annoying was not a good enough reason to treat someone the way I did him. Travis was not a good enough reason either, which I was still trying to convince myself of.

"Nice seeing you again," he said.

"Yup."

"You disappeared for a while, huh?"

"I had to do some soul-searching." I don't know where that came from, but I didn't know what else to say.

"I missed you."

"I figured."

He laughed. "You figured, huh? Well, I guess it would make sense for me to miss you, considering how I was so in love with you."

Shit. Why's he always gotta take it there?

"No hard feelings. I can't be mad if you don't feel the same. It was kind of pathetic for me to keep pushing it, I suppose. But I never regretted being there for you when you needed me. And I hope I can still be that, as a friend."

"Where is this coming from? Or going, for that matter?"

"It's coming from my heart. I'd like to say it's going wherever you want it to, but I'm trying not to be such a pushover anymore; it doesn't seem to be getting me anywhere." He looked down at the ground, blushing. "Well, I'll be back later to pick my mom up. There's no alcohol in there, is there?"

"A bit."

"Well, watch my mom. Don't let her get drunk, will you? She's on some medicine, she's really not supposed to drink at all, but in moderation she should be alright." He started down the steps.

"Why don't you keep an eye on her yourself?" I asked him.

He turned around. "Are you inviting me in?" he asked with raised eyebrows.

"Not really. Unless you'll accept."

He smiled. "Tell me honestly, Cleo, do you think I would ever turn down anything you offered me?"

"Shut up," I said, opening the door. I could feel eyes on us as Derek followed me into the kitchen. He took a seat at the table while I searched the junk drawer for a deck of cards. We played simple card games like Go Fish and I Declare War and talked and laughed for the remainder of the demonstration, which was an hour or two. By the time we finally left the kitchen, the living room was empty except for Deena, my mom, and Derek's mom. They were just chatting. I was kind of disappointed that I hadn't seen Kina off, but she hadn't come into the kitchen to say goodbye to me either, so I didn't sweat it.

"Nice to see you two together," his mom said, "just like when you were little kids."

I looked at Derek, pleading with my eyes that he wouldn't embarrass me by telling them what had been going on between us for years. It was still just too close for comfort, his mom and my mom, sitting on the couch, having been friends before Derek and I even existed. For them to know the "intimate" relationship Derek and I had been having for so long, I would have just died of embarrassment right there on the living room floor. Way too much information for them to know.

"We were never really friends," I said with a nervous laugh, trying to cover up. "I mean, you two are friends, so we were more like friends by default."

"Wow," Derek said, placing his hand over his heart. "Harsh."

I laughed nervously. "I'm kidding! I mean… sort of." I could feel my face growing red and hot. No, Derek hadn't embarrassed me, but I'd managed to embarrass myself, didn't I? "Well, I hope you had a good time here," I said, hoping to invite an end to the visit. They followed my lead and got ready to leave. Derek leaned in for a hug goodbye, but I dodged it and reached for the doorknob. "See ya."

He rolled his eyes and shook his head. "Okay, Cleo. Whatever you say."

I could not have been more relieved to get them out of there. What was wrong with me? I wanted to laugh and cry at the same time. I was losing my mind. I wanted to open the door and watch him drive away with his mother. Luckily Deena started calling me from the kitchen, screaming about how much money I made.

"How much?" I asked, taking a seat at the table.

"Don't get your hopes up, because this is probably never going to happen again, but you have a nice nine-hundred fourteen dollar order to put in. Which means four fifty-seven for your bank account."

"Wow. So when do I actually see this money?"

"When they get their stuff, duh. It will be here in exactly a week from today. But you need to go online and put in the orders and stuff, and then deliver it all, and then do all the money stuff." She handed me the forms. "Put the orders in now, before something comes up and you forget for whatever reason I will be *pissed* to hear about."

I took it up to my bedroom and logged onto the website. I was already tired of this business. My mind continually drifted to thoughts of Travis. A few thoughts of Derek trickled in here or there, but then it would just lead back to Travis one way or another. I'd been sort of busy, so I hadn't had time to really sit and sulk, but at this time the house seemed extremely quiet, like a vacuum of noise. All I could hear were my own thoughts, and my own thoughts seemed to want to be only of Travis. Why hadn't he called me? I'd gotten up the nerve to dial his number a few times, always hanging up right before the voicemail would pick up because I just couldn't stand to hear it anymore.

Enough was enough. I had to do something to keep from driving myself insane. I grabbed a brochure and headed out to Janine's house. I wondered if she'd even gotten my invitation. I should've followed up to see. Roy hadn't shown up with his girlfriend either, I noted. Oh well. I didn't know where they lived, and even if I did it wasn't that important to me anymore.

I knocked on Janine's door and waited. The sun was low in the sky, giving warm, summer light to the girls playing double dutch in the middle of the otherwise empty side street. I heard the door open behind me as I was watching them, wishing I'd learned how to jump when I was younger. Instead, I had been inside with my sister, putting our magazine together. I always thought I was way ahead of the girls who played double dutch when I was that age, but now I found myself wishing I had spent more time having fun with them. I mean, where was my magazine now?

"Hey, Cleo," Janine's mother, Miss June, said to me. She gave me a hug. "Haven't seen you since the shower, and you were gone from there in ten minutes."

"Yeah, sorry about that." I stepped inside. I had to scoop my jaw up from the floor when I saw Janine sitting on the couch with a baby in her arms. "No way."

"Yes way," Janine said, rolling her neck. "Don't tell me you didn't know I had the baby?"

"How would I have known?! I haven't spoken to you in so long." And I was feeling terribly about it, trust me. To not know that she had the baby, my God, what a shitty friend. I sat beside her. The baby was cute and androgynous, but wearing all pink so I figured it was a girl cuz I'm smart like that. "Wow. I can't believe you have a baby."

"I know. Isn't it incredible?" She kissed the baby's forehead.

"What's her name?"

"Chloe."

"Are you kidding?" I raised an eyebrow at her. "You practically named her after me."

She thought about it. "Yeah, I guess your names are kind of similar, but I wasn't thinking of you at all when we decided on it. Junior has a cousin named Chloe and he always liked the name. But since she's been born, he's been M.I.A. like a—"

“Shut yo mouth,” her mother said from the recliner.

“What’s wrong? Is he scared or something?”

“He’s a good-for-nothing son of a bitch, that’s what he is,” Janine said. “I knew he would dip out as soon as she was born.”

Miss June rolled her eyes. “She never mentioned her thoughts about that at all during the pregnancy though.”

“Anyway, if you didn’t know the baby was born, what brings you all this way? Just a friendly visit?”

“I was wondering if you got the invitation to my Bloom thing,” I told her.

“Yeah, I got it.” She stared blankly.

“Okay… so I was wondering why you weren’t there.”

“I wasn’t there because I have a baby.”

“Which I can now see, but I didn’t know that before. But I did bring a brochure over in case you did want to get something.”

“Let me see that.” Miss June held her hand out to me.

“No thank you,” Janine said. “I’m tight on money as it is. And so are you, Mom! You shouldn’t be buying anything, we’re already out of diapers.”

“And? I’m not the mother.”

“Don’t be like that, you know I need your help!”

“I know, I know.”

I was getting tired of sitting there already. “Well, if you see anything you want, just call me. My number is on the back.” I got up and backed toward the door.

“Oh, I see a couple things already,” she said, nodding her head. “Will you hand me my glasses from the coffee table before you go, Cleo? Thank you, doll.”

To think that this girl that I had been friends with for so many years had produced a child just blew my mind. I still thought of us as children our damn selves. We were still fighting over stupid things, then becoming friends again, however estranged. I was nowhere near being ready to produce a child, which had me really reconsidering how I'd always put my mother and sister down for having kids while still in high school. Yeah, okay, maybe they didn't do other things that they could've done, but they hadn't exactly done horribly with their lives either. Maybe, in fact, it was pretty incredible that they were able to take this situation and make the best of it, and be mothers to the best of their ability, and do everything they could to provide for their kids despite all the adversity they faced as young mothers. Maybe, just maybe, I didn't know *every* single thing, and maybe I didn't give them enough credit. Maybe.

Good for them, yes, but that was not me. But what I was, at this point, I was beginning not to know.

"CLEO!" my mother shrieked from the bottom of the steps. "CLEO!"

I kicked the blanket off and dragged my feet to the door. I poked my head out into the hallway to find that she was no longer standing at the bottom of the staircase, but there was a litter of boxes all over the floor. Shit. Years of watching Deena sort through her Bloom orders had taught me well what all those boxes were full of and how long it would take to finish the job. There were nearly twenty boxes, which meant lots of money, but also lots of time to spend.

I could hear Deena's mouth going a mile a minute in the kitchen, while my mother probably sat quietly, drinking coffee and nodding along. I threw on something comfortable and headed downstairs.

Deena cringed when she saw me. "Did you forget to wrap your hair last night? It's a mess."

"Thank you."

"Did you forget to wash your face, too? Your make-up is all over the place."

"Thank you!"

"What's your problem?"

"She just woke up," Mom answered for me. "Let her be for a minute. She woke up to me shouting for her, all these boxes all over the place. Would you like to wake up to this much work to do, and your sister's nagging voice on top of everything else?"

"I'm here to help," Lele said. "Mommy said I can read off who gets what."

I pushed the coffee table right next to the sofa to get as much useable floor space as possible. The four of us sat in the living room, filling bags and writing receipts. I really hoped they didn't expect a percentage of my pay for helping me. Shitty of me to think that, right? But really, I didn't ask them to help. Yeah, I expected it, but I didn't ask.

"Now... deliver it," Deena said, wiping her hands as if she'd just finished a dirty job.

"By hand?"

"Yes, by hand, you lazy bum."

"Are you going to drive me?"

"Do you want me to drive you?"

"That would be nice."

"Yes, it would, therefore you could ask nicely."

"Deena, could you please drive me around to deliver this stuff?"

"Of course, I had already planned on doing it; I didn't want anything getting messed up, marring my good name. Under one condition though: do something with yourself."

"I wasn't gonna go out in sweatpants and a t-shirt, genius."

"Yeah, but how about you let me straighten your hair and fix your face?"

"I'll take care of it, Dee. My God."

"My God, too, and He don't like ugly," she laughed, pointing at me. Lele giggled.

"Meaning ugly personalities," I said, pointing back at her. I took a shower, changed into jeans and a tee and pulled my hair into a ponytail. Deena started to say something about my look, but waved it off. Lele waited in the house with my mother while Dee and I loaded up the car and then drove off. It took nearly an hour and a half of driving around, handing over bags and bags of junk, collecting money, and then driving off before the back seat was finally empty. I held Kina's bag on my lap. "You can just drop me off," I told Deena.

She looked at me suspiciously. "Are you sure you don't want me to wait?"

"Yes, I'm sure!" I told her. "I know them well, I've been here plenty of times."

"If you say so."

I waited at the top of the steps while Deena refused to pull away. When Terrence opened the door, I waved to give her the cue that she could leave. "Hi," I said to Travis's father.

"Hey, Cleo." He seemed confused. "I didn't know you were coming over."

"Oh, yeah, I told Kina I would bring her stuff to her. Is she here?"

"She moved out," he said.

"Oh… wow." Shit. "Is Travis here?"

"Yeah, he's upstairs."

I carried Kina's white paper bag up the stairs with me. I could feel Terrence watching me climb the stairs, then I heard him sigh loudly and walk off. I knocked on Travis's door and waited. I thought about trying the knob but decided against it.

Travis opened the door, standing before me without a shirt, wearing low-slung jeans with white boxers showing. "Cleo?" Not so thrilled to see me.

"Hi," I said, smiling.

"What?"

"I just wanted to visit, see how you're doing and everything. How are you?"

His room was smokier than I'd ever seen it, and reeked of marijuana. It was messier than I'd ever seen it, too, like he hadn't left his room or picked a thing up in about a week. It never smelled that way when I visited so many times before. There were fast food bags, pizza boxes, cups, and soda bottles everywhere. I also noticed a pile of used condoms and wrappers next to his overflowing wastebasket. "I'm cool… but you look different. You don't fix your hair anymore? Or wear any make-up?"

"Well, I didn't straighten it today. And I'm just not wearing make-up right now. I was just doing a quick run, handing out some of my Bloom stuff that people ordered. I didn't really bother to put myself together like I normally do. Well, your mom ordered some stuff so I brought it over but—"

"But what? But she doesn't live here anymore? But she and my father were both fucking other people for years and now my mother moved out?"

"Well, I didn't know about all of—"

"Yeah, well that's what it is." He covered his face with his hand, and then used that hand to punch the door. "So what's the use in having relationships if every fucking person in the world is just gonna be a lying bastard who can't keep their fucking pants on, not even to spare the feelings of someone they say they love?"

"Wow, yeah, I didn't know about all of that."

"Now you know. Clearly you didn't get the hint when I stopped calling you and stopped answering your calls, but here it is right in your face. Is that what you wanted? For me to be mean to you? You know I didn't wanna talk to you. Didn't you realize? And I thought you were so smart..."

I hated myself. I hated myself because I thought he was right about what he was saying. Then I hated myself for believing him, and hated myself more for not being the old me, the one who would not have given a shit about what he had to say, or at the very least would've had it in herself to tell him to shut the fuck up, or something more clever than that.

My throat was burning with the lump that was growing there. It was like a burning lump of coal, blocking my breath and burning the tissue. I tried to hide that I was gasping for breath as I stood there trying not to cry. I wanted to run, but I was concentrating so hard on not crying in front of him that I feared any movement I made could bring an onslaught of tears. Luckily, he slammed the door in my face. At that point, I dropped the bag and ran downstairs and right out the front door. I stopped when I got to the stoop, because I didn't want to take the chance that Travis might be looking out his bedroom window and see me running down the sidewalk like a silly, little girl. I hate silly, little girls. I was hurt and embarrassed.

I walked calmly down the stairs, taking deep breaths to soothe myself. I stood at the bus stop, pacing back and forth. There was no one at the bus stop with me, which I was relieved about because my mouth was running a mile a minute as I berated myself and cursed him.

Exhausted, I took a seat on the stoop that was closest to the corner. I leaned back on my elbows and looked up at the sky, which I imagined would be a relaxing vision of infinite blue and puffy, white clouds. Instead, there were power lines and a phone pole sticking right up in the middle of my sky. Just like a big middle finger, saying, "Fuck you, nature! Fuck you, happiness! Fuck you, love! Fuck you, calm and tranquility!" All I wanted was to look at the fucking sky, and instead I had this mess of cords and wires colliding with one another against a big, ugly telephone pole. Like a busy intersection, they all headed in one direction, got to the mid-point, and then dispersed haphazardly wherever they chose. How was I supposed to figure any of this out if everything just got to a certain point and decided to change on me? What the fuck could I possibly count on if I couldn't even count on a power line continuing on its direct path along the sidewalk? No, it has to get to a telephone pole, fuck everything up, and *cross the street*! What could I count on—if anything—if I couldn't even look up and get a clear piece of the sky when I needed to? *What?!* This little thing had me so riled up in that moment that my hands were shaking.

By the time I took my seat on the bus, I could no longer console myself or keep my sadness quiet. Here I was, crying on the bus again. I pointed out this silver lining to myself: maybe it was a good thing I didn't have make-up on, with all those tears that were pouring down my cheeks. I wiped my face with my hands and shirt. I leaned forward, burying my face in my hands, and bawled. I didn't once raise my head during the ride for the fear of seeing people watching me. I kept my eyes on the ground as I walked home from the bus stop, and then I went straight up to my bedroom. There, I took off my clothes and crawled under the covers in my bra and underwear. I cried and cried and cried and cried, until my eyes had no tears left. Even by that point, I was still too hurt to live, so I slept.

When I woke up, I looked at the clock and then forced myself to sleep some more. I woke up again at two in the morning and figured it was safe to leave my bed. I crept out of my bedroom. The hallway was blue from the light of my mother's television, but I could hear her snoring. I stood in front of the fridge in my bra and underwear, and I thought about what that might look like. The thought made me cry.

Is this why? I asked myself. Is this why he doesn't want me? Because I look like this, standing in front of the fridge at two fucking something in the morning? Am I disgusting to him? I should have straightened my hair and put make-up on like Deena told me to. Maybe then he would've seen me today and thought I was beautiful. Maybe then he would want me. I was darker than him; maybe he didn't like that. Maybe I should've worn sun block all those times I walked to work or stood at the bus stop, then I wouldn't have gotten so tan this summer. Maybe then Travis would like me. Maybe he got tired of the fact that I don't go to the salon to get manicures and pedicures like other girls do. I shouldn't have eaten that third ham and cheese sandwich that my grandmother warned me about when I was at her house last summer. Maybe then I wouldn't be so fat. Maybe then Travis would wanna be with me.

I slammed the refrigerator door shut. A few of the magnets fell to the floor. I kicked the door with my bare foot, and it hurt, and I welcomed the pain. I beat the door with my fists until they hurt, too. I was just too furious to even understand what was running through my mind. I sat on the floor and stared at the refrigerator door for at least half an hour. I'd already known it was happening for a while, I knew our relationship was well on it's way to crashing and burning, but I was trying so hard to put it off. I just thought I could think it into being happily-ever-after. I was blind. I was my mother. I was my sister. I was all of the women I hated for not shunning that vulnerable part of themselves. But as much as I claimed to love myself, how could I really have known what love is if I didn't allow myself to feel it's lowest lows?

I got up, fixed myself a bowl of Neapolitan ice cream, and poured the rest of the potato chips over it, which were mostly crumbs by then. My mother always saves the tiniest bits of anything leftover. I grabbed a serving spoon from the drawer and carried my snack up to my bedroom. I sat in my bed, with only the light from my window to see by. Once your eyes adjust well enough, you can see almost as much in the dark as you can in the light. It's when the lights come on that your night vision is ruined. When I finished my ice cream and chips, I cried myself back to sleep.

It was early in the morning when I woke up, before seven o'clock. I was on a mission before I even realized it. I took every pot of eye shadow, every liner pencil, every brush, every shimmery gloss and everything else, with the exception of a colorless lip balm, and dropped it in the trash. I picked up the flat iron, a pair of scissors, and cut the cord. I dropped that in the trash can as well. I could practically hear the blood-curdling screams of my sister, but they kind of sounded like a chorus of angels. I looked at the wide-open range that was now the top of my bureau and I felt like I could breathe for the first time in a long time.

I went to the bathroom and turned on the shower. I opened the cabinet, but reached for the regular, old moisturizing shampoo instead of the sleek-n-shine shit. I may have been a bit rough as I scrubbed my head, but I felt like I needed to rough it up a bit, you know, like women in villages that wash the clothes down by the river and beat it against the rocks to get it completely clean, to get the fabric back to its original, untarnished state. I wanted to wash every kink and every curl back into my locks, to wash every silky, straight strand down the drain.

I returned to my bedroom, locked the door, dropped my towel, and set up my camera on its tripod. Sexy was not the goal on this morning. Purity. Baring my soul, that was my aim. And I felt that I achieved it, as I barely posed on my bed, naked, kinky hair just everywhere, unable to stop the silent tears from flowing. I wasn't even mad at myself for the tears, I just let them be.

I let myself be.

I picked up my phone and dialed Derek's number. He answered promptly.

"Yes, beautiful?"

"Nothing," I replied, because that was all I wanted to know. I hung up without saying good-bye, which boys do all the time, so I figured Derek wouldn't think it to be rude if he noticed at all. I picked up my notebook and began, writing, and doodling, and crying.

You know that thing?
Maybe you didn't even realize
That you had it for so long,
But that thing was brand new.
You know that thing?
That thing that I gave you
That you held close to yourself
And made it think you loved it?
That thing that swelled
Every time you looked at me?
(No, not that thing.)
That thing that beat
Almost exclusively for you?

That thing that you used?
That thing that you squeezed the life from
And then tossed aside when you needed no more?
That thing that you crushed?
That thing that you defiled?
That thing that you blatantly and
Unapologetically beat to death
With words that I never expected to hear
From a mouth that spoke, that kissed,
That caressed, that licked
So kindly from the start?

That thing, that thing
Was my heart that you shit on,
And I was just wondering:
When can I have it back?

How did I let this happen? How did I get this way? I know better. How could I let someone in? When did I become so enthralled, let my own person become so wrapped up and dependent on him? It was only a few weeks.

Yes, a few weeks, but what is time when you meet that person who stimulates you on all levels? What is time then? What is time when you find that rare person who, dare I say, completes you? Like a puzzle. A puzzle fits, and that is all. Does it fit any better on the second day than it did on the first? Or the third, fourth, tenth, or thousandth? No, it just fits.

I checked my website activity. Normally, new pictures, especially nude ones, would create a serious buzz. These nude ones of me, puffy-eyed and crying, I guess did not warrant that kind of attention. One message: *Girl, you're going through it.*

Yes, I am.

Somehow, I dragged myself out of bed. Well, what was left of my motivated self dragged me out of bed. The other part of me wanted nothing more than to sit and wallow.

“What happened to your hair?” my sister asked with disgust. She closed the magazine she was reading just to stop and stare. Then her expression softened. “Are you okay?”

I tried to stop my lips from quivering, which only made them shake more. The tears began pouring out as my whole body convulsed. I tried to say something, anything, to explain myself, but all that came out was incoherent blubbering.

“Oh, shit.” My sister wrapped her arms around me. My first instinct was to back away, and to tell her to get off of me. But it felt good in a strange way, and I knew I needed it, so I let my sister hug me. “Well?”

“Stupid boy stuff,” I sniffled, sinking into the corner of the couch.

She raised an eyebrow. “*You* have boy problems? My, how the tables have turned.”

I hated myself for it, but I began sobbing into my hands.

“I’m sorry, I guess this would be a bad time to say something like that.” She rubbed my back and stared at me, making me feel completely pathetic and helpless.

For two days, nothing but water, tears, and perhaps my pillowcase touched my lips. I gave in to my weaker self and stayed in bed for most of the hours of the day. Every once in a while I would sit up in bed to check my email and stuff. Claire, my women's literature instructor, wrote an email saying that we could come find out our grades, which would be posted on her office door. We should also feel free to pick up our projects, otherwise she was just going to throw everything out.

Did I really want to go pick up a report that he and I worked on together? I mulled it over, and over and over.

My mom, apparently home for lunch, swung my door open. "That's enough," she announced. She pulled my curtains open, burning my eyes with sunlight. I could practically feel my pupils contracting. "Cleo, you haven't been downstairs for two whole days."

"So?"

"So? Deena, come talk to this girl!" My mother passed my sister in my dooray.

Deena sat on the edge of my bed. "So who was this boy?"

"I don't wanna talk about it."

"You don't wanna talk, you don't wanna eat, you don't wanna shower, and you don't even wanna get out of bed."

"Nope."

"You know what they say? The best way to get over a man is to get under another one." She laughed, then turned serious. "That was a joke, you better not heed that advice."

Too late.

"Good. Now get up."

Easier said than done. I cried my way through a shower, but felt a little better afterwards. Considering how I was basically being forced out of the house, I decided to at least go have a look at my grade, even if I didn't bring our report and visuals home with me.

This whole shitty ordeal was beginning to get on my nerves. Why did I have to feel like I did? We'd only been whatever-the-fuck-we-were for a few weeks. We hadn't had sex in a few weeks. Ugh, what is it with me and breaking down into tears while riding public transportation?

I took a slow walk through the campus to get to Claire's office. I was basically torturing myself, because every landmark I saw made me think of Travis. The pizza place where he bought me a slice more than a couple of times. The tree we leaned against while making out in a warm summer rain. Why was I clinging so desperately when it hurt so bad? It was kind of like when someone gets electrocuted, and they can't let go of whatever it is that's conducting the current. I mean, I guess that's what it's like, I've only ever seen that shit in cartoons.

"Come in!" Claire called from the other side of her door after I'd knocked too loudly. She smiled when she saw me. There were three desks in the small, cluttered office, two with computers. It was pretty clear that she shared this office with another instructor. The other person had lots of stuff as well, but the junk was in piles. Claire's junk was scattered. "Cleo! You know, I've always felt a connection through our names."

"Oh? Um, thanks."

"Close the door. Have a seat."

Oh God. She totally caught me off guard. I took a stack of notebooks from a rickety, wooden chair and put them on the only clean horizontal surface, which was the floor. "I just came to see my grade."

"Yes, I figured. I said I'd post them on the door but I haven't gotten around to it. Shit. Where is..."

I spotted the poster Travis and I had made stuck in the corner. My eyes kept wandering back to it.

"Here we are! So, you got an A, as I'm *sure* you were expecting. I had to give you and a Travis a B+ on your report though. It could've been better researched, for sure. Not your typical work." She put our report on her desk with the big, green B+ scrawled over our title and names. "You don't have to dumb it down to work with other people, okay? Let them step it up."

"I didn't," I lied.

She rolled her eyes and then fluttered her lashes, smiling at me. "Whatever. It's over, right? You wanna take this shi—excuse me."

"No thanks. I just wanted to see my grade."

"Okay, you got it. Taking any of my classes in the fall?"

"Spring," I replied.

"Cool beans. Well, I'll be seeing ya."

"Yep. Bye." I put the notebooks back in the chair and left. Claire was an awesome teacher, I should've thanked her. She was an awesome person in general. I should've talked to her more, responded to her friendliness. Instead I'd given blunt responses and constipated smiles. I should've— "Ow!"

Rounding a corner, I ran smack into someone, bone-to-bone contact, on my left side and his right. And who was *he*? No, it couldn't be. I felt lightheaded.

"My bad," he said, and kept it moving, barely noticing me.

I took the stairs down. I couldn't risk waiting for the elevator and seeing him again. My stomach was doing cartwheels. The stairwell was a never-ending spiral, taunting me all the way that I'd made the stupid decision to walk my ass down instead of taking the elevator. I staggered down the last few flights and burst out through the door to the outside, panting. But, shit, it was hot and humid out there, almost no air. My mind skimmed the thought of getting a ride home with him, but I didn't contemplate it too long. I took my bottle of water from my bag and gulped most of it down, then headed for the subway.

At the end of the block was Travis's car. There was a reflection of the trees and sky covering the windshield, so it wasn't until I was right alongside the passenger side door that I realized someone was in the front seat. That someone was Alicia. My eyes welled up, then my stomach started acting up. She was playing with her phone, so I don't think she saw me. Well, I pray to God that she didn't see me as I ran behind the nearest building and started puking. It was nothing but water at first, then it was nothing at all, just dry heaving. Loud, painful, dry heaving. I was glad that anyone who may have passed by spared me the embarrassment of coming to check on me, but now I have to wonder *why didn't anyone bother to check on me?*

For a *fleeting* moment, as I was bent over at the waist, vomiting water against the side of a concrete wall, I fantasized that my puking was because of a pregnancy, and wondered how that predicament would change Travis's feelings for me, and maybe positively affect the outcome of our relationship. Fleeting, I said. For a fleeting moment. But, even for that fleeting moment, and I can't even describe how I hate to admit this, but I understood how a girl could even consider such a thing. Such a stupid, self-deprecating thing. But also selfish. Bringing a baby into the world to keep a guy so you don't have to deal with heartache? And even I considered it, if only for a few seconds. Even I. Sometimes I hate my thoughts.

I peeked around the corner. No change in scenery. No sign of Travis. As weak as I was feeling, I made a dash to the subway station.

"Of course you feel like you're gonna faint; you haven't eaten in days!" My sister shouted over me as I lay on the couch. "Lele, can you make your aunt some toast please? And bring an apple and a glass of water." She squeezed onto the couch beside me, shaking her head. "Yes, you almost fainted, but chalk it up to malnutrition. Don't give his ass the credit."

"Since when did you start drinking the independent women punch?"

"Since when did you stop? My God, I thought your condescending who-needs-men attitude was a bitch to deal with, but this is much worse."

"I know, I know. I should be over it. But it's like… I don't know. I miss him." And he obviously misses getting head from a stalker-type chick who roughed you up in a corner store, I tried reminding myself. Ugh, just the thought of him being with her made me moan in agony.

"I'll see you later, I have things to do," my sister said, throwing her hands up in defeat.

Lele brought me my toast, an apple, and a glass of water. She placed the water on the coffee table next to me and the toast and apple on my lap. She leaned into my ear and whispered, "Guess what?"

"What?" I didn't mean to snarl, but I wasn't in the mood for stupid, little girl secrets.

She was covering her mouth with her hands, but I could tell from her eyes that she had a crazy grin on her face. She cupped her hands around her mouth and my ear and whispered. "I'm quitting pageants."

"*What?!*"

She nodded, totally giddy.

"Does your mother know that?"

Terror struck her, and she shook her head, shushing me.

"Do I know what?" Deena called from the kitchen.

"That Lele used a butter knife to butter my toast."

"Lele! I've told you, no knives!" I already knew how my sister felt about this. "Spoons and forks only! And no really pointy forks either."

"She can't butter toast with a spoon or fork."

"Of course she can!" my crazy sister replied. "It's margarine, it's soft. She only uses spoons at home."

"You poor thing," I said quietly so that only Lele could hear me. I zipped my lips, locked them, and threw away the key. "So what now?"

"Skateboarding," she said with childish wonderment and a light in her eyes.

"For real? Why?"

"Have you ever seen them, the really good guys? It's so cool. And plus, I think they need more girls." At least she had a vision.

Mom walked in from work, carrying a few plastic shopping bags of what looked to be groceries. I felt embarrassed for her having chosen to wear those bright yellow scrubs that made her ass look so fat, and not in a sexy, rest-your-drink-on-her-booty kind of way. "Hello, ladies," she said cheerfully. "You can fend for yourselves for dinner, because I've got a date."

Oh, God. God! Now this shit? Be happy for her, be happy. It doesn't have to be weird and awkward. Remember, she's more than your mom, she's a woman. Be happy for her.

"What?!" Deena came into the living room, mouth agape.

"A patient was released from the hospital yesterday, and today he came back. He told me he's been waiting days to ask me out, but didn't wanna do it while he was staying there, just in case I turned him down." She laughed to herself.

"But you said yes?" I still couldn't believe it.

"Yes, I said yes. To be honest, I'm not into him all that much, but I figured I could at least give it a shot. He's not a horrible person. Well, actually he seems like a really nice person. Expensive shoes, too. Anyway, girls, how was your day?"

Deena sighed. "Boring. Lil' Mama doesn't have another pageant for another month and a half. I've been here watching TV all day."

"That's nice. Well take this stuff in the kitchen." She handed the bags off to Deena. "I need to go get ready." Mom marched up the stairs.

I could see that Deena was practically spilling over with comments, but I waved my hand in the air dismissively. As sorry as it is to say, I preferred to lay there and contemplate my own depressing love life rather than discuss something so alien to me as my mother's newfound dating life. I stared blankly at the TV, at whichever stupid kid show Lele was watching. I didn't even see my mom leave, just heard the door close behind her and her car pull off. Deena made grilled cheese for dinner, which she all but force-fed me. As if my lack of an appetite and nausea weren't bad enough, it was the worst grilled cheese I'd ever eaten, black in some places, white in others, and a layer of cheese so thin it nearly disappeared into the bread. Her sandwich and Lele's looked a little better.

"Yeah, well, you're not hungry anyway," she said. Bitch.

Before she even left for work, my mom came into my room. “Get up,” she said, swatting my behind.

“It early,” I groaned.

“Yup. I want you up and living your life nice and early this morning. Honey, you can’t lose who are over a boy. Do you want to turn into me or your sister?” she teased. I felt kind of bad that she knew that that would be the death of me. At least she could joke about it though. “You’re lucky to have Deena, helping you out with your Bloom stuff and everything. I know you’re hurting, but you do need to get a move on. Getting out and doing things will help to get your mind off of things anyway. I understand the mourning period, but I think that time has passed.”

“I feel like there’s nothing to do in my life right now.”

“Make things to do! Your party was a good start, but Deena did that for you. And now look. This is only going to go as well as you make it. So…” She pulled the covers off of me and opened my curtains. “Get up, get out there, make some money, have some fun, and stop thinking about that asshole."

After showering and dressing, I sat at the kitchen table and made a list. I very rarely sit at the kitchen table, but I wanted to avoid comfy chairs, couches, and beds at all costs. So I sat at the kitchen table and made a list of all the people I would hit up to peddle my wares. The first names I wrote down were Janine and her mom. I wrote Kina's name, but crossed it out because I didn't have her private phone number, and of course I was not about to call Travis to ask for it. Okay, I'll admit, I thought it would be a good excuse to call him, but I remained strong, and simply crossed Kina off of the list. Who else had I personally invited to the party?

I realized that I don't really have friends. I know people say stuff like that a lot, but it's actually true in this case. Throughout school, I'd always kept the company of a few girls here and there, different ones each year, with the exception of Janine. Janine is the only girl who ever slept over my house, and vice versa. I was always unsure if my school friends ever really liked me, or if it was just convenient because I was right there in their classes, not smelly, and not a weirdo. Yeah, that's sounds about right, so I'm not exactly sure that they would even really be called *friends*.

The list still only had Janine and her mom, after staring at the paper for ten minutes. There was Roy, from Keiman's. He was kind of my friend. And he had that girlfriend, with a name like a cartoon... Anamae, right. She hadn't even bothered to come to my party, so I doubted that it would even be worth my trouble to track Roy down and have him let her know that I wanted to sell her some stuff.

Giving up on that one, I started a new list:

Deena

Mom

Janine

Lele

Roy

Five friends. That's a nice number. It's surely not zero, and it's not twenty, but it's a nice handful. I crossed Roy off. I hadn't made any effort with him lately, it was selfish of me to use his name just to lengthen my list. Oh.

Derek.

Hmm, not too bad. Back to five, and without any fluff. Not that Roy is fluffy, he's a good guy, but it's clear that neither of us cares enough to make any attempts at building. *This* five though, is a good, solid five. A five that I can depend on. Obviously, no list of five, especially not this one, is going to make me the top seller of Bloom products for my district, but so what?

I packed up a few campaign books and headed out. Maybe I would even stop some people on the street and give them a book or two. My name and phone number were stamped on the back, anyone could get in touch with me… if I even gave my book to anyone, which I didn't.

I knocked on Janine's door and waited. I could hear the baby wailing inside. She opened the door with her screaming daughter on her hip, her hair a mess. "Take her!" she bellowed, holding Chloe out to me.

I took the baby in my arms as I stepped into the house. As soon I did, Janine dashed up the stairs. I closed the door behind me and then cleared a spot on the couch with my one free hand. The living room was kind of a mess. There was laundry all over the place, and dirty dishes and trash. I rocked Chloe in my arms, singing what I could remember of *Hush Little Baby*. Miraculously, she began to mellow out.

Janine returned around ten minutes later with her hair gelled back into a bun and a new set of lounging clothes on. "Thank you," she said, beginning to straighten up a little. Then she stopped and looked at me. "What are you even doing here?"

"Just came by to visit," I said. "And to bring my Bloom book over again."

She picked up every piece of garbage and dropped it into a big, black trash bag. "I've been reading your blog on the regular," she said. "What is up with you? You seem depressed."

"I'm not," I said. "I just got dumped... or something."

"Or something?"

"Yes. I don't know. I mean, I guess, I got dumped. I've never been dumped, and I mean, I don't even know if what we were doing would even be considered *dating*. He just abandoned me. And then I saw him yesterday with this other girl who threatened me in a corner store because she was jealous that I was dating him, this really nasty chick that he told me he couldn't stand. I just..." My breath started getting caught up in my throat, tangled up in a good cry that was just begging to come out, and I was so damned tired of crying.

Janine tied the garbage bag and sat on the couch with me. "These things happen. Boys are stupid. Look at me."

Yes, look at you. I'm supposed to be smarter than you.

"I know, and I know you know. We both know, and he knows it, too, that you'll find someone new, someone better. All this tough shit will be a thing of the past."

"But he's so smart and funny and cute and tall and sexy and so many other great adjectives that I can't even think of right now. He's things they haven't even made *words* for!"

"I think you're getting carried away, but there are other guys like him," Janine insisted.

"Do you know how hard it is for me to genuinely like a person? And as much as I hated him at first, I really *liked* him! I met his family and I loved them! Do you know how hard it is for me to change my mind about someone?"

"Yes. Actually, Cleo, my feelings have suffered at the hands of your disapproval a lot more than a few times."

"Sorry."

"Whatever, girl. I know how you are. Fuck him."

I raised my eyebrows in disbelief.

She sighed, exasperated. "No, don't *fuck* him! Ew, Cleo, and he's with that other girl, and you know she probably lets him all up in her ass and everything else. No, fuck him as in *forget* him. You're so much more than this."

"Am I though? Look, I sit around and cry all day and it doesn't even matter cuz I have nothing better to do. I have nowhere to be and nothing to do."

"Please, girl, that's all temporary. You'll be back in school *full time* in about a month. And you have this shit." She held up my Bloom book.

"Yeah, and I'm a fraud for that. I really hate make-up. Look at me, I'm not even wearing any. I was just doing it for everyone else."

She swatted my leg with the book. "Do you use lotion? Do you brush your hair? You damn sure wear a lot of lip gloss. Maybe you don't eat black-eyed peas either, but you worked in the supermarket! Girl, get over it. You are being way too hard on yourself."

"I know. I just feel like… I'm more than a Bloom lady."

"Bitch, who *isn't*? We're all *more* than just one simple part of ourselves." She paused for a moment, looking skyward. "Shit, that's deep."

Surprisingly so. I sat there and played with Chloe while Janine looked through the book, circling only a tube of lip gloss.

"Can you believe this girl?" Janine asked, turning up the volume on the television. "She had *sixteen men* tested and hasn't found the baby's father. Shit like this just blows my mind. Unprotected sex with *sixteen men*, all around the same time? Are these people attending orgies or what? Shit, when I got pregnant, I knew the exact day and time it happened, cuz I don't be having enough sex to not be remembering who or when it was. Nymphos, for real." She cut her eyes at me. "I bet you be having sex like that, don't you?"

"No!" I exclaimed. "What would even make you think that?"

"I don't know, just the way you be talkin'. You used to talk like you can't stand men, but I know you ain't gay, and I *know* you ain't celibate."

"But sixteen different men all around the same time, Neen? You really think I would do that?"

"We've drifted, you know. I don't know you like I used to. People change." Suddenly she started cracking up laughing and hitting me, again, with the Bloom book. "Girl, I'm just playin'. So how many have you been with at one time?"

"One!" I shouted at her.

She threw her head back and laughed so loud that I couldn't hear the television as the host announced whether or not this seventeenth man was the father. From his gleeful reaction, it seemed he was not. "Okay, so how many *total*?" she panted, trying to calm down.

"You first."

"You first! I asked the question, dammit."

I thought about lying. I thought about my number. If she wanted to know exactly, there was no way I'd be able to figure it out in my head—there were things I had to work out on paper, like what exactly I did with each specific person. "Nine."

"That all?"

"Yes, that's all," I replied, somewhat offended. "Why do you think I'm such a freak?"

She shrugged. "You avoid relationships, for the most part, but you seem very sexual. And like, *free*. I've always been kinda jealous of your freeness."

Freeness? I didn't know if that was a word. "Oh." I didn't know whether to thank her for her jealousy or what. "I like sex, yes, but I'm not an addict or anything."

"I wasn't tryna say all that. I was just saying…"

"Okay, okay. Now you. How many?"

"*Three*," she said very slowly. That was low. I knew she probably had not been with as many as me, but I definitely thought it would be more than three. "What you lookin' like that for? I keep a boyfriend, you know."

Yeah, I guess that would cut back on the number. But three? I felt like three was enough to forget about. I could probably have forgotten three on my own list. "Did you love them?" My question surprised me.

"Not all three." Did she have to keep saying the number? "I thought I did at the time. But *that's* love." She pointed to Chloe. "Shit, I don't even love her daddy. I thought I did. You know he's only been over twice in the past few weeks since she was born? I don't love him though. When I realized he wasn't gonna be in the picture, I wasn't even sad. Well, I was sad for Chloe, but not for myself. I was mad as hell, don't get me wrong, I just wasn't sad to lose him though. He's an asshole."

"That sucks."

"Sucks for him, that he can't be a man. Anyway, what about you? Have you loved any of them?"

"Yes."

"Ooh. Which ones?"

"Oh, God, don't even make me think about which ones."

"The last one, duh, moving on…"

"Um, I don't know."

"Cleo, you know!" Out of nowhere, she lunged toward me with a white cloth. "She got you."

I looked down to see that Chloe had puked all over me and I hadn't even felt it. Not until I looked at it did I notice it was kind of warm. The warmth was actually kind of comforting. I cleaned my skin, but my shirt had a huge blot on it no matter how much I wiped. "Great."

"Welcome to my world," Janine said, holding her arms out to invite me.

I shook my head. "No thank you."

We sat and watched TV for well over an hour. I looked over to find both Janine and Chloe asleep on the couch. I got up to my feet. I was unsure if the laundry was clean or dirty, so I just put it into neater, more manageable piles. I took all the empty boxes from the baby stuff and placed them, one inside of the other, by the back door. I also cleaned the kitchen, washing all of the dishes and wiping down the counters and stove. As I was turning to leave the kitchen, Janine's mom startled me from the doorway.

"What the hell are you doing?" Miss June asked.

I laughed, relieved. "I didn't know anyone was watching me."

"What are you, the house-cleaning fairy godmother? You just swoop in while people are sleeping and clean up for them?"

"No, actually I was just hanging out with Neen, and she fell asleep. It looked like she had been trying to straighten up earlier, so I just decided to help her out."

She gave me a hug. "Thank you, baby. I bet you don't even do this at your own house. Let me call your mother and tell her."

"You're right, I don't. She would be pissed if she knew, so please don't."

She laughed and smacked my butt. "Go in there with your girl. And don't you ever come cleaning up in my house again, you hear me? Crazy thing."

Janine was just waking up. "You cleaned up? You're crazy."

"I know, you're mom just told me."

"She's right. Thank you though. I've been so incredibly tired lately. Chloe won't sleep at night. I feel so bad trying to keep her up during the day though. Anyway, babies this young need to sleep a lot."

"Yeah. I guess I'm gonna go."

"You are so weird, always leavin' and shit. Oh, but you forgot to show my mom your book. Mom! Come here a minute!"

Miss June came into the living room, looking annoyed and drying her hands with a Puerto Rican flag towel. "What? You know I just got home. I'm tryna cook some food and I'm *tired.*"

"Cleo is tryna leave, but the main reason she came over is to show us her Bloom book, and I know you said there was some stuff you wanted to get this time around."

"Cleo, you ain't goin' nowhere," Miss June said, waving the towel at me. "You heard me say I'm cooking dinner. You cleaned my house, so I'm damn sure gonna feed you."

Obediently, I took a seat on the couch. "Haven't you had enough of me?" I asked Janine.

"Oh, is that it? You're tired of me?"

"No. You should be tired of me though. I came in here, crying about my boy problems, complaining about my life."

"Shut up. You're my girl, we're supposed to do that shit. I'm thirsty." She stood up to go to the kitchen. "You want some juice?"

"What flavor?" I asked her.

"Red," she replied. She brought me a glass, although I insisted that I didn't want any.

Miss June never could cook very well. I don't know why the spaghetti sauce was so watery because I'm pretty sure she poured it straight from a jar. The garlic bread was actually really good though. I slurped through my spaghetti quickly so that I could really take my time and enjoy the garlic bread towards the end.

"How is it?" Miss June asked, eyeing my empty plate.

"Good," I replied. I wasn't lying, she just didn't know I was talking about the garlic bread alone. Now when could I leave? It's rude to eat and run, right? So, considering I'd been talked into staying for dinner, it seemed only right for me to stick around for some time, maybe offer to clean up the kitchen, even though I'd done it once already that day.

Miss June was flipping through the Bloom book and writing down her order as she ate. "Have you tried this mascara?"

"No," I told her.

She nodded and kept looking.

"You can go," said Janine. "I'll call you with our order when we're done looking at the book. I know you're itching to get out of here."

"Why would you say that?" I tried to sound shocked.

"Because I know how you are with visiting people and stuff. I'll talk to you later."

With that said, I felt kind of like I *had* to go. Or I could just sit there and feel like an embarrassed, ungrateful guest. "Okay. Thanks for dinner, Miss June."

"Just June," she said. "I told you to stop calling me that."

I have a difficult time calling her just June to her face. I know she wants to stay young and everything, but she's my friend's mother. I picked up my bag from the couch and left the house, relieved not to be anyone's company any longer.

I was just watching television alone when Deena stormed into the house. She threw her bag into the recliner. "Where is Mom?!" she demanded.

"Not home. What's wrong?"

Lele came through the door, looking very different from her usual self. She was wearing only her own hair, no weaves or extensions, pulled into a less-than-tidy ponytail, with no curls or other decoration. She wore blue jeans, a white tee, and pink shell-toe sneakers that she'd covered in black marker graffiti. She was smiling though. She flopped down on the couch beside me. "Hey, auntie," she said.

"What's wrong?" I asked Deena again.

"Look!" she shouted, holding her hands out toward little Leslie. "You'll never guess what she told me this morning. I was setting some schedules so we could get back on track with pageants and *she says*..." Deena stopped and just shook her head in disbelief. "Where is *Mom*?!"

"She's not here. She went to the store or something. I'm pretty sure

I just said that. How many times are you gonna ask?"

Deena went into the kitchen. I could hear her slamming cupboards and fixing herself a glass of something much louder than necessary.

"I told her," Lele said, giggling. "Grandpa and I were hanging out yesterday, and he took me to the toy store, and he said I could pick out *whatever I wanted.* So guess what I got."

"I have no idea," I lied.

"A skateboard!" she exclaimed. "So, of course, I had to tell Mommy that I want to be a pro skater now."

"And your mom went crazy?"

She shrugged. "Kind of. She was really mad at Grandpa, not so much at me."

"Why can't you do both pageants *and* skateboarding?"

She shrugged again. "Mainly because I don't want to." Simple enough.

Mom stayed away long enough for Dee to sit and clear her head a little. By the time Mom did show up, Dee wasn't the tornado that had ripped through the house earlier, but was still shaken by the news. She called everyone into the kitchen. Mom, Lele and I sat around the table while Deena paced back and forth in front of the sink.

"Family meeting," she announced. "The real culprit isn't even here."

"Who's the real culprit? Wait... what is the crime?"

"*My father,*" she hissed, "bought *Leslie* a *skateboard.*"

My mom looked at me, then back at Deena, clearly confused. "I take it you think that's a bad thing?"

"Yes, Mom, it's bad! She's a little girl, a *pageant queen,* mind you. And now she doesn't want to do pageants anymore? She wants to *skateboard*? She wants to wear those dirty, ill-fitting jeans and draw with *markers* on her *shoes*? She *refused* to go to the salon this weekend!"

"I guess she grew out of the princess thing," Mom said, rubbing Lele's back. "I wouldn't say that this is *bad*."

"Would you say it's good?" Deena pressed.

"I would," I told her. "She needs to figure out on her own what she likes to do. You don't want her just liking things because you or anyone else told her she should."

"Honey, sit down," Mom said, pushing out the other chair with her foot. "This is not that serious."

Deena took her seat. She couldn't even look at Lele. Lele was still smiling. "We've worked so hard though," she mumbled.

"I know, babe. And it was a beautiful thing for the time being. Now she wants to do something else. Who knows? She may hate it."

"No way!" Lele exclaimed.

"Or both of you may come to love it."

"What about all of your pageant friends?" Deena asked Lele. "You won't be competing with them anymore."

"They weren't my friends, Mom," Lele said. "And their moms weren't your friends either. Can I go now?" Lele led me out to the porch, where her skateboard was sitting. "Mom wouldn't let me bring it in the house. She said she hates this stupid plank of wood. I love it." The design on the bottom was one of pink and purple flowers, which I thought I should've satisfied Deena. Lele scooted herself back and forth across the porch. It was a pretty narrow space, but she was pretty good already. "There are these boys who are always skating near my house. Look what they're teaching me to do." She attempted a very messy ollie.

"Wow, good job," I told her.

"Thank you. They even have a ramp they put out there. One of the boys, his name is TJ, he said he has a *half-pipe* in his backyard! They said when I get better, maybe they'll let me have a turn."

"That sounds cool."

Lele stopped skating and sat next to me on the step and leaned on my lap. "I hope she won't be mad at me forever."

"Of course not!" I assured her. "She's not even mad at you right now. I think she just expected you to do pageants forever. Speaking of which, when did you stop liking them?"

"When I stopped winning."

"You never stopped winning."

"I didn't win the big crown. And the girls with the big crowns looked so happy for real. And I had to just *look* happy."

"You might not always win at skateboarding," I warned her.

"I know, but I still like it, so far anyway. Skateboarding is just fun! You can skateboard by yourself and have fun without worrying about who is the best. Nobody walks around in goofy, sparkly clothes and big, fake hair by themselves for fun; the only reason to do that is to win." She did have a point. "I hate fake teeth, I hate fake hair, I hate getting my nails done, and I really hate wearing a bathing suit when I'm not even swimming!"

"What did you draw on your sneakers?"

"This is a skateboard. So it's *I heart skateboard*. That really means *I love skateboarding*. This is my name, duh." She pointed to the scribble beside her name. "This used to say *hearts TJ*." She giggled. "But I crossed it out because I don't want my mom to know that I like him."

"You're silly. And that looks like a butterfly."

"It is." She got very serious. "That's something I'm dealing with."

"What ever do you mean?"

She took a deep breath and put her hand on my forearm. "I'm terrified of butterflies. The way they fly is so crazy. They're all over the place, going here and there, up and down, all crazy." She used her hands to illustrate their haphazard flight path. "And they're so light that I think they could just get blown in the wind and fly into me. But I know they're not as scary as I think they are. I even held one on my finger at the zoo one time. So, I wanted to put that on my shoe, so if I'm ever scared while I'm skateboarding, I can look at the butterfly and remember that I can conquer my fears."

I'll admit, I was never a fan of butterflies myself, and I realize that it had been for precisely the same reasons. I wasn't so much scared as I was bothered. It just annoyed me that they were always all over the place, and I've always felt like I have to alter my own path to avoiding colliding with theirs.

Deena came out of the house, sniffling and teary-eyed. "Let's go. Bring your thing with you."

Lele grabbed her skateboard and ran after her mom, waving goodbye to me. I got up and went into the house. Mom was still sitting at the kitchen table, flipping through a clothing catalog. She looked up at me. "Oh, I thought you were Deena with something else to say."

"No, why? Did you guys fight?"

Mom laughed and shook her head. "Talk about living vicariously through your kid. I didn't say that to her in those words, but I tried my best to make her realize that continuing the pageantry would not be in Leslie's favor."

"And she didn't want to hear it?"

"Not at all."

"So she's gonna put her back in there?!"

"No, no. She's just gonna have a hard time dealing with her *not* being back in there. She's not gonna force Lele to do anything she doesn't want to do, but she insists that she doesn't have to like this whole skateboarding fad."

"Of course she doesn't, but it's not really about her."

"That's what I said." She handed me a slip of paper, a grocery list. "Could you go pick up a few things? I completely forgot to stop at the supermarket."

"Why didn't you ask Deena? She drives."

"Please, Cleo. Deena does not want to hear from me right now, and I have a terrible headache. I was gonna make seafood pasta later on, but right now I really just need to lay down. And thank you for not cursing me under your breath!" she shouted after me as I left the house.

The last thing I wanted to ride the bus, alone with just my thoughts. Something about the forward movement of vehicular transportation just had me on edge because it was always stirring up something inside of me. Waiting and riding, I just couldn't keep myself from thinking, and once I got to thinking, there was no hope in keeping myself from crying. I noticed a middle-aged lady who kept stealing glances at me. She had an open magazine in her hands, but there was no way she could've been really been reading anything, as much as her eyes rolled my way. It was getting really annoying.

"Can a girl cry in peace?!" I exclaimed.

She adjusted her blond wig, turned her nose up, and looked away, as if I was the rude one. The bus driver looked at me through the rearview mirror and a few other passengers turned to see who was shouting on the bus. I sunk into my seat.

The supermarket was not crowded at all. I was hoping that it would be, so that I could blend into the crowd if I saw Paul or something. I wished there was a supermarket closer to where I lived, but I didn't feel like riding way across town just to pick up a few things for dinner. I held my breath as I rounded each corner with my cart, praying that I wouldn't see Paul there. I didn't.

I did see Roy though. He came up behind me as I was paying for my items. "Hey, Roy!" I said.

"Hey." He forced a smile. It didn't seem that he was quite as excited to see me as I was to see him. He and the girl with him began putting their groceries onto the conveyor belt.

"You still work here?" I asked him.

"Yup." He showed me his discount card.

I showed him mine. "That doesn't mean much," I joked. I gestured toward the girl behind him. "Is this Anamae?"

"This is my mother." Upon second glance, I realized she was well into her fifties, at least. But her hair was long, shiny, and red, and she was wearing flared jeans and a plain blue t-shirt, which could span many age groups. His eyes welled up with tears. "Anamae dumped me."

"Oh, I know how that feels. Trust me." I paid the cashier, Christine. I never really talked to her when I worked there. She never really talked to anyone. She hadn't even said a word to me the entire time she was ringing up my things, not even to tell me what the total had come to. I had to look at the screen and figure it out for myself.

"We were together for *three years*!" he banged his fist on the counter to emphasize how long they'd been together.

Okay, maybe I didn't know what that was like.

His mother stepped in between us. "Excuse me, do you want to get your things and *go*?" his mother asked me.

I grabbed the couple of bags that I had and took my change from Christine. The bus wouldn't be coming for at least ten minutes, so I waited around outside the store. When Roy came out, he tried to make a sharp turn and dodge me, so I ran up to him. "I'm sorry!" I blurted at his back.

He stopped and waved his mother on. She looked at me with a suspicious eye and then kept on towards their car. "It's not your fault. You didn't know."

"No, I didn't. And I don't know what it's like to be with someone for three years either. My situation is trivial compared to yours."

"Not trivial..."

"Anyway, what have you been up to?"

"Trying to get over her," he murmured.

I wanted to ask how long it had been, partially to see if my mourning period was getting a little ridiculous in its length, past it's season of reasonable time. "Work is good and everything?"

"Work is work."

"I hear ya." I rubbed his shoulder. He gave me a look like didn't understand why I would do that, so I removed my hand because it was a pretty unnatural gesture for me anyway. I was just trying to be nice. "You'll be better off someday."

"You never met her." His lip quivered.

"Oh, I meant the job," I said, pointing to the building. "I meant one day you'll never have to come back here."

"I don't mind it that much," he said. "It's better than sitting at home doing nothing, thinking about her. Anyway, my mom is waiting for me. I'd better go." He headed for the car, then stopped and turned back. "Would you happen to need a ride?"

"I would appreciate that, thank you." I climbed into the first row of the minivan. His mom was in the passenger seat, filing her fingernails. She turned and faked a smile. I reached out to shake her hand, but she just blew some dust off of her fingernails and turned back around. I guess it's hard to forgive someone who made your grown son cry in a supermarket. There was a lot of junk on the floor of the car. Every time we turned a corner, at least one of about four soda bottles would roll out from somewhere and hit my foot.

"So you worked together?" his mom asked.

"Yes," Roy and I answered in unison.

She glared at him for having said a word. "Where do you work now?" she asked me.

"I sell Bloom," I said, trying to sound aloof and bored about it.

"You do?!" She turned all the way around to face me. "You wouldn't happen to have a book on you, would you? They have this stuff that I used to use on my hair all the time. I used to get it from a lady on my job, but she died."

"Oh, wow." I reached into my bag and found a book at the bottom. "Got it." I handed it to her.

"Oh, thank you! Your number is on the back and everything. There is probably a whole list of things I'll need to get, so I'll give you a call by tomorrow."

"That'll be great."

She hit Roy on the arm with the book. "You didn't tell me you knew a girl who sold Bloom. I told you I've been looking for that hair serum."

"Mom, like I know anything about that."

"Thanks for the ride," I said as he pulled up in front of my house. "Nice meeting you." I held out my hand, and she shook it this time. I went inside, found the scrap of paper I'd written my friends names on, and added Roy's name again.

To be honest, I kind of missed the amount of time that the pageants took up in Deena's day. Since Lele had officially quit, she and Deena were around the house *constantly*. During every daylight hour, you could hear Lele skateboarding and trying out new tricks on the porch or the sidewalk directly in front of the house. Deena just sat, watched television, and talked on her cell phone to customers, writing down their Bloom orders and chit-chatting.

"Have you ever been to a club called *One Thousand Eleven*?" I asked her as soon as she hung up the phone.

"You mean *Club Ten Eleven*," she said. "Yes, I've heard of it, why?"

I didn't know whether I should go into it with her or not. A few hours prior, Jason had sent me a text message, saying that he wanted me to accompany him to some party that a local radio station was hosting. He was a VIP, and there was going to be press coverage, so he felt like he should have a date. For some reason, he wanted me to go. Personally, I didn't think it made much since, considering the title and theme of his latest and only single.

"Yes, I've heard *Ain't Ma Girl*," she said, laughing. "What, is that song about *you* or something?" She was joking, I could tell. She didn't believe me.

"Why do you think I've been sitting here researching this lame ass club for an hour?" I gestured towards my open laptop. "Because I just wanted to go shake my ass this weekend? No."

She was laughing really loud by this point. "I can't believe this, it's too funny! Wow, Cleo." She took a deep breath and tried to calm down. "Okay, so… Yes, I've heard of this club. What did you want to know about it?"

"Well, J. Cru wants me to go with him. And I've never been to a club before. So I was wondering if you might come with me?"

Dee's mouth hung open in shock, and moved up to the edge of her chair so fast that her notebook and pen fell on the floor. "Are you serious?"

"What's the big deal? Yes, I want you to come. I don't want to be out with him by myself or whatever. I don't know the protocol of these sorts of things."

"This is the last thing I ever expected you to say to me," she laughed. "Okay, yes, I'll go! One thing, though. You need to invite someone else to come with us, because I don't want you running off with this rapper and leaving me to stand in a corner all by myself."

I picked up my phone and dialed Janine's number. Chloe was crying in the background and Neen was practically screaming in my ear to make up for it. After repeating my dilemma several times, she agreed that she'd come along. An hour later, she called me back.

"Chloe's asleep. So, what were you saying? This weekend?"

"Yeah. You know J. Cru?"

"Vaguely."

"He's a friend of mine, wants us to come to his party."

"Us? He doesn't even know me."

"Okay, he wants *me* to come to his party. And I want you and Dee to come with *me*."

"Did he say you can invite guests?"

I hadn't even thought of that. "I mean, it's a *club*. He doesn't own the place."

"But there are guest lists and stuff, especially for VIP. Look, Cleo, I don't wanna get there and be all embarrassed and shit because they won't let me in. You know I'll go off on somebody, and you better hope it's not you."

"Okay! I'll look into it," I lied. Well, it wasn't an entire lie. I did text Jason back just to say: *I'll be there +2*. He confirmed receipt of my acceptance of his invitation, with no discrepancy about the +2 that I threw in there, so I figured it was all good.

Deena was still laughing to herself and grinning from ear to ear. It was getting to be a bit ridiculous. Yes, it was very unusual for me to invite her out somewhere, but she was acting like a little kid, or like I'd just asked her to be my bridesmaid. "You have no idea how bad I need to get out. And to a VIP event? Do you have any idea who might be there?"

"Considering *J. Cru* is the *guest of honor*, I can't imagine there will be too many big celebrities there."

"Yeah, but you never know. So what are you gonna wear?"

"I have no idea."

"I was thinking of that black sequined dress that I have, and those silver, strappy sandals."

"Do you think I keep inventory of your wardrobe or something? I don't know anything you're talking about."

"Come to think of it, maybe *you* should wear the black sequined dress."

"If you think so..."

"Can I flat iron your hair?"

"Um, I don't have a flat iron anymore."

"What do you mean? Oh my God!" She jumped up from the chair and ran to the door. "Leslie! I can see you right through the window! If I ever see you skateboard down the steps again, I will wear your ass out!" She slammed the door. "Yeah, anyway, what do you mean you don't have a flat iron?"

"I threw it out."

"Why?"

"I don't know. What do I need it for? I like my curly hair."

"Yeah, it's okay when it's actually *curly*. Most of the time it's a mess though."

"Why are you such a bitch?"

She put her hands on her hips and scowled at me. "Fine, wear your hair just like that and see if he wants his picture taken with you."

"Like you know anything about what men want. You haven't dated a guy in how many years?"

"Uh, I'm the bitch?"

"Go home."

"You know what, Cleo? I was just about to, but because you had to *say something*, now I'm just gonna stay here! How about that?" She took her seat again and started scribbling in her notebook.

"Fine, stay." I closed my laptop and carried it up to my bedroom. Now she had me worried about what to wear.

"I'm leaving!" Deena shouted up the stairs. "See you Saturday!"

My sister was pissed off at me already. "You threw every-thing in the trash?!" she screamed at me. "So when you agreed to let me come do your make-up, what were you thinking?"

Well, I was thinking that Janine was supposed to be there well over half an hour earlier, so I had planned on just using some of her make-up. I didn't have time to say this to Deena, because she had already stormed downstairs, and I wasn't about to go running after her to explain myself.

I had decided to wear the black sequined dress as Deena had suggested. I wore it with a pair of tall, black, patent leather heels, which were a tame version of stripper heels. My hair was in a big, curly ponytail, as I had absolutely refused to let Deena flat iron it. Deena said it wasn't her time to shine, so her outfit was more low-key: a pair of black jeans and a teal halter top with braided straps and gold, strappy sandals.

Janine rang my phone, explaining to me that she was on her way. Chloe had been crying her head off and Miss June wouldn't let Janine leave until she calmed Chloe down. She showed up at my bedroom door, panting. She wore a teeny, tiny, black mini-dress and black heels that laced halfway up her calves. Her hair was out in crispy curls with her baby hair gelled down around her forehead. Her facial features were extremely strong: penciled-in eyebrows, dark eye make-up, and dark-lined lips. Big, gold, doorknocker earrings framed her face. I was kind of worried about whether or not her look would satisfy the dress code.

Deena came into my room as Neen was dumping her make-up out on my floor. "What look are you going for?" she asked, her arms crossed over her chest.

"Have you ever been in a limo?" Neen asked Deena.

"A simple, yet somewhat dramatic cat-eye, I guess. I don't want a whole bunch of shadow or anything," I answered Deena.

"Yes, when I went to the prom," Deena said. "Why do you ask?"

"Apparently this J. Cru is coming to pick us up in a limo," Neen said.

"Are you serious?!" Deena screamed. "Oh my God!"

"Calm down," I said. "Yes, he said he's picking us up in a limo."

Not exactly a limo, but a stretch SUV. Deena, Janine and I were waiting in my living room, and there came a loud honk from outside. I jumped and looked out the window. My heart jumped up into my throat when I saw that abomination of a gas-guzzling monster idling outside my house. Deena and Janine were jumping up and down, squealing and laughing. I was mortified.

Jason opened the door for us from the inside. I let Dee and Neen climb in before I did. There were two other guys in the back, which I was not expecting. I don't know why I expected him to have this huge ride all to himself. Jason and I did the introducing of everyone to one another. The two guys were trying to make small talk with Janine and Deena. Jason and I sat and didn't say very much to one another, which may have looked awkward from the outside, but we never did say very much to one another.

"So," Deena said loudly, trying to open up the conversation to the rest of us. "What is tonight in celebration of?"

"This nigga right here," Dave, the one next to Dee, said, pointing at Jason. "We're about to blow up, for real."

"And who are you two, exactly?" Janine asked, removing the other guy's hand from her knee. "I know you're Dave and Peanut, but what do you have to do with J. Cru?"

"I'm his cousin," Dave said, "and I produced *Ain't Ma Girl* and a few of the other tracks on his latest album."

"I rap, too," Peanut said.

Deena gave me a look like *what the fuck have you gotten us into*? I knew she had pepper spray in her bag. I had to agree with what I knew she was thinking, that we were not in the highest class of company. All three guys were dressed in jeans, boots, and white tees, with different jewelry and head gear to differentiate between them. At least I knew that if they could get in looking like common hoodlums, Janine should be okay with her trashy look.

Dave started pouring shots of vodka and passing them around. I threw mine back immediately. "Yo, slow down," he laughed. "You wanna wait for the rest of us?"

"Oh." I held out my glass. "Pour me another then."

He filled my glass again, but this time I waited. "To J. Cru," he said. We all clinked our glasses together in the middle of the cab and took our shots. They all stared at my outstretched arm. "Another?"

"No, no! That's enough." My sister took my shot glass from my hand and put it on top of the mini bar. "Calm down."

"Calm down?" J. Cru laughed. "I don't want anybody calming down!

I want y'all getting wild!"

"Yeah, wild," I said, poking out my bottom lip. "I can't get wild if I can't have another shot."

"*One more.*" She gave Dave my glass and stared me down as I took my third shot.

There were people waiting on line when we pulled up in front of the club. I was so embarrassed to have to climb down out of that big-ass limo in front of everyone. J. Cru jumped out before me, soaking up the attention that he imagined he was getting. I could tell by the faces of the people waiting out there that they had no idea who he was. The six of us went directly inside, escorted by some girl who worked the VIP section, who introduced herself as Dylan.

It was really dark in there, with flashing, colored lights that did little to nothing to help me see where I was going. I just followed blindly, holding onto J. Cru's hand in front of me. Dylan led us to a booth where there were three bottles of champagne waiting for us on ice. "Have fun." She kissed him on the cheek and sauntered off into the crowd.

"This is dope!" Janine said, sliding into the booth beside me. "I never been up here before. I've been down *there.*" She pointed over the railing, where the main dance floor was for the general public.

J. Cru took me by the hand and led me away from our booth. We stopped in front of another booth where J. Cru began shaking hands with some people. A few of their voices sounded very familiar. "Cleo, these are my radio friends, DJ Kam Q and Chandy."

DJ Kam Q didn't look like I expected him to. Considering his somewhat high voice, I expected him to be short and skinny. He was high yellow with a big gut, and really needed to shave. His hair was gelled back into a little ponytail at the nape of his neck, and he was wearing sunglasses in a dark place, at night, which I thought was ridiculous. He actually took them off to get a better look at me. "Nice to meet you," he said, shaking my hand. "But you look very familiar."

Chandy reached out to shake my hand as well. "Nice meeting you, also. Excuse him, he's a horny dog. He tells all the girls they look familiar. Don't let him talk you into anything." She gave me a pat on the back. "She's a cute one, J. Cru. What did you have to say to get her to come here with you?" She laughed and led him off a few feet away.

"Don't listen to her," Kam Q said. "You really do look familiar." He took a seat and invited me to sit beside him, which I did. "I hope you don't take this wrong way, but do you have a website?" He filled my glass with champagne.

"Actually I do." I gulped it down and held it out for more.

"I knew it! And your name, I recognized your name, too. I'm not like a stalker or anything, I just have a thing for the thick ladies, and in my search for some plus-size porn, I came across your pictures one day. I'll admit I was drawn in by the photos, but your smarts and creativity are what keep me coming back." He was feeding me exactly what I'd hoped someone would say to me about my website. "I mean, to be honest, if porn is what someone's looking for, your site definitely isn't the place to be." I needed him to tell my family that.

"You actually read my stuff." It was more of a statement than a question. I wasn't sure whether to believe him yet.

"Yeah, I read your poetry and blogs every once in a while. I'm not gonna sit here and blow smoke up your ass like I'm your biggest fan, but I check it out every once in a while, when I remember. There's one in particular I liked about how you're proud of your body and you feel like the world tells you that you shouldn't be. That shit was deep! Matter of fact, why don't you write down your web address for me, and when I get on the air, I'm gonna talk you up a little bit."

"Are you serious?"

"Yeah! I go on the air in about an hour. I'll put in a word about you. How long have you been modeling?"

"I'm not a model," I said, blushing. "I'm definitely more of a photographer… whose favorite subject just happens to be myself."

"Wow! So you're just overflowing with talent and substance. J. Cru is a lucky man."

"Yeah, but I could never be his girl."

"Why is that?" He took a moment to think. "Oh, the song! Ha, you're funny."

Chandy and J. Cru returned. It looked as if Chandy had given him a very quick make-over. He was now also wearing sunglasses, with his blue baseball cap askew, no chain, and his shirt halfway tucked in on the left side.

"I told you I recognized her," Kam said to Chandy. "I'm a fan of her writing."

J. Cru took me by the hand and led me back our own booth. Janine was dancing with Peanut. Deena snatched me by my arm and pulled me down on the seat.

"Where did you go?!" she hissed.

"Just to talk to some people," I said. "I met DJ Kam Q and Chandy, the radio personalities. Kam Q recognized me from my website. Can you believe that?"

"Ugh, that's disgusting!"

"What's disgusting about it, Deena? I do more than take pictures of myself, and the pictures really aren't that bad if you'd give them an honest look instead of just listening to what Mom told you. I write poetry, and blogs about shit. And Kam Q said he likes my writing!"

She rolled her eyes. "He was probably just saying that."

I grabbed a bottle from the bucket on the table. "Can we pop this shit open now please? This bitch needs a drink!"

"You're pushing it," Deena said, grabbing me by the arm again.

I yanked myself away from her. I stood up, wobbled a bit, got steady, and handed the bottle to J. Cru. His back was to me, and at first I didn't even realize that there was some girl grinding herself against his front side. She was bent over anyway, so he just popped the bottle over her head and handed it back to me. I poured a glass for him, for myself, and for Deena. "Drink up," I said to her, and drank mine quickly.

Not long after that, I lost count of how many drinks I'd had. I vaguely remember doing more shots and drinking more champagne. I remember lots of dancing, walking barefoot on a wet floor at some point, standing on a table, standing on the booth seat, making out with someone, and my panties being half off. I also remember waking up in the booth and throwing up in the bucket of ice where one of the champagne bottles had been. From what I could piece together it was a pretty good night.

I woke up on Deena's love seat. Janine was lying on the couch, messing with her phone. Deena was in the kitchen, cooking. My head was pounding. "She's awake!" Janine sang in an opera voice.

"Enough of that," I said, holding my head as I sat up. On my phone was a text message from J. Cru, simply asking *what the fuck?* Whatever that meant, I didn't really care. "Can I get like ten ibuprofen? What time is it?"

"About twelve. My mom has been calling and texting me all damn morning. I need to get home, but I will definitely be having some Belgian waffles first."

"Well yours is done," Deena said. "Strawberries and whipped cream?"

"Hell yes," Janine said, jumping up and heading into the kitchen. She was wearing a big t-shirt that I figured Deena had loaned her. I was still wearing the sequined dress but my shoes were on the floor. The bottoms of my feet were black with dirt. I feared what my make-up might look like, but took a deep breath to prepare myself before I looked in the bathroom mirror.

It wasn't nearly as bad as I thought it might have been, but it looked nothing like it had when Deena put it on me. Dee had more painkillers in her medicine cabinet than a drug store. I laid out four ibuprofens on the coffee table in front of me.

"Four?" Janine said, cutting up her waffle. "Do you have a problem?"

"Me? You should be asking Deena. You should see how many pills she has in her bathroom."

"Hey!" Deena shouted, bringing me a waffle with strawberries and whipped cream on top. "When you wake up with a headache, I'm sure there's no place you'd rather be."

I looked at the waffle with its neat, little puddle of strawberries and pile of whipped cream. I'd never had a Belgian waffle before and was feeling really iffy about the toppings. I wasn't big on fruit. I mean, why not just eat a regular waffle with plain, old maple syrup? I cut myself a big piece, stabbed my fork through the strawberry and the waffle, scooped up some whipped cream, and shoveled the whole thing into my mouth. It was to die for.

Janine laughed at me. "Are you *moaning*? Are you having an *orgasm*?"

"Shut up," I said through the waffles and strawberries in my mouth.

Janine used her fork as a squeegee and cleaned her plate completely. "Okay. Let me get out of here." She carried her dishes into the kitchen, then rushed into the bathroom to change her clothes. "People are going to think I had a one night stand, wearing something like this out in the middle of the day."

"Do you want some shorts or something to throw on under that?"

Deena offered. She took a seat on the couch with her own plate.

"Since when do I care if people think I'm coming home from a one night stand? Shit, I wish that was the truth. Thanks for the breakfast, Dee. And you went so hard last night, Cleo."

I paused with my fork halfway to my mouth. "What do you mean?"

Janine looked at Deena with raised eyebrows. "You might want to fill your sister in. Anyway, I'll see you bitches later." She closed the door behind herself.

"Fill me in?"

"Yes, Cleo. As per J. Cru's request, you definitely got wild." Dee went on to describe the rest of my night. I drank and danced nonstop for quite some time. Both Dee and Janine had each caught me making out with at least two different guys and had to pull me away from them. I was very unsteady, leaning and falling all over the place, but instead of sitting down as Neen, Dee, Jason, David, Peanut, Chandy, Kam Q, and several other people suggested, I just insisted that it was my damn shoes that were tripping me up. So I took the shoes off and continued enjoying my night. At one point the crowd had cleared a small circle so that they could see me doing a split and twerking my ass cheeks one at a time. (Dee and Neen had no idea I could do that. "I did," Jason told them.) I danced on tables and chairs (which I did recall) and even gave someone a lap dance with my dress pulled up over my hips (which I did not recall). Once my sister saw that, she had had quite enough of me, so she dragged me back to the booth and blocked me in until I fell asleep in there.

I was pretty shocked to hear all of this… and quite embarrassed… and, as messed up as it is, a little proud. I made a mental note to check the Internet for any pictures.

"To be honest, I went out last night feeling quite sure that I could expect some shit like that from Janine," Dee told me, "but I never expected to be half-carrying your incoherent ass up to my apartment."

"That's not fair," I said. "She gets to go out and have a free pass to get drunk, but I'm expected to be responsible?"

"No, it's not fair. I just never thought I'd ever see you like that."

"Don't tell Mom."

"I'm not going to tell Mom," she said mockingly. "We're grown. I mean, some are clearly more grown up than others, but we're certainly not children here."

"Thank you."

"How was the waffle?"

"Delicious. I'd never had a Belgian waffle before."

"Really? Maybe you should come visit me more often."

I felt kind of bad that she felt she needed to say that. But what, honestly, would I want to visit her for? She was always visiting Mom and me, she lived at the top of a million stairs, and we usually didn't even get along. "You're right," I lied. "Sorry."

"It's okay."

"And I'm sorry about last night, too."

"It's okay. You probably needed it anyway. You got enough male attention to get your mind off of that Travis boy twenty times over. And, although I'd rather not see you be such a drunken slut, it was much closer to the Cleo I like to see, not crying or caring about some boy. I know it's such a cliché statement, but you're so not that girl."

"While I wish I could say how right you are, I think everybody is 'that girl,' even if it's just a little bit. Even boys."

"You think boys are that girl sometimes?"

"Definitely."

"I don't know."

I knew it for certain; Derek was that girl. She'd never seen a boy turn bitch-like over a female? I began to wonder how much she even knew about men. I decided to be bold and just ask her. "What's your number?"

"My number?" She was completely confused.

"How many guys have you had sex with?"

"Cleo! Please, I am not telling you that." She paused, then looked at me. "How many guys have you been with?"

"I asked you first."

"Ugh, okay. Of course Leslie's dad was my first. A couple years after he died, there was another guy, then another guy I was sort of dating, but not enough to tell you and Mom about. Then there's this other guy, who comes over occasionally when Lele is at Mom's or my dad's."

"Four?" She seemed to be misreading as my scrunched-up face to mean that that number was way too high. "I'm way over four," I said to calm her worried expression.

"Way over?! How much way over?!"

"We're talking as friends here, right? Not big sis, little sis. It would help if you could sound a little less judgmental."

"Okay." She cleared her throat and put on a very fake, pleasant voice like a tour guide. "Way over? How much way over?"

"Ugh, I can't talk to you like this."

"Okay, okay," she said, getting serious. "It's just kind of hard to hear that your little sister had more sexual partners than you have, especially in today's world, what with all the disease and everything."

"Deena, my God, I've been tested many times! I'm not just going around having raw ass sex with a bunch of men I don't know, leaving my health up to chance!"

"Okay, okay. Tell me about it. I'm calm."

"Are you sure? You're not gonna give me another lecture?"

"I didn't *lecture* you but, yes, I'm ready." She took a deep breath and held it. When I told her my number, she let it out very loudly. "That's not as bad as is it could be. It's not forty or something."

"It's nowhere near forty!"

"I know, I know. It's just… remember when we were younger, we wanted to have that magazine, and I was supposed to be in charge of all the men and relationship stuff?"

I thought she'd forgotten all about that. I was pleasantly surprised, and my heart was touched lightly.

"Well, now I couldn't even do that. *You* would have been in charge of that department. What could I even do anymore?"

"Hair, make-up, fashion. Although I don't know how in-style ball gowns are in everyday life. And it's very rare that a woman in a bathing suit wears high heels in the real world."

"Ha… ha… ha. Who put your look together last night? Me. And I think it's quite safe to say that you looked pretty hot. It may have been your loose and overtly sexual antics, but guys were clamoring to get next to you. Not that you realized any of that."

"It was probably a combination of the two. How come Janine got to sleep all comfortable on the big couch in a t-shirt and everything, while I was cramped up on the loveseat in a sequined dress from last night?"

"Because you were too drunk to give a damn. Were you uncomfortable? Did you even notice where you were?"

"No."

"Then stop complaining and shut up. And since I cooked, you should clean the kitchen. Thank you." She left her dirty plate, fork, and cup on the coffee table and went towards the back of the apartment.

I washed the dishes, wiped the counters down, cleaned the Belgian waffle iron, and then flipped through the television channels as I waited for Deena to finish up in the bathroom. I took a shower and put my clothes back on from the night before. Deena offered to give me something else to wear. "No, why? Is this inappropriate?" I asked her.

"Yes, quite. It's early Sunday afternoon."

"Janine walked out of here in that little, tiny dress."

"Okay, yeah, but Janine is a little, tiny girl, no offense." How was I not supposed to be offended by that? "And what do you think Mom is gonna say if you walk in the house wearing that right now?"

I really wasn't bothered about what Mom might say, but she obviously was, so I took the clothes she offered me. I put on her noisy running shorts and family reunion t-shirt, both of which she told me I could keep. She definitely wanted the flip-flops back, and I was to take them off as soon as I got home. It had been a while since I'd been in Deena's car. On the radio, they were talking about how the party the night before had been poppin', and how J. Cru had come out with a few of his close friends.

"That's us!" Deena exclaimed. She didn't even know him, but whatever. I changed the station as soon as they started playing his song. "You don't like that song?"

"No, I don't like that song," I said. "Why would I? I don't even like *him* that much."

"That's rude."

"You may think so, but you don't know him. He can be a real asshole. I just wanted to go because I'd never been there before."

"User."

"Whatever. You were there, too."

As soon as I got home, I stepped out of Deena's flip-flops and left them by the door. Mom and Lele were playing Chinese checkers at the kitchen table. I peeked in, waved to them, and went right upstairs. I closed my bedroom door and went back to bed for several hours.

When I woke up in the early evening, I started combing the Internet for pictures from the party. I could smell someone grilling outside and it smelled delicious. I figured it was the people next door, who used their grill about five days a week. On the radio station's website were snapshots from the night before. There was a picture of me talking with DJ Kam Q in his VIP booth, and although I wasn't too far-gone yet, I hadn't even realized that picture had been taken. There was a photo of J. Cru, nuzzling my neck or whispering something in my ear as I held my drink off to the side to keep from spilling it. I was in several other pictures just dancing in the background. Then there was one picture of me, barefoot, on the floor, doing a split in my sister's sequined dress. Thank God I'd chosen to go with black boy shorts for underwear. I'd never really noticed I could splay my legs like that.

I went to my own website to put a link on there that would direct my own visitors to the party images. I figured they might like to see that newfound freak side of myself (or *freakier*, depending on how you look at it). When I got to my page, there was a flood of new messages and comments on my poems, blogs, and pictures. At first I was stunned, then I remembered that Kam Q had promised to mention me on the air. And I was still kind of stunned. I had gotten about a thousand new visitors within the past eighteen hours or so. Of course there were those who wanted to know who the hell I was, and why I thought I was so special, and how I got air time. For the most part, the reaction was overwhelmingly positive. I went back to the radio website to write Kam Q a thank you.

My phone rang. "Girl, did you see your pictures from last night?!" Janine screamed in my ear. I couldn't tell if she was proud or disgusted.

"Yes, I happen to be looking at them now."

"I can't even talk right now. I'm sitting here with my mom and my brother. My brother said he had no idea you had it in you, and he wants you to know that he means that as the highest form of a compliment."

"You're looking at it with your mom and brother?! Are you trying to humiliate me?"

"They just happened to walk over when I screamed. I think he's revisiting that crush he had on you in middle school. So you better believe that next time you come over, he'll be here." I could hear him tell her to shut up as she laughed loudly.

"I never thought I could be so embarrassed over the phone."

"Girl, get over it. You did it to yourself. If you have no self control, you should've never gotten so drunk."

"I know that *now*. Where were you last night?"

"Pulling your ass up off the floor and off of every male in the place. Boo, you know I was looking out for you. You're a grown-ass woman; you can drink what you want. Me and your sister wouldn't let nothing bad happen."

"I can't deal with this right now. I gotta go." I hung up the phone, closed my computer, and put both of them on the floor. Just a few moments earlier, I had been slightly giddy over my pictures. Now, just from having Janine talk to me, I was completely over it. Why was I like that, happy about something until someone else got in on it? And then, out of nowhere: thoughts of Travis. His eyes, his touch, lying in his bed… I groaned loudly to myself and slid down under my blankets and tried to fall back asleep. I couldn't, so I took out my notebook and started writing what I felt.

Restless
About life
About love
About nothing to do

About anything
About what this all means
And that I'm afraid it means nothing.
Nothing but striving and heartache,
Goals unrealized,
Life not lived,
Love lost,
Life lost.
Restless.

I almost stopped there, but it didn't feel right. It felt pessimistic to stop there. And though I was agitated about so many different things, I was not beaten down.

But restlessness
Is that yearning for something
Further than what's in front of our eyes.
A grasping, a grabbing,
For something more.
Something better, something bigger.
Something like walking into
A warm hug from someone you love
When you've been thinking
You were unhuggable.
Something like freedom.
Something like finding yourself.
Something like thriving,
Instead of merely surviving.
Something like hope,

Which brings you through that time of restlessness,

When you think that that restlessness

Could be your demise,

But it's not.

It's the fire, the drive.

So how dare I think that

This all means nothing

When I feel so restless?

I closed my notebook and made a mental note to put it on the blog later. I know poems can be hard to understand in some cases, but mine aren't *that* deep, at least I don't think so. They're short, they have nice rhythm and stuff, so I don't see what's not to like about them. I think they're very accessible. Despite all of what I think about the poetic baring of my soul, the readers don't care that much for it. Of course, if I write something about relationships or, more specifically, sex, the readers jump all over it. Especially when I give tips to the guys, they love that shit. In any case, Janine is typically the only one to respond to my poetry, although it's rare that she gets what I was trying to say. (A while ago, I contemplated just keeping my poems in my notebooks, and I know this is strange, but I felt bad about not giving them room to breathe.)

Leslie opened my door and poked her head in. "You sleep a lot."

"Thank you for closing my door on your way back downstairs," I said to her.

She opened it up completely and walked in. "Cranky pants. Grandma's friend is here, grilling. It's almost ready."

"Huh?"

"You heard me. And then, after dinner, I want you guys to come out front and watch me do a new trick. Grandpa built me a ramp, and it's *in-*

credible. You have to see me jump it."

I was still wearing Deena's shorts and t-shirt. I went downstairs in my bare feet. The back deck was smoky, and I couldn't see the face of the man who was standing over the grill. Mom was standing with her ass poking out of the refrigerator. "What's going on?" I asked.

Deena was at the sink, washing lettuce. "Where have you been?!" she exclaimed. "You missed everything."

"Everything?" I repeated. "And, anyway, you know where I was. I'm hung over."

The sliding door opened and the gentleman walked in from the deck. He wore a pale, yellow polo shirt and khakis, a nice-looking brown belt with a shiny, brass buckle, and brown loafers. He was balding around the top and had a tidy goatee around his mouth. There were equal amounts of black and gray on his head and in his beard. His skin was milk chocolate brown, and his eyes were black but bright. He gave me a toothy, white smile and held out his hand. "You must be Cleo." I could totally see him as a professor, instructing one of my courses in college. He was pretty dapper and looked smart. Nice watch, too.

"And you are…"

He laughed a deep, warm laugh. "Oh, excuse me. My name is Ted. I'm a friend of your mother's."

"Ted is the guy I met at the hospital, the one I went out with the last time," Mom explained, as if I didn't know that, as if she was dating so many guys that I couldn't keep track of them all.

"I hope you like cheeseburgers," Ted said.

"She loves cheeseburgers!" Mom told him.

I liked them.

"We should eat out on the deck," she suggested.

"I don't know," I said, peeking out there. "That table has been in all kinds of weather. I can see the splinters from here."

"Shush, Cleo. We'll just be careful." She smiled at Ted and squeezed by him as she carried napkins, plates, and flatware outside. Deena followed her with the condiments and a huge bowl of potato salad. Lele followed her with two two-liter bottles of soda.

It was just Ted and me. "How old are you?" I asked him.

He laughed. "Do you guys have any pickles?"

"Probably." I opened up the fridge and peered inside in a way so that I wouldn't have to turn my back on him. It's not that I didn't trust him as a person… but you must understand I'm a little wary of a man in the house. I handed him the jar.

"Bread and butter," he read from the label. "No dill?"

"Bread and butter's not good enough for you?"

"Why do I feel like I'm talking to Denise's father?" He laughed some more. "I'm just kidding around. Bread and butter is plenty good for me. I'd better get back out there." He rushed for the door to step out and handle the grill. He seemed like a really nice guy. I figured I should stop hassling him. He carried the plate of burgers and hot dogs over to the table as I took my seat next to Lele. I wished I wasn't wearing shorts because the wooden bench was quite prickly. Ted and my mom sat on the same side of the table with a good amount of space between the two of them, enough so that they wouldn't be bumping arms "accidentally".

"Ted is—get this—a *meteorologist*," my mom said. "Isn't that cool?"

"What's that?" Leslie asked, not looking very impressed.

"They predict the weather, among other things," Ted explained.

"You predict other things? Like a fortune teller?"

Ted laughed… again. He was quite the jolly fellow. "No, I mean we do other things besides predict the weather. I mean, that's the main thing I do though."

"Do you have any kids?" Deena asked.

"Nope, no kids. Can't say I never wanted any, but I never had any." He looked down at his plate, nodding. Mom gave her the eye. "I've got a slew of nieces and nephews though," he said, perking up. "They're the little lights of my world. Some aren't so little anymore, but you get the picture."

"Sure do," Dee answered. "So how tall are you?"

"Six feet even," he chuckled. "Boy, am I getting the third degree here or what? Denise, you have some very protective daughters."

"I'm sorry," she said, eyeing both of us. If looks could kill...

"No, no, I really don't mind. It's good that they feel they need to watch over you, it must mean you've very precious to them. If they didn't give a crap about who you were dating, then I'd be a little suspicious." They laughed together, though my mom's was kind of forced.

Ted didn't stay very long after dinner. Mom assured him that we didn't want him helping to clean up the kitchen, but he did, and promised to leave immediately after, which he did. I watched from the window as Mom walked him out to his car. They hugged, gave each other a quick peck on the lips, and then she walked back into the house.

"Were you spying on me?!"

"No," I lied.

"You weren't sitting by the window when I left," she said. "That's not right, Cleo. I give you all the privacy in the world."

"Like it matters. I don't bring boys around here."

"Because you're afraid I'll be like you, spying. I don't do stuff like that."

I followed her into the kitchen, where Deena and Lele were sitting at the table, arguing about skateboarding. "So do you like this guy?"

"He's nice," Mom said.

"You don't like him," Deena said.

"I do!"

"Not enough," Dee replied. "Yes, he's nice, but he's kind of just… *blah*. I mean, a *meteorologist*? Please, come on."

"I think that's cool!" Mom said. She leaned against the counter and crossed her arms over her chest. "Okay, you're right, I don't like him that much. He laughs at *everything*. At first I was pleased that he was so good-humored, but now it's getting annoying."

"I think you should give him more of a chance," I said.

Deena and Mom both looked at me as if I'd just suggested that Mom should run naked down the sidewalk.

"Yes," I said, standing by my statement. "He's a nice guy. He's not the guy you typically go for, and maybe that's why it rarely works out. So give the other guy a shot."

"Since when did you become such a romantic?" my mother asked.

I couldn't answer that because I didn't know. I was trying to figure it out for myself.

"Enough of this boy stuff," Leslie announced. "Everybody come out front and watch me do my thing."

Dee and I took a seat on the stoop while Mom stood in doorway. Lele set up her ramp, which was only about three inches at its highest point. Even so, Deena cursed the thing. "What was my father thinking, building her this death trap?"

"It's hardly a death trap, Dee. You're way overreacting. I think it's cute that he's helping her do something she's really into."

"I *used* to help her do something she was really into."

"And no one forgets it, especially not Lele," I assured her.

Lele, wearing her knee and elbow pads, strapped on her helmet and walked down to the end of the block with her skateboard in hand. She kick-pushed her way up the sidewalk at her top speed, which was not fast at all. I could definitely walk faster. Deena actually had her eyes covered, but I don't think Lele noticed. Lele went straight for the ramp with no hesitation, up the incline, and down the other side, catching the tiniest bit of air. She wobbled a little bit, waving her arms out in front of her and to the side, but steadied quickly and landed it perfectly. "I freaking did it!" she screamed, jumping off the skateboard and running up to the porch to give hugs all around. "*I did it*!"

"Watch your language!" Deena said, then cracked a smile. "I'm so proud of you." She hadn't even been watching, but I guess she was proud enough Lele wasn't crying and covered in blood.

"That was the first time I got it right! Every time I've been practicing, I kept falling, or I would get scared when I got to the ramp. I knew I was getting closer, so I just told myself I was ready, and I told you guys I was ready, and I did it!"

My mom went out with Ted again. They were supposed to go out to dinner and dancing, but I went to bed around one in the morning and she still wasn't back. I woke up about eight and a half hours later, and she still wasn't back. Another hour or so and she came in wearing the same clothes from the night before.

"Good morning," she said as if it was just like any other day. So I decided not to acknowledge it either. She was my mother, not my child; she deserved her privacy. "I think it's going to rain. The sky is so dark."

"Great. I had planned on delivering my Bloom orders today."

"Now you have all day to chill and watch movies with me," she said, hugging me tight. "That's what I had planned on doing today anyway. I'll help you sort them. Let me put my comfy clothes on first."

I sat on the living room floor and opened up the Bloom boxes. With the remote control, I selected an independent horror movie to watch, but didn't dare start it until my mom came back downstairs. She sat on the floor with me and helped me fill the paper bags according to what my few customers had ordered.

"What is this?" she asked, gesturing towards the television with a nod of her head.

"Something scary." I changed the subject quickly before she could protest, as I knew she would. She would probably try to talk me into putting on some lame romantic comedy that only she would enjoy. I knew that, deep in her heart, she secretly liked horror movies though. "You didn't buy anything from me this go-round," I pointed out.

"I'll get you next time."

"It is next time."

"Well pick something out and I'll pay for it. Only up to twenty dollars, though. Your hair has been looking a little frizzy lately—maybe you should get some of that moisturizing serum, define your curls some." My mother and Dee insult me so casually and carelessly that I sometimes think they have some wicked plan to slowly but surely break me down.

I chose not to fight this battle. "How does Deena sell so much stuff? She's like a machine."

"She sells to anyone and everyone. When we go out to the store or something, she's handing out cards and brochures to absolutely everybody."

"I've never seen her do it."

Mom shrugged. "Do you really go anywhere with her? No." Were they in on this together, too, trying to make me feel guilty about not spending enough time with my sister? "How are Janine and her baby? I still have to get over to see them."

"Good. I don't even know if I told you the baby's name. Did I?"

"If you did, I don't even remember."

"Chloe," I said. "Sound familiar?"

"No, who's Chloe?"

"It sounds just like Cleo!" I exclaimed. "How can you not hear that?"

"I mean, yeah, but… it's not."

"Whatever. I'm trying to watch this movie." I turned my body to face the screen completely and continued bagging items. I felt kind of bad about getting huffy with her. I kept glancing over to make sure she didn't look hurt, but she was contentedly filling the bags, paying me no mind.

Out of nowhere, she spoke up a few minutes later. "You're kind of self-centered."

"Ugh! What?"

"Yeah, it kind of sounds like your name. Forgive me if that's not the first thing I realized."

"Well, excuse me, I thought it was pretty obvious."

"Maybe to *you*, because your mind is always going *Cleo, Cleo, Cleo.* Maybe the rest of the world thinks about other things."

"Whatever, Mom. Can I please just watch this movie and get my work done without being put down constantly?"

"Please, you're the strong one, too strong to care what anyone says to you. You definitely have a greedy portion of confidence. I only put you down to keep you on a tolerable level. With an ego like yours, if I only ever built you up, your personality would be *unbearable.*" She laughed and tried to assure me that she was only kidding. Maybe she meant it to be funny, but she wasn't kidding. They say there is some truth to every joke, and while I don't think that's a steadfast rule, it definitely rang true there.

As I stepped out of my house, I had to make a prompt change of direction to my left to avoid stepping on the box that was placed on the porch, directly in front of the door. It was a little bit wider than it was deep, and only about five inches in height. The top of the box was white with no images or type. The side of the box showed a sleek DVD/VHS player combo. I couldn't believe my eyes.

I looked around. There were a couple of people walking themselves to wherever, but no one was watching me. I'm not entirely sure what I expected to see—maybe my father peeking out from a behind a bush or something, but he wasn't. There was no trace of him, except for this box. Upon coming to terms with this, I told myself to calm down and think about who I was dealing with. Yes, the box was taped up securely, looking nice and new, but who's to say what was really inside? It could be empty.

I bent over to pick it up. It was heavy. Like DVD player/VCR combo heavy. I still tried not to get my hopes up. It could've been bricks. Or a large quantity of dope that he wanted my mom to hold onto for him while he was hiding out from the cops. With him, who ever knows? I carried it into the house and placed it on the coffee table. I walked around it for a while, looking at it from different angles. The picture looked nicer than the old machine I'd had. If that was what was really inside, I was kind of excited to see it. Again, I had to remind myself that there were no guarantees.

As much as I wanted to rip the thing open, I was also dreading the impending disappointment. I went to the kitchen and took the scissors from the junk drawer. I cut the tape on each side, then straight across the top. Under the four cardboard flaps was a large mass of Styrofoam, which was difficult to get out because it fit so snugly. But once I removed that, I was relieved more than happy to find that the picture on the outside depicted exactly what was on the inside. I got up, ran to the phone, and dialed my mother at work.

"Yes?" she answered. I was so relieved that she just happened to be sitting at the nurse's station and I didn't have to have one of her colleagues fetch her or, worse yet, wait for her to call me back.

"Guess what?"

"What? Calm down. You're screaming in my ear."

"Someone left a DVD player/VCR machine on our porch!" My voice kept going up and down as I tried to refrain from screaming into the phone.

"Someone?" she repeated. "Now, honey, who do you think that someone could be?"

I didn't want to say. "I'm shocked."

"Trust me, so am I."

"I gotta go, I wanna hook it up to the TV right now."

"Okay. See you when I get home. Love you, babe."

"I love you, too." I hung up the phone and crawled onto the floor. I began taking out the cords and manual and laying them out in front of the TV. While I was doing this, I noticed a yellow index card on the floor. The handwriting was beautiful and feminine, flowing over the blue rules of the index card like the steadily flowing water of a creek.

Meeting in the Chinese food place like that was messed up. I understand why you acted like that, and I understand why you wouldn't like me. But I think it's cool to know that Quincy has an older sister out there. Not to sound too corny, but it makes me feel a little less alone. I wish I could've gotten this to you sooner, but I've been saving up. Please try not to hate me.

So this gift was not from my father, but from his twenty-one-year-old baby mama. How did she know where I lived? She was on stalker mode for real, or I guess she could've easily found out from my dad. At least she was considerate enough, despite the fact that I'd humiliated and exposed her family in public. That was pretty big of her to look past all that.

Suddenly I was not so excited to stick yellow, white, and red plugs into their corresponding, colored sockets. I put the note in my pocket, left the mess on the floor, and walked out of the house.

The fresh air felt good, and I took deep breaths to fill my lungs with it as I walked. I picked up a fallen tree branch to use as my walking stick. Without really knowing where I was headed, I took myself to the regional rail train station, and climbed up the hill beside the tracks. There was no one on the platform. No trains either. I said a quick prayer and then jumped down onto the track. I walked out to the middle of the bridge and looked down at the street below me. It wasn't that far up—three stories, I could tell by looking at the building next to the tracks. My neighborhood looked small though, like a doll village. I held my walking stick out over the wall at arm's length and let it go. I couldn't see because the wall was too high to look straight down, but there was silence for what seemed like forever, then the wooden clatter. Luckily a car hadn't been coming, or I would've felt terrible for dropping that somewhat heavy stick onto it. That thought didn't even cross my mind until it was too late.

I continued across the rest of the bridge, to the hill on the opposite side of the street from which I came. I sat there and looked out over my neighborhood and toward the city skyline. On the other side of the skyline was Travis's neighborhood, which seemed a world away now. In a lot of ways, it really was a world away. The heartache was not yet that far, but at a more tolerable distance. It was getting to be ridiculous how I still couldn't go an hour without thinking about him, even if it was just something small, like seeing a pair of shoes that reminded me of the ones he wore, or seeing someone about his height, or smelling something that brought up a memory of something we did together. I caught a whiff of garbage once and it reminded me of the time that he and I walked to get water ice, and we passed by a really stinky dumpster on the way there. We both looked at each other and started cracking up laughing at the hysterical faces we were each making because it just smelled so horrible. Now I hate that memory.

My random, aimless walk reminded me of high school. I used to do stuff like that all the time back then. I would just go out and walk, sit somewhere and think about stuff for hours, then come home well after dark. My mom was very suspicious of my whereabouts at that time, worried that I might be getting into drugs or something. She would swear me down that my eyes were bloodshot and droopy, but you know how teenagers are always tired—if I wasn't out walking with nowhere to go, I was in my room, taking a nap. She even called the school a few times to make sure that I had shown up for class. Of course she had nothing to worry about though, as I was never ever the type to get in trouble. I hated it at the time, but now I can understand and appreciate her concern.

A butterfly approached me. Weird as it was, I immediately had a sort of fight or flight mentality that struck me. I remembered what Lele had said about being afraid of butterflies. It was beautiful, yes, very high contrast with bright orange and black, but it really did look crazy. It's general path was towards me, but it dipped and dived and bobbed and weaved all over the place, like a drunk person stumbling towards you as you just pray that they'll fall off to the side before they get close enough to put a hand on your shoulder and ask for a few dollars or a ride somewhere.

It didn't come for me. Instead, it went right by me and landed on one of the wildflowers a few feet away from where I sat. I felt sort of bad for judging it, comparing such beauty to an unpleasant encounter with an alcoholic. Kind of like life. You know how people say stuff like "life's a bitch, then you die"? That's when people look at life like the run-in with the alcoholic, who doesn't care about the discomfort or pain he causes others and just continues his destructive path with no particular goal in sight. I don't believe that, though. Life is absolutely more like the butterfly; it takes many twists and turns, and you can never be sure where it's headed, but I think there is an ultimate goal, one comprised of more good than bad intentions.

I carefully walked down the hill. There were lots of rocks and glass bottles, things I could easily hurt myself on. My mom had freaked out back in high school when I told her about my thinking spot, claiming that I could easily fall down and bust my head on a rock or cut my face open on a broken bottle, *or* be crushed to death by a derailed train.

I made my way home, intent on taking a nice, long nap. It was a luxury I needed to indulge in as much as possible now, as I would be back in school in a little over two weeks. At least I wouldn't be hauling ass from class to the supermarket anymore since I could work from home and create my own hours. I had to give Deena credit for suggesting that whole thing. As I walked through the living room, I made sure not to look towards the junk on the floor. Yes, I was glad to have it, but I just didn't want to deal with it yet. I took the note from my pocket and put it in the box where I keep special things like that.

Derek insisted on picking me up from my house, and I almost gave in. Instead, I kept running over in my mind the response my mom would have to seeing me get into his car, and I just couldn't deal with it. There would be so many questions and inferences and great expectations. No, I told him he could just pick me up at the train station. He was there waiting for me. I got into his car and turned the radio off because I just didn't feel like listening to any stupid music, especially since they seemed to be playing the very same songs over and over again, and one of those songs was still J. Cru's. I mean, good for him and everything. Neither of us had spoken or texted a word to each other since that text I got from him the morning after the party.

"Haven't seen you in a while," Derek said. "What have you been up to?"

"The same stuff since the last time you saw me," I replied. "And you?"

"Well—I thought you might be proud of me for this—I'm enrolled to start school for the fall semester. Just at community college, but it's a step, right?"

"Yeah, that's awesome."

"I had to cut back on work though, so I'm down to two jobs now. But it's cool because I have a good stack of money stashed, not including my regular savings, so I'm paying for this semester outright."

"Wish I could say that. I got an education to get a good job, now I need a job to pay for my education. I'll be paying for college for the rest of my life."

"Aw, don't say that. It'll go by quickly, trust me. You'll be making lots of money when you graduate, as talented as you are. Anyway, what would you like for dinner? I'm really in the mood for Italian. Have you ever been to Angello's? That's my favorite Italian place."

"I don't really feel like sitting in a restaurant right now."

"No problem, they have take-out. Does that sound good to you?"

"Sure." I told him I wanted lasagna, then got out of the car and headed for the bookstore, which was just a couple stores down in the shopping center. We had a while to wait before the food was ready, at least twenty minutes. I browsed the clearance section, picked up a few books I'd been wanting to read, ever since they had been regularly priced. I carried them with me over to the couches and began looking through the photography book I'd picked up.

Derek found me about fifteen minutes later. "What you got there?" he asked, sitting on the arm of the chair.

"I don't think you're allowed to sit there," I said, and he immediately moved to the seat beside me. "It's just a photography book, a bunch of self-portraits from different photographers."

"You love yourself some self-portraits," he said, nudging me.

"This isn't really about me. I just like photography. And self-portraits are very telling."

"I know, Cleo, I was just messing around with you. And that book?"

For some reason, I don't like when people ask me to explain books to them. People get paid to write the summary on the back of paperbacks or the inside flap of book jackets, and everyone I know can read, so I don't know why they ask me. "It's about a girl and a guy, and she kills him… because he asks too many questions."

He rolled his eyes. "How much are they?"

"I actually found them on clearance, which I'm psyched about. This one is five dollars and this one is ten. Ten dollars… it used to be forty-five!"

"Wow. Can I buy them for you?"

"No," I said. "I found them, I want to buy them for myself."

He poked out his bottom lip. "Come on… I just want to do something nice for you."

"Why? I never do anything nice for you."

He took a moment to think about that. "I just figured it's not in your nature, so I wouldn't want you to go too far out of your element." He stood on his feet, scooped the books off of my lap, and proceeded toward the cash register. Of course I wasn't going to make a scene in a bookstore, snatching them back from him and running to the check-out counter, so I just followed quickly behind him.

"Why are you doing this? I don't need you to buy me books."

"You don't really need me for anything, Cleo, but I just want to do it. Can you just let that be okay with you?"

I crossed my arms over my chest and remained quiet. He handed me the bag after he'd paid for them, and I really didn't like the feel of it, like my daddy handing me my goodies. I waited in the car for him while he got our food. The food didn't bother me, we were both eating the food, but the books… I don't know, I just felt some kind of way about it. The books were *mine*, and I wasn't too keen on the idea of having him shove himself into such a personal spot in my life.

After dinner, we sat and watched TV without exchanging words for a while. I was flipping through my new photo book on the side while he flipped through the channels. Suddenly, he turned the volume down on the television very low. A girl was crying as her family hugged her, relieved that she was agreeing to go to rehab.

"I was seeing this girl for a few weeks," he sighed, sounding like he was confessing his darkest secret to me. "We had to break it off though, it was pretty dramatic. I don't know, I shouldn't be talking about this with you." He took his glasses off and put them on the coffee table.

"No, go on. Friends talk." It was actually pretty weird to hear him talk about another girl. I had talked about other guys with him quite a few times, when I was really upset about something, but he had never mentioned any other girls to me. I always figured there weren't any other girls.

"She reminded me a lot of you, except—I hate to say this—*nicer.*" This girl left Derek to go back to an emotionally abusive ex-boyfriend. Not only did he call her every name in the book and constantly tell her how useless and ugly she was, he even hit her once. By "hit" her, I'm saying he knocked a tooth out. "She said it was already loose anyway, for whatever reason. I don't know what to think of this whole thing. It's such a messy situation. I mean, I was sad for myself that we can't continue down the great path we were on of becoming great friends and maybe more, but I feel even worse for her. She's—and I hate to say this—kind of pathetic. I feel so sorry for her."

"I think sometimes people are drawn to others who hurt them. Like the pain is familiar, so it's almost nurturing in a very warped way." As soon as I said it, I realized that it was kind of the same situation between him and me. I had to make a much better effort to be nice to him. "This is an amazing image, huh?" I showed him the page I was looking at. "Thanks a lot for this book." So contrived, right?

"No problem. How about a zombie flick?"

"Absolutely."

He turned off all of the lights and joined me again on the couch. Five minutes into the movie and I was in his arms, burying my face in his chest whenever I couldn't bear to look at the screen anymore. You can always tell when some shit's about to go down because the music changes. That's when my heart starts pounding and I know it's time to start watching the movie through the tiny cracks between my fingers.

I was literally clinging to him by the time it was over. He was laughing at me as I followed him from the couch to his bedroom, gripping his t-shirt in a tight fist. "It's not funny," I said. "Can you turn a light on?"

"You can turn it on," he said.

"Then I have to let go of you to find the switch. No."

He stopped walking in the middle of the bedroom. I was nervous. Had he seen something I hadn't? Was he still Derek, or something undead? His hands wandered over my body, up to the back of my head, and he kissed me on the mouth. I wondered if I needed to close my eyes, since we were already in the dark. We kissed with closed mouths, long kisses, three times, then started going at it with ferocity. My hair had come undone from its tight ponytail because he was pulling at it so hard and crazy-like. I'd removed his shirt and mine, and then we were on his bed, removing our pants as well.

As passionate as we were in the beginning (I guess it was the zombie movie that got us all riled up?), once we really got down to business, it felt disconnected. I guess we were both thinking of other things, other people. He finished early—not early by most standards, but—earlier than usual. I, on the other hand, was taking forever to get there. He insisted that he didn't want to quit on me. I wanted to be done, chalk this one up to a good romp with no climax… so I faked it. Derek got me a warm washcloth and came back to bed.

Lying in the dark, maybe twenty minutes later, he put his hand on my shoulder and moved very close to me. "You don't have to fake anything for me." My back was to him, so I didn't say anything, hoping that maybe he'd think I was asleep. He didn't push the subject, so he must've figured I was.

After lying there for nearly an hour without falling asleep, my body and mind fully awake, I got up and went to the living room. I turned on a light and took a seat on the couch to continue looking at my new book. I was scared to death, still unable to get those zombie images out of my head. I sat at the far end of the couch, in the corner of the room, so that I could see all around me. Nothing could sneak up on me from that vantage point. Yes, I could see the entire room, and every time I looked down at my book, I swore I saw some dark shadow in a doorway or rounding a corner. There weren't many doorways or corners there, by the way, but in my unstable frame of mind, I felt like I was in a haunted labyrinth of zombie hiding places. It was too much for me. I turned off the light, ran back into Derek's bedroom, and jumped into the bed.

"Are you awake?" I whispered.

"Yeah, why?" he asked.

"I'm scared."

"Of what?"

I didn't want to just come out and say that I was afraid of zombies; that sounded completely ridiculous. "That movie just has me a little freaked out, I guess."

"Come here." He wrapped his arms around me, and I really did feel so much safer (as long as I could rely on the fact that he wouldn't turn into one of them while he was holding me). It took me some time, but I was finally able to fall asleep.

I was still in Derek's arms when I woke up in the morning. His eyes were closed, but I could tell he wasn't asleep. "Good morning," I said, rolling out of his grip.

"Good morning." He yawned towards the other side of the bed to spare me his morning breath. "Sleep well?"

"Yeah, after… you know."

"No, after what?"

"Like, when you were, like, holding me and stuff."

"Aw," he said, just to poke fun at me. "You're the mushy type."

"Shut up, I'm really not. I'm just a scaredy-cat."

"Something's different," he said, sitting up and putting a t-shirt on. "Let's see, what could it be? Oh, I know! You're not trying to run out of here! Now why is that?"

I shrugged. "Why should I? Do you want me to?"

"No, no! Don't get me wrong, I love for you to stay. It's just very rare."

"Well things are more greatly appreciated when they're rare. Or would you prefer I make this a common occurrence?" I propped myself up on my elbow with my body turned towards him.

Derek took a deep breath and sighed, leaned his chin on his hand, like the statue of the Thinker. "Cleo, I know you. And you know me well enough to be certain that I appreciate you for the rarity that you are, whether you choose to make your presence a common occurrence or not. And you also know that I would greatly prefer for you to make this a regular thing. But, like I said, I know you."

"And what does that mean?"

He mumbled something that sounded like, "It means that what I want doesn't matter." I didn't ask him to repeat himself, because if that's what he had really said, I didn't want to hear the words clearly. I would have felt horrible. He got up and went to the bathroom.

I went to the kitchen. There were eggs and cheese in the refrigerator, but no breakfast meat. At least there was toast and butter. I made omelets, arranged them on plates with buttered toast, and poured each of us a glass water, since there was no juice of any kind. I could hear as soon as Derek stepped out of the shower.

"What's that smell?!" he hollered from the bathroom.

"A surprise!" I shouted back.

He came out to the front of the apartment, wet with a towel around his waist. "No way."

I nodded. "I can cook."

"I never would've guessed." He sat at the table where his place was set and began eating before I'd even gotten my own plate to the table.

"Is it good?"

He nodded. "A little heavy on the butter for the omelets, though. My omelet is practically caramelized."

"Shut up," I laughed. "I'm always unsure of how much to put in there, but I'd rather it be too buttery than to stick to the pan and burn."

"I'll teach you how to do it right with the perfect amount."

"Let's talk about this other girl. What did you say her name was?"

"I didn't. I don't really want to talk about her either."

"Oh." I waited thirty seconds, then tried again. "What was it about her that made her nicer than me?"

He shrugged. "She liked being here."

First of all, I didn't like the way he said that, that she was there, in my spot. "I like being here," I said defensively. "You think I just come over because I like getting head? No, I come over because, on some level, I like *you.*"

He laughed. "On some level. Well, she had no problem admitting she liked me on all levels."

"Are you trying to pit us against each other?"

"Cleo, no. Look, you asked about her, remember? I just said I didn't want to talk about her. She's a nice girl, she's clearly fucked up in the head though and what would I wanna deal with that for? No. I want a girl who's got her mind right, like you. And maybe you're not always nice, but you're always interesting. You make me want to make myself better than I already am. Because of you, I'm enrolled in college, and I never imagined that would happen."

"Oh. Thank you."

"Another thing is the sex was wack. Sex with you is always amazing. Well, except for last night."

"Was it not good for you?"

"It was great for me! I'm sorry it wasn't good for you, though."

"It felt great for me, also. Just because I didn't have an orgasm doesn't mean it wasn't great. Everything else felt *so good.*"

He smiled. "Oh. I'm glad to hear that. I was kind of worried. Well, with that being said, I think it's safe for me to say that even our off nights are better than my best nights with her."

"Ick. That wouldn't work out in the long run."

"I could teach her things, just like I taught *you* things."

I guffawed. "You mean like I taught you things! I came to you with my head and riding game on lock."

"Oh please. Let me call up your other boyfriends and see if you've been trying that thing I told you how to do."

"I certainly don't remember you teaching me that. What about this other girl? I bet I could call her and recite play-by-play how you went down on her."

He shook his head. "I didn't."

"You *what*?!"

"She wouldn't let me. Said her boyfriend had never done it for her, and she was too shy to let anyone get that intimate with her down there. Not yet, anyway."

"Wow, she *is* fucked up in the head."

Derek nodded. "I was kind of disappointed at first, but now I don't mind. At least I can say I saved that part of myself for you."

"Aw. Aren't you the mushy type?"

Derek tried to help me clean the kitchen, but I refused to let him. I pointed him toward the couch and cleaned up everything myself. As I was getting through all those dishes and pans, I sort of wished I had let him help, but I knew I had to do something nice for him that was not related to sex, at least this once. I joined him on the couch with my dry, wrinkly fingers. He was watching some boring superhero cartoon and was way too into it for a man his age. I put my hand in his and laced our fingers together.

"Look at your fingers," he said. "Now I feel so bad for making you do all that."

"Like you could make me do anything," I replied. "I wanted to do it."

He kissed my hand. "And I thank you." He made a trail all the way up my arm. "And I thank you, and thank you…" The parade of kisses ended with a finale of licking and sucking on my neck. But the finale of the parade is what kicked off the main event.

It seems kind of funny now that that was the first time we'd ever had sex on his couch. He had no roommates, so we could've been having sex all over the apartment for months. He was pulling my hair a lot again. I figured that was something he learned from that other girl, and I wasn't mad at her if she'd asked him to do it; I really liked it. We were much more in sync this time, and perfectly paired in assisting each other to reach our highest highs.

I guess our whole reunion could've been sweeter, more platonic and pure, if we'd just spent time together, talking, watching movies, and eating Italian and breakfast foods without the intermittent sex. I guess that might be so, but I'm sorry, I like to have sex. Actually, I'm not sorry. I like to have sex, and no, I'm not sorry.

From her seat on the couch, my mom stared at the wires and DVD player that had been sitting on the floor for days. "Are you going to set this thing up or what? I'm tired of looking at this mess. It's just been sitting there for days."

"You can't do it? The plugs are color-coded."

"Cleo, come on, you know I don't know anything about that."

I got down on the floor and plugged the stuff in. There wasn't much more to it than that, since the time and stuff set itself once I plugged it in. "There." I put all the manuals and stuff back into the box and carried it all to the kitchen.

"You're not throwing the instructions out, are you?" she called behind me.

I had planned on doing just that, but just because she said something I took them out of the box and threw them in the junk drawer. I still hadn't told her that the gift was not from my dad. How would I explain that? Would I go all the way back to that day in the Chinese restaurant, where I met the woman who was his newest baby's mother at the time, at least as far as I knew? Then she would be asking me why I didn't tell her about it as soon as I found out, and I wasn't even sure yet why I'd kept it from her. I guess to spare her feelings or something. On the other hand, I absolutely hated to let her go on thinking that my father had done a good thing by replacing what he'd stolen.

My refusal to let my father get any sort of credit he didn't deserve won over. "Dad didn't buy that thing," I said as she fumbled with the remote. I don't know what she was trying to do, just watch a DVD, I think. I took the remote from her and pressed play.

"Who did?" she asked, not sounding particularly engaged.

Okay, I still hadn't decided how to answer that part of the question. I shrugged.

"You don't know… so how do you know it wasn't him?"

"When is the last time he did anything nice?"

"He bought us those hoagies and cooked breakfast the next morning." She laughed at her own joke, shaking her head. "That's pathetic, right?"

"Definitely is. And considering that, what makes you think he would buy us something so nice?"

"I guess you're right. So who's it from? If not him, who would know that we needed it? You? Deena?"

"Maybe he gave it to someone else, and she felt bad about it," I said, still shrugging.

She looked at me with squinted eyes. "You know something."

"No, I'm just guessing." When had I become such a bad liar?

"Then why did you say 'she'? How do you know it wasn't a man? You know there's another woman, otherwise you would've said 'maybe *they* felt bad about it.'"

"No, I was just guessing. First of all, 'they' is a plural word, so I wouldn't have said that. Secondly, we know him well enough to be sure that there's most likely another woman involved; let's be realistic here."

She figured that I was right about that. I ran up to my room before she could ask anymore questions about how much I knew. Even if she was ignoring the obvious, she had to have known that there was at least one other woman in his life, and I doubted that it was just the one. I took the note out of my keepsake box. Before I had stuffed it into a tight corner of the box, I had tried to fold it into such a tiny rectangle that it wouldn't lay flat. I just put it on my bed and watched it slowly open up, but only partway. I had manually open it up completely.

There were ugly creases in the paper, but the handwriting was still beautiful. It looked like she had taken a calligraphy class or something. I was kind of jealous that I couldn't write like that. My dad probably didn't even know she had such great handwriting. He probably didn't know anything about her, except that she liked sweet and sour chicken with fried rice. She hadn't left her name or a phone number or anything. She wanted to do something nice, replace what he'd taken, and she appreciated the thought of her son having an older sister, yet she didn't want to give me any way to get back in contact with her. So why had I even bothered to save the note at all? Well, whatever. I ripped it up and tossed it in the trash can.

My blog's readership had been on a steady incline since my free promotion. Kam (he said I could call him that) and I had written back and forth a few times, and each time I thanked him for mentioning me on his show. People were even reading some of my older blogs, especially the ones about my thoughts on sex and relationships, of course. But there was more activity around my poetry, which I was pleasantly surprised to see. I hadn't really expected that.

There was one poem in particular, the one in which I talked about my heart being shit on, that a lot of ladies seemed to really respond to. But there was one comment from a boy. I recognized the email address to be Travis's. All it said was:

SRY

-T

That's it. He hadn't written *I'm sorry*, but *SRY*. What, did he type it while Alicia was giving him head, so he didn't have the time or patience to write out the whole thing? Was he typing it in from his phone while he was driving, just narrowly avoiding a head-on collision? Was he too upset and distraught to type out full sentences? *SRY?* How *SRY* was he if he couldn't even say it, not out loud, and not in full sentences? Couldn't call me to say it, or even text me, as if he didn't have any way to contact me by phone? He only had the balls—or lack thereof—to leave it as a comment to one of my poems on my website and blog? And not even type it out completely? That's it. *SRY*.

I guffawed, laughed out loud. It was pretty pathetic. If the only thing he had to say was that, something so insignificant, such an afterthought of an apology, I would really have preferred if he just didn't say anything at all. I wanted to call and say that to him, but I restrained myself. I held my tongue. I didn't hold my fingers though—I blogged it all out of my system, and just hoped that he was still a regular reader. It would be so satisfying if I could go back to school, see him on campus, and know that he'd read each scathing word.

I reread it completely, edited my spelling and grammar. I posted the blog, read it again. It felt so good to see those words in front of me. Really, really good. Then I deleted it. What difference did it really make? I already felt better. He was insignificant from that point on in the grand scheme of things. Would it really make a difference if he read it or not?

Would it reverse everything that had happened? Would he ditch Alicia and realize that I was so much of a better catch? Would he call me up, crying and apologizing in full sentences with non-abbreviated words? No, none of that. Even if he got it through his thick skull that he had definitely been an asshole, he would probably just go on with his life as if he'd never even read it. So I just deleted it, and I deleted his irrelevant, five-character comment as well.

What would *really* be satisfying would be to go back to school, and not even see him. Not that I wished he'd die—or worse, drop out—but to be like *yeah, he's there, but I don't even see him.*

I closed the browser window on my computer. I'd downloaded the picture of me doing a split in the middle of the dance floor and set it as my desktop background. It made me smile. I played some music from my computer and took a seat on the floor, leaning my back against the side of my bed. I doused a cotton ball in nail polish remover and started working on my fingers and toes. I then painted my fingernails bright yellow, and used black nail polish with a thin brush to paint smiley faces on my thumbnails. My sister would probably tell me it was unsophisticated and that I should stop wasting my time and just go to a nail salon. Sometimes I couldn't give a shit what my sister had to say… other times she was kind of alright.

My phone vibrated beside me. "Hello?"

"Hey. I'm coming over."

"Shut up."

"I'm not kidding. I'm around the corner."

I was absolutely certain that he was full of shit, just trying to get a rise of out of me. But no more than five minutes later, there was a knock on my bedroom door and Derek poked his head inside.

"Knock, knock," he said.

"What are you doing here?!" I whisper-yelled. "Is my mom downstairs?! Did she see you come up here?!"

"No, I broke in." He sat on the floor in front me. "Is it really so bad having me over?"

I realized that it wasn't. "I guess not."

He took me by the ankle and put my foot in his lap. "You have such cute toes." He picked up the hot pink polish. "I love this color on them." He shook the bottle, as I instructed him to do. Then he hunched over my foot and got to work, painting my toenails. It was kind of cute the way he stuck his tongue out the side of his mouth as he concentrated. Just when I thought he was finished, he went back for a second coat. And when I thought that was done, he insisted on a topcoat. "It's so messy," he said, sounding a little disappointed. "How do you make it to neat?"

"I'll just wipe off the excess with a little nail polish remover on a cotton swab, like I usually do," I explained.

"Can I?" Of course I let him. He was giddy over the finished product. "It's weird, right?" he asked me. "I did such a good job, I wanna show somebody, but then again, I'm not too eager for people to know I painted some toenails."

I laughed with him. "They never looked so good," I told him. "For my toes, I usually just do one coat and call it a day."

"Don't expect to have them sucked now, cuz I don't wanna be messing up my handiwork. And you better not have anyone else sucking on them either."

"No, never that," I said, then thought for a moment. "I don't think you've ever done that to me."

"Nah, I haven't. Just thought about it."

I slapped him playfully on the shoulder. "Nasty."

"Nasty? How about whipped? What wouldn't I do to you or for you?

The list is very short, if it exists at all."

I didn't know what to say to that, so I just changed the subject. "What made you come over here anyway?"

"Don't tell her I told you, but your mom invited me."

"Oh great."

"What's the problem?"

"I just don't want the pressure."

"What pressure? We're up here, she's down there, paying us no mind."

"She could be listening at the door, for all you know."

He got up and opened the door to the empty hallway. "Are you done being paranoid? What were you doing, smoking up here before I came in? Paranoia."

"I'm not paranoid, just being realistic. She'll try to meddle."

"Moving on from Paranoia Villa..." Derek sighed. He picked up my poetry notebook. My hand was twitching to reach out and snatch it back. "Poetry, wow." He flipped through the pages. "*Lots* of poetry, wow."

"Yeah, don't read anything, please."

He closed it right away. "As you wish. Don't you put it all on your blog anyway?"

"Yes, but... sometimes I edit things... *a lot.* And I don't incorporate my little side margin notes when I put the poems online. And, I don't know. It just seems too intimate for you to read it in my bare handwriting."

He nodded and put the book in my lap. "Will you read something to me, then?"

"Uh..." I looked around for something, anything that could give me an answer. There was nothing, just the same room as always. "I guess. But, you can't look at me." I got up on my bed. "Lean your back here." I patted the side of the bed. "And don't turn around to look at me. Promise?"

"I promise," he said, turning to take the spot I had been sitting in on the floor.

I looked for something that wouldn't be too embarrassing. I definitely wouldn't read the one where I said I lied about loving him because I liked the attention. That would definitely be a mood-killer, not that I mentioned his name in it or anything. Anyway, I had written that quite some time earlier, and I didn't even know if it was true anymore. I mean, it wasn't true anymore. "Ready?"

"Yeah."

"I look up in the sky...It is night... And there is a full moon... No wonder my feelings have been unrecognizable... Things I thought I knew... Have changed... People I thought I knew... Have left... The me I thought I knew... Has become a me I thought was meant for someone else... And I realize, then... That it's not a full moon... But a plastic bag... Caught high in a tree."

Derek gave a few quiet moments to process it. "What is that about?" he asked.

"Well, I wrote it back in middle school, when I felt like I didn't recognize my body as it changed, and how I felt pulled in two different directions by my feelings about boys and men, and I was mad at my sister for liking boys more and more... I felt like I was being lied to a lot. My world was going crazy, you know, like they say weird things happen under a full moon."

"I can sense that." He nodded. "Can I look at you now?"

"Yes."

He kneeled at my bedside. "Do you still feel that way?"

"No, it was more of an adolescent thing. I still like the poem though. Every time I get a new notebook, I copy it in there because it was like my first *real* poem, ya know? I read it often when I'm sad about something, or feel abandoned."

He put his hand over mine, which was laying across my open notebook. "I wish you would never have to feel that way again."

The following day, I received a call at 8:20 in the morn-ing. Who could possibly be calling me so early? I used to expect these sort of interruptions back when I had a credit card, but since I'd paid off my debt from that damned thing, I thought I was free of morning wake-up calls from people I didn't even know.

"Good morning," a woman's voice replied to mine. "Is this Cleo?"

"Yeah," I yawned loudly to be sure that she would hear it.

"Hi. I'm sorry, were you sleeping?"

"Yeah."

"I'm sorry. This is Erin… your dad's fiancé… we met at the Chinese food place… I gave you a DVD player a few days ago…"

"I get the idea," I said. "Well… did you want something?"

"Yes, actually. I was wondering if you would be at all willing to meet with me this afternoon. I know this out of nowhere, but I really don't want things to be awkward between us, you know?"

I grunted something.

"How about one o'clock? We can get lunch or something."

"I don't eat lunch," I lied, just to object to something.

"Okay," she snickered. "Well, near the Chinese food place, there's this park I always take my son—your half-brother—to play at. You wanna meet there?"

"Yeah, okay. I'm going back to sleep now."

"But you'll meet me there, right? At one o'clock?"

"Yeah, see you." I hung up the phone and was pissed off that I couldn't get back to sleep. I had wanted to sleep until like eleven at least, just because I could. Time was winding down until I'd have to get up at the crack of dawn every morning to be at class on time. I stomped down to the kitchen, where my mom was having a half of a grapefruit before work.

"Good morning," she said.

I mumbled back to her.

"I have a confession to make," she said. "I invited Derek over yesterday."

I gasped and threw my hand to my forehead with my palm facing outwards. "You're kidding!" I made myself a bowl of cereal and sat across from her at the table. "But why would you go and do a thing like that?"

She shrugged. "I guess I wanted to show you that I respect your privacy."

"Kind of a backwards way to show it, don't you think?"

She nodded. "You could say that. But I wanted you to see that it's not awkward to have a boy over here, because I won't be all in your business. There's nothing to be embarrassed about."

She was right about that: for all the sexual freedom that I claimed, it still made me uncomfortable to display any sort of relationship, platonic or otherwise, between a boy and myself in the presence of my family. I was definitely immature in that sense.

"Well, since we're confessing things here," I sighed. "A little less than a month ago, I ran into Dad and his new girlfriend at Chinese restaurant. They have a two-year-old son." My mom was much less bothered by the news than I thought she'd be, and I was relieved for that. "That DVD player was actually from her. And she called me this morning because she wants to meet with me this afternoon."

"*She* bought that?! Well that's big of her."

"Yeah, I thought so, too. But what's with her wanting to meet me?"

"I don't know. What did you say?"

"I told her okay, but I have no loyalty to her. I could care less if she's disappointed that I don't show up."

"I think you should go," Mom said. "You have a little brother out there, it couldn't hurt to get to know him. Take your pepper spray though, and keep your eye if she has too many friends standing around, and don't let anyone get up behind you."

"What? Do you think she really wants to jump me? I'm the daughter, not the ex. I'm not *you*."

"I'm just saying, you never know with some of these bitches nowadays. If anything happens to you, well I haven't been in a fight in a long-ass time, but I will kick somebody's ass. I will rip that damn DVD player out the wall and smash her ass with it, if I have to. Be cordial, but not necessarily kind. And don't get too close. I don't care how nice she is; don't be doing any favors for her." She kissed me on the forehead on her way out of the kitchen. "I gotta get to work. Good luck with that, I hope it goes well."

She's kind of cool, my mom.

The clock seemed to be moving extra slow. I decided that I would indeed go and meet this Erin girl, this girl who was only a few years older than and *engaged* to a man old enough to be my father. Yuck. What could she possibly see in him? Her looks were neither here nor there; she wasn't cute (I think it was her face that was the problem) but she wasn't exactly hideous, so it's not like my dad was the best she could do.

I felt a need to look cuter than her, so I tried on several different outfits before settling on a white tank top and jeans with white flip-flops. It was simple and clean, because I didn't want her thinking I'd put time and effort into coming to see her. I wanted it to look like I was just sitting around the house in this outfit, looking as cute as I always do, and then I looked at the clock and though to myself, *Oh, yeah, I'm supposed to go meet that girl right about now.*

The titties were sitting up high and on display in my tank top and drawing a lot of attention at the park. Moms gave me dirty looks while most men admired them. I wished I'd brought a hoodie or something, it's not even like it was really so hot that I needed to be outside in just a tank top.

I'd gotten there early, as I often do to most places. Two guys were walking by, talking to each other, and casually stopped to take a rest on the bench I was sitting on. They each took a seat on either side of me. They were about the same height, but one was kind of husky while the other was of more average build. They were both dressed in the regular urban, summertime uniform for young Black males: a white tee, jeans shorts so long that they may as well have worn pants, and fresh, white sneakers. The smaller one wore a red durag and talked a lot though.

"You waitin' for somebody?" he asked me.

"Yes," I replied.

"Who, your man? If he got you out here waitin', maybe you need to leave him for somebody better? Like me or my brother." He and his brother laughed.

"No, not my man."

"Oh, you don't got a man? You should date my brother then."

I looked over at him. He wasn't bad-looking, but why the would I want to date him? He walked up to me as I sat on a park bench and had his brother do all the talking for him; I felt like we were back in elementary school. He may as well have said *can you pass this note to her? Tell her to check "yes" if she likes me and "no" if she doesn't.*

"Thanks, but I never said I don't have a boyfriend."

"Oh, my bad." He stood up, took his chubby brother by the arm, and walked off.

I could see Erin coming from a mile away. She was wearing gold high-tops and a cobalt blue baby tee that fit her top half as tight as her gold, metallic leggings fit her bottom half. I'll admit she had a nice figure—I wouldn't be caught dead in that outfit, and not only for the fact that it was a tacky mess. She had a friend with her, who was pushing little Quincy in the stroller. Her friend turned off toward the playground while Erin headed straight for me. Her make-up was very Chola-inspired, with a very dark lip-line, high, dark eyebrows, and dramatic eye-liner. Unfortunately, her cover-up did nothing to hide the devastating craters that either crystal meth or a horrible case of adolescent acne had left across her cheeks.

She used her hand to shield her eyes from the sun as she looked toward me, and the rhinestones on her fingernails nearly blinded me. "Oh, hey!" she said. She leaned over and hugged me, which was as awkward as it sounds. I sat there, stiff as a board, and just let her do it. "You been waiting here long? I'm not late, am I?"

"No, you're not late." I couldn't stop myself from just staring at what she looked like. It was one in the afternoon! No wonder my sister had tried to stop me from going out in that sequined dress when she drove me home the morning after that party. Seeing Erin, I completely understood. I closed my eyes and took a moment to recuperate. "Well..."

"You know your dad's in jail, right?"

"No…"

"Oh my God." She lowered her eyes. "Oh my God. I thought you knew! I'm so sorry, I didn't mean to just blurt it out like that."

"Look, I really don't care. I know he's your *fiancé* and all, but I really don't know the man from a can of beans. So what are you saying? What did you call me out here for? You need bail money or something?"

"Of course not! You think I would come out of nowhere to hit you up for something like that?"

"Well you are of unsound enough mind to date my father."

"Low blow. But he can be quite the charmer, you know."

"He can also be quite high, quite drunk, quite desperate, quite a deadbeat…"

"Okay, I get it. I will admit, he gave me your number and address because he wanted me to ask you and your mom for bail money, but I didn't. Instead, I held onto the address and brought that DVD player to you. How's it working?"

"Well enough. Is that all this is about?"

I could tell that her patience was wearing thin. She was being pretty nice to me and I was just shoving it back in her face. "No. Do you even wanna know what he's in for?"

"Who? What?"

"What your dad is in jail for?" She didn't wait for my response, which was smart because I was going to say *no*. "He had an illegal gun on him and some coke. He could be in there for up to five years."

"Wow," I sighed. "That's fascinating."

We sat in silence for a moment, listening to the traffic, the distant sound of children playing, and a few birds chirping back and forth at each other. "I hate to even ask this, but what's your name again?" she asked me.

"*Cleo*. And yours?" I already knew her name, but I didn't want her thinking she could just forget who I am and I would remember her.

"Erin." She held out her hand to shake mine. I shook it, even though I thought it was stupid because she'd already hugged me. "I don't know if you read my note, but I mentioned in it that it makes me feel good to know that Quincy has a big sister. I kind of feel like, if anything ever happened to me—"

"Whoa! Stop right there! Are you crazy?" So this is what my mom meant about not doing this bitch any favors.

"I'm not asking you to be his legal guardian in the case of my death. I'm just saying… oh, I don't know. I don't really have much family, so I just like knowing that Quincy has more family than just me, you know? I really wanted you to meet him. Is that okay? Do you even like little kids?"

"Yeah, sure." I got up and followed her over to the playground. I noticed some of the moms giving Erin the stank eye, too. We must've been a sight: me with my endless cleavage, Erin with only a thin layer of Spandex that left nothing to the imagination. I waited by the slide while Erin went to collect Quincy. I wondered what possessed her to name him Quincy.

Quincy followed a little behind his mother, reaching out before himself to hold onto her hand. He had very light brown skin, with medium brown hair of a texture common to Black folk. His eyes were beautifully hazel, and big and bright in that child-like way. He seemed too cute for either of his parents to have had a hand in making him. His mother told him to say hi to me, and he did.

I got down on my knees. "Hi, Quincy. My name is Cleo." I looked up at Erin and whispered, as if he couldn't hear me, "Can I tell him I'm his sister?"

She nodded, smiling. "Please do."

"My name is Cleo," I repeated to him, "and I'm your sister. Do you know what that means?"

He shook his head.

"It means that your daddy is my daddy. So it means that you and I can be best friends, and whenever you need me you can call me, if you want to play or anything." Unsure of what else to say, I took a cue from his t-shirt. "You like robots?"

"Yeah!" he exclaimed, with wide eyes. He let go of his mother's hand. "Do you like robots?"

"Who doesn't?" I replied. Of course he was only two and a half, so he wasn't exactly keen on rhetorical questions. Quincy pointed to Erin in response to my inquiry. I waved it off. "Don't worry about what she says. Robots are awesome."

"Don't worry about what I say, huh? I guess I'll leave you two alone." Erin went to sit on a bench alone. I don't know where her friend had gone off to.

"What's your name?" he asked me.

"Cleo. Can you say that?"

He nodded. "Cleo," he laughed. "I'm Quincy."

"I know."

"Slide?" By the time I turned to look at the slide, he had already darted off to get on it.

Erin waved me over to her. "He likes you," she said.

"You think?"

"Yeah. He doesn't talk to everyone."

He didn't talk much anyway. I took a seat. "Why did you name him Quincy?"

"Your dad wanted to. He *loves* Quincy Jones. His favorite movie of all time is *The Wiz*, largely because of the music. He can recite every word of the entire movie. He says Quincy Jones is his inspiration."

"How is that?"

"He just loves music. He can play his ass off, too, on guitar, piano, and he dabbles with the sax. He was in a band a couple years ago, while he was clean and sober, playing guitar. That's how I met him. I was a go-go dancer at the time. That wasn't really stripping, like I do now, it was just dancing on stage in skimpy clothes. In fact, I think I wore this exact outfit my first night. Not with these sneakers, of course, I had some stripper heels on, clear platforms if I remember correctly. I miss those things bad; the strap broke as soon as I walked off stage one day. I wasn't exactly old enough to be in that club, but I was there anyway. Back to the story of meeting your father: I was waiting for my turn to go on, and there was your dad up on stage…"

It was like I listening to some old lady. I didn't wanna hear about the good old days from a few years back when my dad was on the right track and still didn't have half a mind to do right by my mother and me.

"Yeah? That's great. I don't really wanna hear about it, sorry."

"Oh. No, I'm sorry. I get it."

"Do you though?"

"Hey, my dad wasn't always around either. But I think at some point you have to realize that he's not a bad person. Don't you think it's time you should let it go?"

I sat for a moment and tried to think of something nice and mature to say. Nothing came to mind. "I don't need you to sit here and counsel me. He stole our DVD player and gave it to you. Years before that, he stole our TV, too. And those are the only two times that I ever remember seeing him *in my life*. That's malevolence if I've ever heard of such a thing. Let it go? It's not like I'm stuck on it, like I obsess over this every day, but I would think you might understand if I choose to hate the guy. I'm entitled to, dammit. And then how would you feel if your step-mom came into the picture, telling you all kinds of great things about him that you never got to experience? Would that make you feel good?"

"I'm not your step-mom. Hey, I'm only a few years older than you."

"You said you're his fiancé."

"I am." She showed me her ring, which had the *tiniest* rock I'd ever seen. Actually, it just looked like there was a hole in the band, but I'm assuming there must've been a diamond in there.

"So if you're not my step-mom now, you will be soon enough, assuming he actually goes through with it."

Erin sighed. The expression on her face showed that she didn't feel too certain about what I'd just said. Either that, or she was thinking about something else. "So you don't wanna go see him, I'm guessing. I was gonna offer to drive you out there if you wanted."

"Are you joking? Like I would go visit him in prison and he's only visited me—at my *home*—twice in my life?!"

"I see. Look, I really don't want any bad blood between us. I just want you to get to know Quincy, and for Quincy to know you well enough to say that he has a sister he loves and cares about. You can pretend I'm not even in the picture if you want."

"I may just do that." I went over to the slide, where Quincy was on the ladder. "Hey, dude, I'm about to leave."

"Bye."

"Can I have a hug?"

He jumped off the bottom rung of the ladder and hugged me at the knees. I had to bend over to hug him back. It was one of the warmest hugs I'd had in a while. I asked him if he remembered my name. He shook his head and asked, "What's your name again?"

"Cleo," I told him.

"Cle-o."

"Right. Bye, Quincy."

"Bye!" He started back up the ladder.

I waved goodbye to Erin and left the playground. I meandered around the park for a while, making sure to steer clear of the playground where I could see Erin was still sitting. She had some nerve asking me to come meet her and then trying to convince me to make amends with my unrepentant father under the false pretenses of getting to know her son. I felt sorry for Quincy, with a mother like that. Shit, I thought I was bad coming out here with my cleavage showing, but her clothes were so tight she may as well have been naked.

If I wanted to look on the bright side, I could say that at least she hadn't had some of her friends jump me, and I didn't have to take out my pepper spray. Then, of course, there was the obvious good thing of getting to meet Quincy, who was a cute little kid, though somewhat lacking in personality. But he was only two, so I gave him a pass on that.

From a distance, I saw Erin pack up her kid and his stroller and leave. I took a seat on a bench and watched them exit the park. I considered following her to see where she lived. I would've been pissed if she had a place nicer than my house, and for that reason, among others, I decided not to do it. I sat and thought about what I would say to my mom. There was no doubt that she would ask me about it. My stomach growled. I called Deena to see what was for lunch.

"What's for lunch?!" she shouted into my ear. "Go look in the fridge and answer your own question."

"I'm not at home, I'm at a park."

"A park? For what?"

"Never mind that. Let's go to lunch."

I waited on the porch for Deena to pick me up. I said hello to Lele in the backseat as I fastened my seatbelt. She was still rocking her "skater" look. "Where are we going?" I asked Dee.

"I have a coupon to this Irish pub place called O'Neilly's. You're paying for yourself though."

"I know, I know."

"O'Neilly's, yay!" Lele shouted.

We were seated in a booth by a window. It was dark and ugly in there, one of those places with lots of "antique" junk on from sports and other random paraphernalia on the walls. There were a million beers listed on the back of the menu, and the expected steaks, fries, chicken fingers, sandwiches, and burgers inside. Our waiter placed a basket of rolls on the table. Hard-ass rolls. It was clear Deena didn't come here for the rolls. It was also clear that she did come here for the waiter.

"Hey, Deena," he said. His green polo shirt was very fitted, and you could see that he had the body of a man who might've modeled for Ancient Greek sculptors. His nametag said his name was Byron, unfortunately. "Where ya been?" he asked my sister. He had cute, little twists in his dark hair, like mini-dreadlocks, no more than an inch long. His eyes were big and friendly, and so deep and dark that you could just get lost in them. You could, but he kept his gaze bouncing from here to there, which was a good thing.

"Oh, around," Dee said, trying her best to sound non-chalant.

Byron greeted Leslie with a fist bump. "How's the skating?" he asked her.

"Awesome," she said.

Where ya been? Lele hadn't been skating all that long. Dee had to be a regular at this place for him to say that.

"And who's this lovely?" Byron asked while looking directly at me.

"My *little* sister," Deena said. "Anyway, Byron, how have you been?"

"Great, but uh, the boss is watching like a hawk today, so what'll you have? The usual?"

"Yes," Dee and Lele said in unison.

"And for you?" he asked me.

I had hardly even taken a serious look at what they had to offer, so I just went with a cheeseburger. "Cheddar cheese, well done," I said. "And a Shirley Temple to drink."

"Ooh, me too!" Lele exclaimed. "A Shirley Temple for me, too!"

"Is that okay?" Byron asked Deena.

"Yeah, why not?"

"Let's get down to business," I said as soon as Byron walked away. "There's a main reason I wanted to come out to lunch with you. But, first of all, what's up with you and Byron?"

"Shut up," Deena said, cutting her eyes toward Leslie. "There's nothing, he's just our waiter."

"Is he *the guy* you were telling me about? You know, when I stayed over your apartment and we were talking about our numbers?"

"No!" she stage-whispered. "And I wish you would cut it out now. He's not the guy."

I shook my head. "But you obviously wish he was the guy."

"No, because the guy is a great guy, and I wouldn't just boot him out for another guy."

"Yeah, but if things fell off with the current guy, I'm sure you wouldn't mind Byron being the new guy."

"Well, Cleo, who wouldn't? But this isn't up for discussion, so drop it. What was the other thing?"

"I never told you or Mom this, but I met my dad's girlfriend not too long ago, and they—"

"Cut! The one who gave you the DVD/VHS player? I've heard this.

Mom called and told me this woman asked to meet with you today. How did it go?"

I was shocked, but I shouldn't have been. I rolled my eyes, annoyed that Mom had already told her half the story. "She wanted me to meet my half brother…" I said, with a tone that I hoped would hint that there was more to the story. Apparently it did.

"And?"

"And to tell me that my dad is in jail for illegal gun charges and cocaine possession."

Leslie looked up from coloring on her placemat with a worried expression.

"Wow," Deena said.

"That's what I said… but with much less sincerity. I could care less where he is, it's not like I was gonna see him anyway, not as if he would've done anything for me if he were a free man."

"True… but nobody wants to be in jail."

"What is with people feeling sorry for this man? He's screwed up more times than he can probably even count. Erin, that's the bitch's name—excuse me, Lele—the *woman's* name, was trying to get me to quote let it go unquote. I was like, *Bitch, I'll let it go when I'm good and ready.*"

"You said that to her?"

"No, but something along those lines."

Byron put our drinks on the table, winked at Deena and walked off.

"That's crazy. What's their son like?"

"Cool, I guess. I mean, he's two and a half, so there's not much to say."

"Does he look like Larry?"

"No, not particularly."

"You think maybe he's *not* Larry's?" Deena speculated.

"Dee, I just went to meet him a little over an hour ago! I'm tryna be a good big sis and now you're gonna suggest he may not even be my little brother? Besides, why would this chick lie about *Larry* being the father? If she's gonna lie about it, don't you think she might've picked a better daddy?"

"You're right about that. This is such an interesting set of occurrences. I never did like your dad very much, and I've known him longer than you, remember."

"Who could? I was trying to figure that out when I was with her. She doesn't seem like the type to just love everyone around her. I mean, the first time we met she gave me straight-up attitude, not that I didn't deserve it. Do you know how they met? He was playing guitar in a club that she was a dancer for."

"Dancer?"

"Go-go dancer," I clarified. "This is before she started stripping."

"That's romantic. But, look, what's the big deal. If she's keeping the trouble over on her own side, away from you and Mom—"

"But he came to visit not too long ago, remember? So what good is she then?"

"You're right about that, also. I don't know what to tell you, Cleo."

"Of course you don't. Cuz you've got a good daddy who comes around and visits you, who buys you birthday gifts, calls you every now and again and shit like that."

"Don't be mad at me for it," she said, shaking her head.

"I'm not," I sighed.

"Heads up! Hot plates!" Byron placed my burger in front of my face. "Enjoy, ladies," he sang. "Anything else you might need?"

I just shook my head because my mouth was already stuffed with food.

After Deena dropped me off at home, I fell asleep on the living room couch. I woke up when I heard my mom come in from work. I tried to sit up and look alert as if I hadn't been sleeping.

"What's for dinner?" she asked me.

"Grilled cheese," I yawned, improvising.

"Yum. Give me two. I'll be back down in a minute." She went upstairs.

I went to the kitchen and started preparing the meal. I was still kind of full from lunch, but I made myself a sandwich anyway because I knew that once I smelled that warm, toasty bread and melted cheese, and saw my mom eating her two sandwiches, I was definitely gonna be craving one of my own. She sat at the kitchen table while I cooked.

"How was it?" she asked.

"Fine. But, before I start, have you talked to Deena today?"

"No, why?"

I turned from the stove to face her.

"I mean, *yeah*, I talked to her *earlier*."

"Yeah, and you told her everything that I said this morning."

"I didn't know it was a secret!"

"It wasn't, but I'd like to know that I can tell you things without the whole world knowing afterwards."

"Okay, okay…"

"So what I'm asking here is if you've talked to Deena since then, because there's no point in me telling you how the meeting went if Dee already told you everything."

"No, she didn't say a thing about it."

Now I knew who I could trust with my secrets. "Well, Erin and I met at the park. She had her friend watch her son on the playground while she and I talked. She told me dad's in jail."

"Pfft."

"Yeah, my reaction exactly. Then she introduced me to her son, my half-brother, Quincy."

"Is he cute?"

"Yeah."

"Two ugly people make the cutest babies."

"You've never even seen her. How can you say she's ugly?"

"Is she cute?"

"No. I think it's her face."

"It usually is."

"For some reason she thought she was my psychiatrist, trying to tell me that I need to get over hating him."

"You don't hate him."

"If you think I don't hate him, you don't know me as well as you think you do."

"Cleo…"

"Okay, maybe hate is a strong word..."

"Of course it is. This is like the most perfect grilled cheese I've ever seen in my life, and I have seen a lot of grilled cheese. Anyway—mm, and delicious! Anyway—oh my God. Anyway—don't worry about him. You're life is gonna go so far beyond anything that has anything to do with him. He's a bum. The best thing he ever did in his whole, entire, sorry-ass life was to make you. And can I tell you something, between us girls? When you were conceived, it wasn't even that good."

"MOM!"

She tilted her head to the side. "Well, honey, I just wanna stress the point that you are the only good thing that came out of that relationship."

"I know that's meant to be a comfort but—"

"Okay, okay, I get it. I'm your mom, not your girlfriend."

The grilled cheese was delicious. "Where's Ted been?"

"Storm forecasting, I guess. We talk. I've just been tired lately, so we haven't gone out. One of my girls quit on me, so I've had to pick up time in her place. She was one of the dumbest girls I've ever met anyway. I don't know how she got that job. How's Derek?"

"Mom, don't..."

"What? You're so uptight. I'm going to bed."

"Already? It's not even eight o'clock."

"I know! I feel like such an old lady but I can't wait to put on my pajamas and just lay in bed, watch TV, and then *go to sleep*." She put her used plate and glass in the sink, then went upstairs to her room.

I sat in the living room alone, watching television and surfing the web. The Internet is a funny thing; sometimes I will feel like there is absolutely nothing on there to interest me—nothing in the whole, wide web—and then there are times when I'll happen to stumble upon an interesting blog or website, and find interesting links to other blogs and sites from there, and so on and so forth. I wonder to myself, *Where was this blog two days ago when I was dying of boredom?* It was right there, in the same spot, of course. Naturally, we don't find these things until we stop looking for them.

Around two in the morning, I finally went up to my bedroom. I locked my door, stripped down to nothing, pulled the bed covers back, and laid on top of my sheets. I still hadn't gotten my window screen fixed, so I had been sleeping with my window closed. Normally, that was fine, but since the summer was winding down and the weather wasn't really heat wave status anymore, my mom had been keeping the air condition off. It was stifling in there. I could hardly breathe, so there was no way I could fall asleep. I got up and opened the window, then got back into bed.

I felt like I'd slept a hundred years, but in a good way. I wasn't groggy or drowsy; I felt refreshed and renewed. My room was super bright from the sun streaming in through the window, so it had to be well into the morning, if it wasn't yet afternoon. I felt my nakedness on my sheets and remembered that I'd been practically sweating to death the night before. It was cooler now, but it still felt good to be naked. I rolled over to stare up at the ceiling and think, and—

"Oh my God!"

Something went flapping by my face in a blur of orangey-yellow and black. The first thing that crossed my mind was a bat. We had a bat in our old apartment once, and it was absolutely the scariest experience of my life. If this was a bat, in my bedroom, what the hell would I do all on my own? I pulled my covers up over myself and hid. My clothes were too far to grab. I peeked my head out and scanned the room. Something stirred over by my dresser, and I saw a butterfly and it's reflection in my mirror.

"Oh," I sighed, loosening up a little. It was not an ideal situation to have a butterfly in my room, but there could have definitely been worse situations to wake up to. Quickly, I just reached for my camera, never taking my eyes off of the butterfly. I changed the settings quickly to capture the light just right, keeping one eye on the butterfly and the other on my camera screen. I snapped plenty of beautiful shots of the butterfly admiring herself in the mirror on my bureau. She allowed me to get very close to her, and then I must've pushed the boundary, because she up and flew away. I tried to capture her flight—on film?... on media card, I should say, but that sounds so much less poetic—but I lost track of her and had to pull the camera away from my eye.

She'd landed over by my bed, on my latest poetry notebook. She flew over to my bookshelf in the corner, where there was a dried flower sitting on top. She was getting restless, feeling trapped, I could see. How would I get her out? I went digging through my laundry to find the netted bag that I always washed my bras and panties in. I bent up a wire hanger, to create the frame and handle, and in conjunction with the netted bag, made an impromptu butterfly net.

I went over to pull the screen up completely. Sure, she had come through that hole in the screen, but there was no way I was gonna try to force her out through such a small space. Only when I got to the window and saw some people out on the street, people who didn't seem to notice me, luckily, did I remember that I had been prancing around my room after this butterfly in the nude. I ran back over to my laundry and pulled out a t-shirt and shorts to throw on. Then I went back and lifted the screen open.

Don't be fooled by my uncommon bravery; I was scared to death. My hands were shaking as I tried to sneak up on this butterfly. I grabbed the photography book that Derek bought me to cover up the open end of the net. The butterfly had moved from the book shelf, back to my dresser, but was sitting on the top now instead of on the mirror. I wanted to put the net down and pick up my camera again, but I felt bad for her. She didn't want to be in my house any more than I did, so I had to get her out of there. I placed the net over her very carefully. She went crazy as soon as she realized she was trapped, and I went a little crazy, too.

"Ew, ew, oh my God, yuck," I groaned as she flew all over the place within the confounds of the net. What would I wash my unmentionables in now? I held the book at the lip of the dresser and slid the net on top of it. I walked briskly to the window and stuck the net out there, throwing the book onto my bed behind me.

She wouldn't get out of the net. She was flapping hard, but she was stuck or something. I knew what I had to do, although I hated that I had to do it: I used my free hand to turn the net inside out. Her wings flapped against my fingers a few times, and I shuddered, but then she was free.

I closed the screen and the window. She drifted off, bobbing and weaving, her flight path looking as haphazard and erratic as any butterfly before her or since. What did it matter though? Who am I to have to know every single turn she's going to make and path she's going take? I didn't doubt she had an ultimate destination, or that she would get there, so I knew I shouldn't be annoyed, as I had been, that butterflies fly in the unpredictable way that they do.

I washed my hands fiercely and then took a shower. I got dressed in own room, then realized that I didn't have any deodorant left. I went into my mom's room to borrow hers, and who do you know is sitting out on the cable wire, right outside of my mom's window? I went to the window to get a closer look, which only enhanced my certainty that it was the same butterfly. She flew over to the telephone pole and clung to it with her wings spread open.

The way the light hit her was gorgeous. I hoped she would stay there while I got my camera, so I ran to fetch it, but when I came back, she was gone. Oh well. I put some deodorant on and went back to my room. It was getting hot in there, but there was no way I was going to leave my window open again. I was lucky it had only been a butterfly in there that time.

I uploaded the other pictures from my camera to the computer. They were more beautiful that I'd imagined they were going to be. Her colors were so bright that I didn't even have to tweak the saturation. I was about to put the best ones up on my website, but then decided against it. These were too personal. Some things aren't meant to be shared, and I wanted to keep those moments for myself.

www.ingramcontent.com/pod-product-compliance
Lightning Source LLC
LaVergne TN
LVHW091030080826
845145LV00002B/430

* 9 7 8 0 5 7 8 0 2 5 3 7 7 *